A CHANGE OF RULES

EPISODE 1
OF
THE MISSING SHIELD

Copyright

Visit the author's official website at

www.llthomsen.com

Contents

Head's up From the Author:

Hi there and thank you for hopping onboard.

I just wanted to let you know that I have deliberated and decided that I would not clutter up this book with the usual array of inventories or glossaries.

Now it's not to say I don't love these things. As a matter of fact, I feel every self-respecting fantasy book should have something to support the narrative – because it's fantasy after all!

So with that in mind, I would like to invite you to my website www.llthomsen.com where you can explore titbits about the world of Dallancea at your own leisure, as well as look up names, terms, information about the series and of course about yours truly, also.

This is just the beginning – I hope you stay for the journey.

Map 1

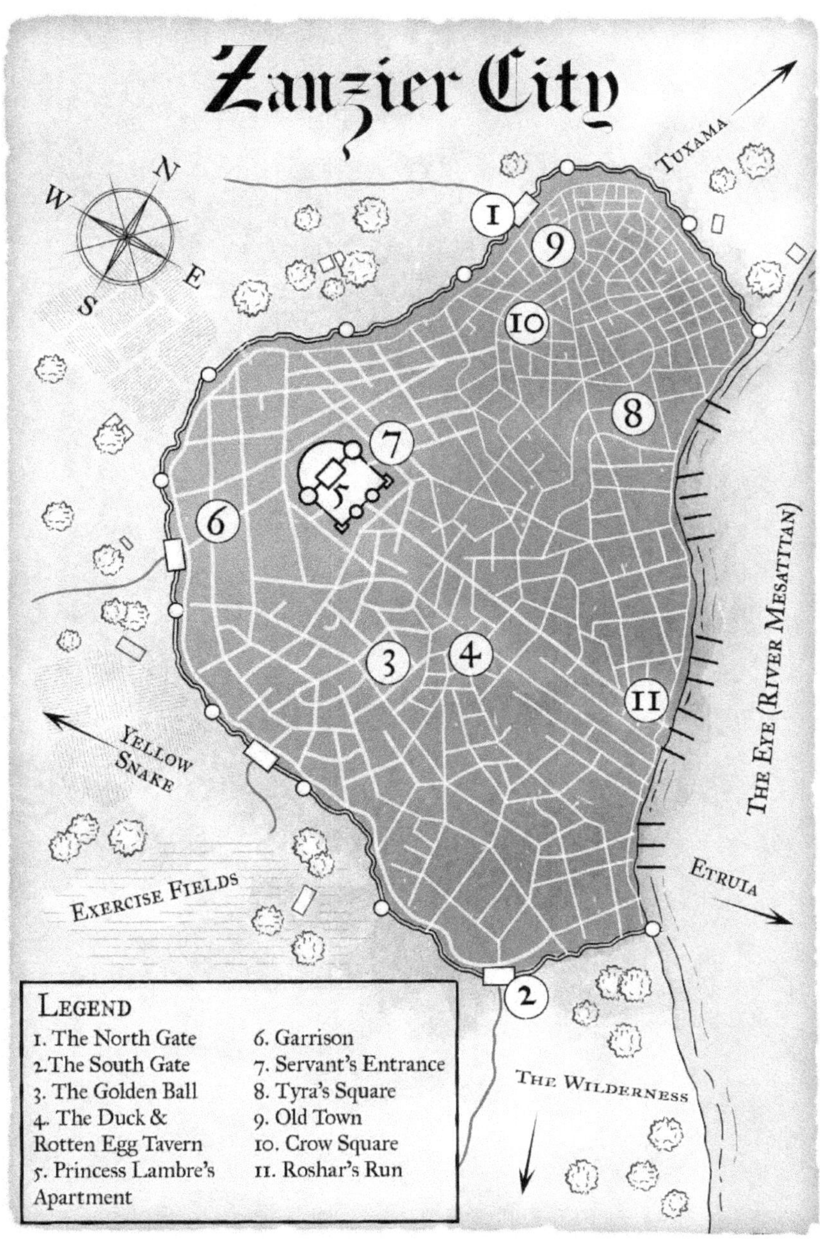

LEGEND
1. The North Gate
2. The South Gate
3. The Golden Ball
4. The Duck & Rotten Egg Tavern
5. Princess Lambre's Apartment
6. Garrison
7. Servant's Entrance
8. Tyra's Square
9. Old Town
10. Crow Square
11. Roshar's Run

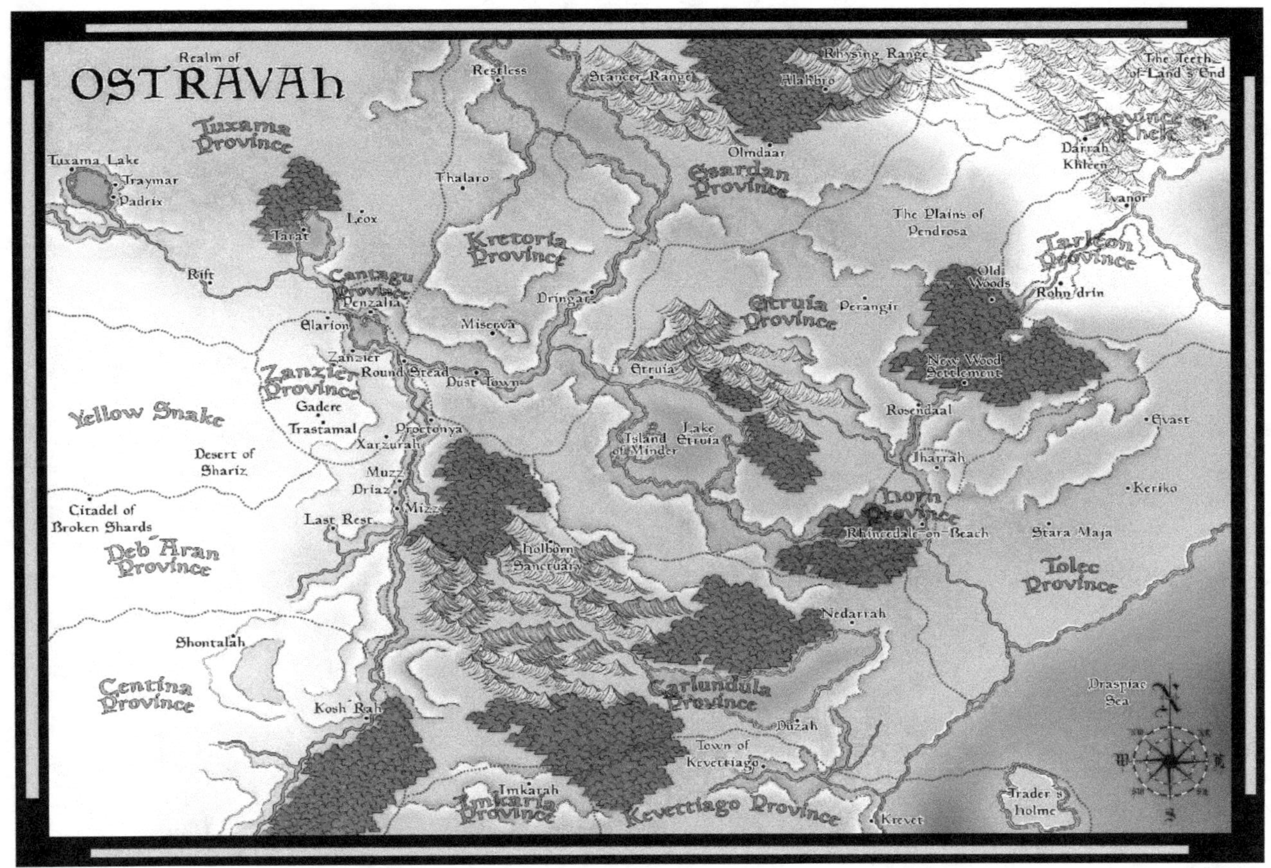

Realm of
OSTRAVAh
Tuxama Province
Tuxama Lake
Traymar
Padrix
Tarat
Leox
Rift
Cantagu Province
Penzalia
Elarion
Zanzier
Round Stead
Zanzier Province
Yellow Snake
Gadere
Trastamal
Desert of Shariz
Citadel of Broken Shards
Deb'Aran Province
Shontalah
Centina Province
Kosh Rah
Proctonya
Xarzurah
Muzz
Driaz
Mizz
Last Rest
Imkarah
Imkaria Province
Town of Kevettiago
Duzah
Carlundula Province
Kevettiago Province
Krevet
Trader's holme
Draspiac Sea
Nedarrah
Holborn Sanctuary
Lake Etruia
Island of Minder
Etruia
Dust Town
Miserva
Dringat
Kretoria Province
Thalaro
Restless
Stancer Range
Rhysing Range
Alahhio
Olmdaar
Gsardan Province
The Plains of Pendrosa
Etruia Province
Perangir
Rosendaal
New Wood Settlement
Oldi Woods
Rohn'drin
Tarkon Province
The Teeth of Land's End
Darrah
Khleen
Ivanor
Province of Khek
Jharrah
Horn Province
Rhinedale-on-Beach
Stara Maja
Keriko
Gvast
Tolec Province

P_{reface}:

Trapped in exile, the Maker Alérathnar's first children – mad, powerful creatures who style themselves 'Gods' – have fought for millennia to break through 'The Veils of Time' in an effort to return to the world of Dallancea.

During their most recent attempt, they almost succeeded.

In an unprecedented event of extraordinary chaos, aided by a blood-hungry, magic-craving race named the Venzoians – the Gods seemed but moments removed from achieving their desire. However, though all was nearly lost, the Veils were saved in the final hour by the fated Twins who thwarted the mad creatures by working the magic-imbued artefact known as 'The Astrolabe'.

This act secured peace for another 1000 years – yet, in victory, the world also experienced great loss, for the event shattered the Artefact, crippling the magic across Dallancea's nine realms, also costing the Maker's Avatars – the Guardians of the Veils – dearly, both in power and supremacy and perhaps more…

$\mathcal{S}$olancei's Memoirs

The Province of Tarléon.
Ocean's End.
Autumn of 780 P. C. W.

Hollow. How does one conquer hollow?

I remember blandly watching the Funeral Adepts lower the two white-lacquered coffins into the carved-out abyss of ice and tranquillity. A detachment much colder than the surroundings wormed like a giant parasite within me, but I embraced the feeling, the anxiety awaiting on the other side, not something I cared to allow foothold back in. *I was seven. Hollow… indeed…*

Pale-lipped and wind-chilled, it took the fur-wrapped young men no time at all to perform their task and as the harsh autumnal sunlight flashed just once across the metal-edged caskets, they gleamed with one final sliver of suppressed splendour – almost inspiring the imagination to hear a wordless plea for rescue ricocheting across eternity. Then the coffins were lost from view, and it was final. My blustery father and austere mother… forever gone.

I was too young to quite comprehend the concept of the wondrous finality of death back then, yet the hollow where emotion might have lived must somehow have fed from something similar, and there was nothing complex about that. *Though as for the reason…*

In my mind, I can still hear how the Prefect mumbled the appropriate words of song and worship as he stood before me, simultaneously beseeching the Gods to lend the dead peace and the living courage; and I watched the man speak, heard the sounds, but they seemed muffled – as though he was talking to the congregation through the layers of silver-white fleece that cloaked most parts of him.

In that outfit, he resembled a bi-pedal snow-fox with slouching tendencies and a paw that possessed independent life to twitch once in a while irrespective of the God signalled to pay heed. It was a picture that would have inspired mirth any other time. A prune, wearing tailored pelts so that he looked as wide as he was tall? A small dry-faced man no bigger than a standard block of ice hewn from cheap stock – yet sprouting barges for feet…

Yes, that was surely hilarious! Or, at least it might have been. *But fun?*

Now there's a concept nigh-on forgotten! On that day I lost my heart for a while. My beautiful friend, Iambre, recovered it; gave it back to me; made me whole. Was I that innocently stupid that I thought I could keep it forever? These days I wonder, but perhaps it matters not. For my cousin, I would give it all. *For Iambre.*

Solancei

The Upper Circle

With a slow ripple of white pleated cloth and robes of ivory silks the Speaker, Sinuhé Sedjem-Alhath'naar, rose smoothly from his Seat of Heritage: an action to cloak feelings of concern that clung to his mind, courtesy of the Long Sleep. The others watched him, a sense of bated anticipation riding his every move, but he needed to take a moment. *The world was different now. His fellow Guardians thought they knew, but…*

The Grand Oratorio's elegance was possessed of a wintery silence that made the beauty of their sanctuary appear cold though it wasn't. In all its smooth architectural magnificence the vast dome hundreds of feet above, allowed him to look to the Void's pearlescent perfection, the familiar 'nothing and all' forever swirling like oil on water, stretched by restless winds that did not exist, drawing new patterns that could never settle.

Am I seeing the dreams of children and the wishes of the dying, come together to hinder the mal-doer and aid the kind-hearted, Sinuhé mused with the same incidental care as ever, for he recalled the old dogma from his childhood with a strange fondness for the superstition that had flourished even then. However, unlike before; unlike any time he'd stood here and looked up, there was now a silvery undertone presented on the tail of every swirling cipher. *Was it part of the problem? Or the solution?*

With a kernel of mild exasperation, he barely daren't speculate and pushed the thought aside for later. The inky marble before his feet, so instrumental to the survival of the Nine Realms and the preservation of the Veils of Time, gave the appearance of polished treacle flecked with base metals, but for a blink within blinks, he saw the tarnishing runnels of filigree imperfection slither within the infinity and quenched a shiver. *It was another strange disturbance. Had the others noticed? Would they?*

Uncertainty permeating his bones in a way that could draw the brown hue of his newly-quickened skin from healthy maroon to ash-smeared clay once more, he fought the idea that the future was already lost and let his seasoned nature cover any show of personal discomfort.

What must come raised in him a weariness that might well invade past strength and fortitude if permitted to grow. It left him ruffled, obscenely stripping the otherwise fine quality of mind and knowledge till these twisted, raising connotations of the way he might have felt in youth, still close to mortality – keen to make a difference at the table of diplomacy, and a certain sense of desperation still riding him to achieve a particular outcome before-

Well, it was a long while since he'd been a youth. Even longer since mortality had played a far-away fiddle in his life. Like his fellow Guardians, he was Reborn by the grace of the Maker, Alérathnar, the Creator, and thoughts of youth and fickle shortcomings did not become his status, nor the task he must steer a way to perform for the good of all.

Burying further whimsical ideas of undoing, he looked around, subtle concerns now pushed into a slight double frown upon a tall brown forehead. In honour of his status, every set of eyes swivelled with what felt like the weight of the supernatural as the Circle offered him their attention, yet respect-earned did not disguise the hungry urgency that seemed to roll off the gathering. They'd been here before. *Yet never-*

Never under such crippling circumstances. This time… this cycle he feared-

Sinuhé raised his chin – the pose in itself a stance of readiness to do battle. Carefully, *deliberately,* he shunned the now empty seat in their midst: an empty seat to match an equally empty slab of dark, spell-wrought quartzite in the crypt. *Though he knew it impossible in this place between time, the air did seem too cold suddenly – quite as if the now redundant magic was leaking up from the rock below his feet, slowly purged from the raised stone chest no longer tied to Purpose and Life.*

It must not sway him, though. Not yet. Sinuhé had awakened with the knowledge that he must gather the Circle to his stratagem, but first things first. *There were ritual words to be spoken...*

He cleared this throat. "Guardians. The Upper Circle is awakened. With the Quickening, we are called. With the Quickening we serve as was sworn thrice to the Maker Alérathnar in Oaths and Blood, to bind and moderate differences under one purpose, one design, to preserve the Realms, to protect the Twins, and to raise the Veils against the Gods and their creatures of Chaos. Raise your right hand to prove heart and mind still bound to the truth of this pursuit. Say, Dai-varon – yes – that we might proceed."

A few blinks of pure, thick silence followed. *Dai-varon... the sacred reference and reminder of their oaths: to the Maker; to the cause.* It permeated the Circle – weighing like a poorly-executed Weave of entrapment against the Speaker's skin. He hoped the others would not notice the sensation; he hoped...

The silence drew long, an imaginary raindrop pulling impossibly against the laws of gravity. Unease peppered the air. *This could be it. Would they own up to the new flaws he alone knew gripped them all from within, or...*

"Dai'varon, let it be known: the Destiny of Ice and Blood stands ready," said Isavelia Cahmerhin of the Ermaron, the smoky, harsh quality of her voice sounding sure to the ear, as – raising a broad leathery hand in solemn response – she retained the appearance of an unshakable mountain.

The remainder of the Circle waited a beat, then voices intermingled as the remaining seven Guardians raised hands and spoke the prescribed words with barely a trace of the inconsistency they'd all awoken to. It must be curling like bands of restraint on their oaths, however – still Sinuhé almost sighed with temporary relief. If they spoke the words, they could make it well. He just needed time. They just needed patience. *Patience to listen and come around.*

Clearing his throat surreptitiously to face the hurdle that must come next, the Speaker raised his right hand, palm open to the Circle, and intoned, "Dai'varon Guardians, Let it be known that I, the Keeper of Chronicles, stand ready. Let it be known that I, the Speaker, have heard and accepted your word as truth. Now, in the Name Of All That Is; in the Name of Alérathnar the Maker, feel the peace of the Circle that binds to rule once more. Let it guide and strengthen you till the final breath of this cycle comes upon us. Let it be known: the council is now in session."

With an echo of designated fraudster singing within his conscience for saying the words that might no longer mean the same as they had done for millennia. The Maker's touch flowed through him and the gifted runes on his skin, with a paltry weakness he'd never before known – it might account for the perception of chill in the air and the detrimental concerns in his core, yet to his relief Sinuhé noted that there was still solace to be found in the way the deep-bass rumble of his voice carried easily even if it hadn't been aided by the Oratorio's impressive acoustics. One of the small tricks from his previous days, that power was still his. It had lent peace on many an occasion, be it amidst the Circle of Guardians or at a conference table, neck deep in negotiations, and it would do so again in this gathering! *Small things. Small things mattered.* This wasn't just a hard misfortune for him. It was going to prove a trial for every one of them. *What would emerge from it all?* He prayed not 'everything'. *Not if he could help it.*

Face smoothed into a mask of serenity that had on occasions been dubbed theatre-worthy, Sinuhé shifted bright azure eyes over the assembly, wondering now if anyone else would prove brave enough claim the floor and make their stand known?

He wanted to speak first, but to appear too eager? To push his point?

Sinuhé rubbed the fingertips of his left hand together with an edge of nervous distraction, but the Oratorio seemed sterile now and he felt overtaken by a sense of impatience. The air was too frigid; no one seemed particularly ready to reveal whether they saw him as a saviour of 'face' or a hindrance. Certain eyes, betrayed by careless disregard, wandered freely to gauge Commander Denarlin's mood rather than centre on the Speaker as might have been expected – or at least preferred. *Was open conflict really still on their minds? It could be disastrous if they would not consider-*

The Speaker mentally bandaged the snake bite of irony – right at the very moment fellow Guardian Thessilia Emara caught his eyes, mouth pulled firmly crooked in a mirthless smile to compliment the persistently raking light of challenge writhing within the depths of her all-too-black gaze.

Like the rest of the assembly she was facing the large sunken circle from the ornately carved cathedra, but unlike the other Guardians, Emara's sophisticated, pointy-posed face showed arched reservation.

Sinuhé nearly opened his mouth to speak, then refrained, suddenly convinced he'd win more favour, were she honoured with attention, not dismissal. It was a tricky allowance, but maybe she'd back down. *Maybe...*

For a heartbeat the set to her black gaze traced the lofty heights of an imaginary parapet as she appeared taken aback by his strategy, then her fine lips twisted: held as though strained by metal wire in a grimace that might have looked a smile to many – yet for those familiar with her antics, could bode only trouble.

It made him rescind the idea that she should be allowed to speak. *When had Emara ever backed down?! If she turned the Circle with her rhetoric...*

Shifting slightly, the Speaker offered her a benign frown though it was far from genuine. *He was on tender alert. Was she bluffing?*

Leaning forward just a fraction of an inch as though she meant to glide to her feet, Emara glared with near-lewd confidence at the Speaker, and he shifted in alarm. In turn, she halted mid-move to flick an imaginary speck of dust from the tight, golden cloth of her left sleeve but the Speaker had already been propelled into action; had already set one foot inside the circle before realising that she'd successfully snared him. *The floor was his and he'd stumbled forward: spooked like a Toledo fawn.*

Gritting his teeth inwardly, he brushed off the deceit. For a Guardian of mostly Human-descent, Emara had ever been wily! Of course, she'd want to know what she'd be up against. Of course! *She'd just made him seem a blundering half-wit, and now – whatever he had to say – she'd be protesting, attacking the format of his appeal from a point of chosen offence or defence as she saw fit. Of course, she would.*

Their eyes clashed. She awarded him just the briefest nod – a gesture somewhere between deference and insult – and with a flare of quickly-drenched resentment for the way she'd so successfully manipulated him into action, Sinuhé inclined his head in her direction.

So throw down the gauntlet then, Guardian Emara! I know what you wish for but you will not win this one without a persuasive argument! Not unless the Commander shares your sentiment, in which case...

"Fellow Guardians," he managed just shy of a hiss as he turned from her, "if you'd be kind enough to let me open the council, then hark my words and grant me patience even when you might find yourselves straining towards opposition. You see… I have a plea. A request of sorts for you to consider. And make no mistake Guardians, for consider it you must, although what I must propose is not of what you might deem 'regular character'."

Sinuhé paused. From the corner of his eye, he saw Guardian Emara move to tap a sharp nail against a front tooth in feinted intrigue, but he pointedly refused to grant her sleep-pale face even a fraction of interest. *She'd pushed him. She'd not throw him again!*

"Fellow Guardians," he carried on with rekindled equilibrium and flourish, "Recent events haunt our footsteps as could only a Blight Rider, and indeed, I feel the eagerness of the Circle that we must now rise to mete out justice directly: as is right; as is fair. However, understand now that this is why, in my unfortunate duty as Speaker and Chronicler, that I must demand of you a moment of patience to reflect on caution in this matter, so-"

A few disbelieving exclamations issued across the Circle, forcing him to pause. As could've been predicted, Guardians Utarion, Orleara and Lucareo already seemed to have grasped the essence of his imminent proposal and they looked unimpressed. *Only one thing for it though…*

"Now, I ask you to recall the root of our Oaths along with the true path of our existence-"

Though he hadn't meant to, the Speaker was forced to cut his own sentence short again, when loud dissent from the very same Guardians met his words, drowning a fair chance to be heard without shouting. It released tension though – and if he didn't enjoy their show of open agreement, he still brokered the interruption with a collected mien and a slightly belligerent frown: an offering of both grace and warning.

Yet if a traditionally cautious Guardian like Lucareo found himself so readily of similar persuasion as the hit-first-make-peace-later Utarion, was his already a doomed process? Truly, would they rather be reckless then? Regardless of the past, regardless of what hidden pitfalls they might face?

Sadly, he could not even pretend at surprise, and though reluctant, the Speaker could not help the reaction then; a quick look at Guardian Thessilia's face told him more than a bunch of scathing words – and once again, it was all but impossible not to look towards the emptiness in their midst.

With a placating mien and a gesture to convey his understanding to the Circle, the Speaker took another step forward, 'casually' removing the vacant seat from his peripheral view. With a voice blooming with tones of reason, he coaxed, "Guardians, please... you misunderstand. I too, appreciate the need to act. Indeed, how could I not? But mark my words, and mark them well; the Long Sleep has revealed to me no further insight by which to cast light upon... *upon the circumstances of our loss.*"

The Speaker lowered his gaze. In deliberate tones of regret, concluded, "Guardians, I understand that what we do next will prove crucial to the way we intend to shape the present, and thereby the future. Regardless of your righteous wrath, please, if you have some tidings to counter my suggestions – nay, if you have any intelligence *at all* – then by the Maker speak of it now to enlighten the Circle or else honour my word with fair reason."

He wasn't proud. This was not the best reprieve but those very words would force them to ponder the unhealthy details of their personal 'afflictions'- and hopefully put a dampener on their vengeful spirits. Of course, it could crack the barrel open in the opposite direction too: could have them all doubly insistent upon action just to hide the extent of the calamity that had robbed them of 'sight' and 'power' during the Long Sleep, but he didn't think they'd openly reveal such weaknesses. *At least… not yet, because for now Guardian Envalair's demise would be considered the priority. It must, and it might just be enough to distract if he could curb this council as intended.*

Leaving the silence to fester, Sinuhé's eyes crawled along the multi-coloured intricate pattern of the Oratorio's unbroken wall mosaic. *This was all about caution. Silence could be as powerful as speech; his next words must be right.*

"Now what the Circle must understand, is that I do not speak lightly of caution," he ventured slowly then, gaze returning to the people facing him. "However, our duty to the Maker stands prime, no matter our personal persuasions or the specific inklings we might once have held before the Oaths. And thus I beg you to recall that we have a duty to take the most efficient action: the most beneficial – *not to us* – but to the Twins, and the Realms, and the Veils."

A smattering of sporadic mumbles met his petition. *They still did not appreciate where he was going, but his appeal to their conscience was taking an effect.*

"Guardians," he pushed, indeed more bluntly than had ever been his style, "what I wish to remind the Circle today is that we cannot confuse the need for retribution with the task that we were given Life to pursue. To do so is to break Oath. To do so is to break Faith."

The statement killed the mumbles and the new, purer silence was telling. Once more stamping himself a jester for speaking on matters of faith, still, he carried on, "I know your hearts pull you one way, but we cannot yet seek confrontation. It is undoubtedly what the Mad Ones expect, and I say to you this: let us now not oblige these imposters-masking-as-Gods. Our time will come, but with good reason, it is not to be yet!”

Conveying her emotional state from across the Circle, the genteel Guardian Arachk'thea found his eyes. The tiny iridescent scales of her normally golden-red skin turning an uncanny tinny colour as she held his gaze, Sinuhé nodded his understanding. Next to Arachk'thea, Guardian Orleara simply devised to frown – a thing of secret complications on the Guardian's dark vulpine features and a sharp contrast with the sudden brooding spied upon Utarion's hard wide face, but they were all telling.

It was what he'd needed to happen, though. They would not enjoy the reminders served, but as hoped – and in spite of instincts – the assembly appeared reluctant to counter his logic. Certainly, Guardian Mehand'Arun seemed to reek of deeper contempt than usual, of course, and even if the stout, pale-haired Isavelia Cahmerhin looked angry with herself to be contemplating the sanity of his words, it was all showing more promise than heartbeats earlier.

In the quiet, Thessilia Emara shared a veiled look with Lucareo who stroked his neatly-cropped golden beard pensively in response. Ever a distraction, the Mazes on Lucareo's wide ornate wristbands whispered for attention, but the Speaker still had enough eye for the rest of the room to note how Emara didn't even dare to look at their Commander. To do so, she too would have to look at Envalair's now-vacant seat on Denarlin's right, and though the Speaker silently urged her to do it, he knew she couldn't.

“So now you preach to us about caution, Guardian Speaker Sinuhé Sedjem-Alhath'naar.” Emara sounded bitter.

As if to emphasise, she offered him a thin smile, the wire stretching. “Well, I suppose it holds a certain logic, so humour me. What would you have us do? Caution never served us before, and yet you now think we'd serve the Maker best by doing nothing? By quelling instinct and stilling vengeance?"

Almost she cast their Commander a questioning look, but her eyes never quite obliged intent and she turned instead back to Sinuhé. "Honoured Speaker, I must be mistaken, but do you speak as though we are not still of sound nature, for a reason?"

Not of sound nature? For a blink Sinuhé's breath caught. Thessilia Emara was watching him with a strangely analytical expression – virtually as if she was as knowledgeable as he, but... *but no! Thessilia could not know! She could not know...*

He opened his mouth to speak.

"Oh forgive me, Guardian Sedjem-Alhath'naar,-" she overruled with dripping sarcasm before he'd uttered a sound, "-you do of course still command the floor so perhaps there is somewhat else you feel a duty to share with the Circle? Something to account for this... *this charade?"*

Shock permeating, this time the Speaker felt the silence directed against himself. *It seemed to trickle from the walls.* From the corner of perception he sensed a flash of unease just as Guardian Rhindarhlar Mehand'Arun's softly-slanted, gem-like eyes seemed to flare: the sudden intrigue, a near physical touch. *This would not do!*

"Guardian Emara," Sinuhé started, "you really must-"

"Must I?" Guardian Emara injected as she gripped the ornate, lacquered armrests of her seat to lean forward. "But are we not the Guardians of the Upper Circle? Are we not *the Plague that Scours?* Guardian Speaker, I'm keen to know now: how did *we* ever serve caution?"

"Guardian, I can assure-"

"It's just that I fail to marry up the intent with understanding." Guardian Emara's tone seemed as physical as a cutting blade. "Tell me

Guardian Speaker, would you have us forget what happened? Is that it? Would you prefer to overlook the fact that Guardian Envalair was cut from our ranks at the pinnacle of events – as though he were not the Maker's Avatar; as though he had no protection? Tell us: would you allow *the Mad Ones* to go unpunished for what they did – because even if it splits the Upper Circle, I will not!"

Solancei's Memoirs

The Province of Tarléon.
Ocean's End.
Autumn of 780 P. C. W.

So here's the thing… I was a goodly mile onto what we used to call the 'grave-ice', my parents were about to swim this sub-zero lagoon for eternity, and for mercy, the Prefect (as old as the ice itself) knew well how to give his crowd a good send-off, but to me, it hardly mattered. I'd been to other funerals, but on that day the man projected only meaningless dross.

You see, my grief lay not where expected: did not have much to do with the two special caskets containing the bodily remains of the people I had named 'parents'. For sure, theirs had been an untimely demise – however, in all of my then-short life, I'd barely known the two adults well enough to address them by anything more than noble titles.

I never minded that. Or at least I didn't think so until later I realised my own lies. Still, back on that day, and for a long time after – by sheer default I could not lament their passing, nor think it more than an odd curiosity. *Yet if wishes had had wings…*

Yet I sensed on this day that the ice would not hide me anymore, and besides: as the only daughter of the deceased Lord and Lady, I couldn't very well have just run off anyway. At least, not this time. *Taliana would-*

Now oddly, this was the moment where the snow-dusted ice at my feet caught a lance of the bitter sun, forcing me to blink rapidly though it hardly cut the eye. *Taliana would do nothing. Ever again…*

As I think back, I believe myself immune, yet in truth, I might never be. The Gods-cursed feeling of loss is as raw now as it was back then, and I pray you understand.

See, I know what it does to a person to lose the thing you care most about in this life. It happened to me on the day that bloody messenger galloped into the lower bailey of Ivanor, flogging his ice-encrusted, steaming courser to run without care for limbs or life to deliver the devastating news that my parents had perished in a coach accident along with several other people, including Taliana.

Sometimes I have wondered if something within me broke that day, or if I was already just simply born this way, but I hadn't been aware of my own cold loneliness until that moment, and now the fact remained that my parents were not the only people missing from my world.

Fleck, how I struggled that day on the ice. I might have harboured little real attachment to either of the deceased we'd all come out to honour, but Gods' mercy on the world, the same could not be said for Mistress Scavino; the name 'Taliana' remained with me at this funeral like a promise on a birthday, simultaneously punishing my efforts in thought and haunting my memories like a curse!

My lady, my teacher, my ally... gone...

I felt my thoughts made the hollow edge sift: threatening to ford the gap between myself and the splinter of grief I'd otherwise managed to bury successfully deep and I feared that were I to let go; were I to allow myself the pleasure, I'd shame myself in front of all these already grieving people.

In result, I must have blinked a dozen times then, burrowing into the hollow; nurturing the gap: widening, deepening. Yet escape was not easy. My mother's handmaid who'd nursed me and kissed my scraped knees and taught me how to plait my too-straight dark hair in a multitude of Iddian designs that would leave it pleasantly wavy upon unravelling; the woman who'd shown me how to conceal a dagger in a sheath attached to the shin, even when in a dress; the lady who'd put me to bed every night and had taught me letters and numbers... *that Taliana... that Taliana...*

For shame I'd realised too late that the 'shades of ceremony' had 'stolen' away the woman's wrapped remains in the early mists on a morning days ago to be unceremoniously incinerated in the castle furnaces – because even in spite of her standing, Taliana had still been a foreigner here and thus not entitled to rest within the ice core of Ocean's End.

Perhaps it was just that I was 'hollow' and alone, my grief as cold as the winter of my province as it clapped its icy palms around my heart and squeezed, but as I fought the tears, I felt… I felt…

Well, needless to say, I felt cheated by men and Gods alike! Sadly, it wouldn't be the first time. Nor – as life would have it – the last.

Solancei

The Sense to Prevail

The Circle erupted in murmurs of subtle question and mild alarm.

As speaker of the Upper Circle, Sinuhé's expression never altered, yet from his perspective of Chronicler and Guardian, Thessilia Emara's rebellious words raised a fundamental need to query her mental state. He could not speak without revelations pulling to life, however, and so, for the greater 'must', he unhurriedly folded his hands within the wide girth of his drooping sleeves.

"I should urge Guardian Emara to choose how she frames the arguments of her desires and bruised feelings – lest she's seen to forget the very oath she just renewed before the Circle and the Maker."

Thessilia tutted as though to dismiss a child's inconsequential comments. Her bristling curls floating wide in a gesture of impatience, she sprawled back on her perch to look up at the dome where from bright iridescent light of the Void ascended like spell-cast sunlight.

Sighing as if over the failure of finding whatever she'd been searching for above, she trained her attention back on Sinuhé, contempt re-loaded in her features like the wrath of a viper on the cusp of striking. "My dear, dear Guardian, take no offence, but how do you see us capable of turning a blind eye to the slight we've suffered?! If we do, are we then not acting against our Oaths; if we do, are we then not truly diminished? Seems clear that you advocate a path where if taken, we might as well offer up our names for destruction, for then we are lost."

Something about her tone worked something under his skin. With a near-bark, he refuted, "Guardian Emara, you give me no credit!"

"And yet there is truth to her word," Paimar Utarion commented, surreptitiously rubbing his heavy fists as though in anticipation of breaking the skull of a Venzoian Drehstragian.

"The Maker bear witness, there is no truth!" Sinuhé revoked with a streak of vehemence, "not yet, anyway!"

Utarion's scarred eyebrow – made striking by the Maker's rune drawn red and gold straight through the old injury – twitched in surprise at the outburst and the Speaker reined in frustration to claw back a strain of his usual aplomb. It partly worked.

"My unreserved apologies to the Circle," he managed, inclining his head just a fraction. "Of course, I recognise your conflict! I was working towards addressing these misconceptions, so if you could please rein in your impatience for just a small time longer, and-"

"Oh, I shall rein in my impatience good Speaker," Guardian Emara interrupted with barbed acerbity, "if you would then remember not to insult our Heritage with pointless chit-chat."

"Guardian Emara, you go too far! This is hardly chit-chat!"

Emara simply smirked. *Hex upon the woman!*

Applying another small trick, this one to create 'space', he said, "You already know that I do not ever knowingly insult, so should you feel wronged by my words, then accept my humble apology. It was not my intention to sow ill-will."

The Speaker found an expression to match the words. It worked. The Circle settled anew and like a touchy queen put upon to share rule, Thessilia issued a muffled sound in her throat but glanced away with an acute gesture of dismissal. She was of course not pacified but he'd managed to temporarily shame her into compliance.

It allowed him the freedom to adjust his stance slightly to catch a furtive glimpse of Commander Denarlin. None of them would like what he'd say next either, but mercifully, personal emotions carried no weight with the Commander and the Speaker expected this to remain unaltered even when it came to matters of fallen brethren. Of them all, the First Guardian had ever been level-headed reason personified; objective and ruthless. *Yet with everything changing?*

Sadly, Denarlin's pale, lean face fostered no notions of assurance nor failure. In fact, nothing in his serene expression hinted at his thoughts or feelings on the matter, provoking instead a stab of unease within Sinuhé. If their Commander spoke the word, they'd all ride to war with retaliation on their minds and destruction in their hearts – and there'd be nothing that he or anyone else could do about it. *Was he doing enough to promote Denarlin's understanding, or…*

He forced personal qualms to rest. The Circle was waiting for him to speak. Rhetoric and grace had won him the right and Denarlin was not rash. *Would that he knew whether the Commander still had the Sight: it would've helped him greatly to know this but… well, there was something else he was not likely to find out.*

Despite his own better judgement, the Speaker offered their First Commander a veiled look of inquiry, but if he'd hoped for a hint of support, hoped for a sign to indicate the direction of the Commander's views, he stood sorely disappointed when Guardian Denarlin simply returned the look without a sliver of emotion upon his even features. *It would be as expected. One challenge at a time. One challenge.*

With a sudden lump in his throat, Sinuhé glanced away. *He'd begun but where would it end?* It wasn't just the failure of the past, which haunted.

It was also the hitherto unknown entity of 'uncertainty' and what they would do without a full Circle.

To top it, the Witches were no more. Their army had reduced to all but a handful of renegades camping on the edge of lawlessness, and no longer might they rely upon the help of mortals as they once had. *How to deal with the issue of magic and the shattered astrolabe? How to win without the use of their usual strength and power? And most bewildering of all: how to search out the Alscara and Tarvia in time without the Sight?* Thessilia sensed that something was amiss. Did the others? Would it make his task easier if he revealed the additional weakness that seemed to have slithered in amongst their ranks like an assassin through the backdoor or would they all resent him for such brute exposure?

Sinuhé Sedjem-Alhath'naar looked up to the dome, perhaps searching for similar strength as Thessilia. Many things he knew, some he suspected, and yet? *Unfortunately, he still had a very uncanny idea of what his fellow Guardians might do, should he speak too frankly on matters of perceived personal character…*

"So Guardian Emara enquired what I would have us do?" This time Sinuhé deliberately looked towards the gaping presence of the empty seat in their midst. *It stood surety to harden his resolve: to validate his arguments! No more dancing round!*

"I do not query whether Guardian Emara is right or not," he relented, changing tactics. "We cannot allow the Mad Ones even half a chance of success! With their boldness, they have injured us gravely, weakened us! And yes they must feel empowered by their success – indeed, if they could do what they did to Guardian Envalair, what's to stop us from assuming they could do the same to any one of us now?"

Eyes on him, no one answered, but their attention never wavered.

Sinuhé sighed, meandering regret leaping forth. "Fellow Guardians, let me speak plainly: there are changes to everything we once took for granted! We face dangers previously unknown to us and the future is at stake – perhaps truly for the first time – and so I must sue for patience until certain questions might be resolved so to grant us insight and surety of success. That is what must take precedence over an outright attack."

"The Speaker is of course right," the willowy Guardian Jonaeus Lucareo allowed, shrugging to himself as he pensively rubbed the contours of his neatly-trimmed beard. Framing each Guardian with a stare of golden eyes, he continued, "As the Speaker says: the changes are indeed countless. In truth, I fear the illusion would be to expect that we must not make alterations to adjust, for as it stands we are still blinded by ignorance and as I see it, new dangers remain hidden beneath these unchartered sands. Slip once and one might adjust, but slip twice and the sink-hole may swallow you beyond retrieval. Guardians, they took one of us. It could happen again. I understand this."

The Speaker nodded. *Precisely.*

"For the first time the path to victory is flawed; unclear," he reiterated, building on the facts, "We need information to form new strategy! Guardians, so many questions beckon! Questions about the Artefact: *how to find it? how to restore it?* But also others; you have probably all made your own considerations – and now is the time to find the answers. Otherwise… well, otherwise I fear we may yet fail!"

Again Lucareo nodded, almost sagely, "Yes, we are faced with a number of conundrums beyond anything we've met in the entirety of the Upper Circle; the Speaker serves up a point! We simply cannot allow ourselves to err in this. Our hearts might yearn for revenge, but our actions must have sound strategic value!"

Faces like carved stone looked at the golden-eyed Guardian one beat longer, then met the Speaker's eyes as he looked around. He knew they 'felt' his words and knew how his logic would grate upon their resolve but it was necessary. He did not like this setback any more than they but he had to build on this!

"We need time but the Maker has granted us just that!" he resumed, "the Quickening has called us early. We have time to bury arrogance and haste: time to resume our investigations where we were forced to leave off. If we can re-fortify our power and understanding; if we can turn over all the details of errors old so better to comprehend them, then we will be armed to act accordingly once the need arises."

"And this passive stance," Isavelia Cahmerhin, their wide-set third-in-command, enquired with studied interest, "What exactly would it entail, Guardian Speaker? We Quicken for a reason! You say we have time? How much? I feel only that the time is ripe for us to act, so explain to us: with everything that's happened, can we truly afford to investigate? What if we waste what's given?"

"Captain Cahmerhin, if those are your only questions then let me counter you with this: what makes you think that we can afford *not* to investigate?" Sinuhé shot her a candid look. "After all, we are at a clear disadvantage right now, are we not?"

Guardian Cahmerhin grimaced just once and unconsciously shifted her powerfully muscled body as though in sudden discomfort. Sinuhé eyed her, exhaled softly, and hid the sentiment that he was secretly pleased she did not currently choose to claim the floor for when the Ermaron woman left her seat she was an impressive sight – nearly a head and a half taller than Sedjem-Alhath'naar himself and hard to broker with for the sheer sense of her 'presence', not to mention the poisonous needles secreted at her wrists.

He was long past believing she might lash out at him, of course, but Cahmerhin had never been friendly. *Perhaps the pins were a comfortable reminder that not everything had changed?*

Cahmerhin considered him numbly for a few blinks more. Then, with a shrug of final surrender, she said, "Your point is sustained, Guardian Speaker."

Sinuhé nodded. *Not friendly, no – but there was understanding now. Good…*

From the corner of his eye he saw Isavelia Cahmerhin flash the First Guardian a look across the wide circle of polished night – as though she sought to weigh her compliance through his reaction – but like earlier, their general gave nothing away. The Speaker suspected that the Commander would reserve his judgement for later. *Either that or else! High time now to push this home…*

"I thank the esteemed Guardian Cahmerhin for her gracious ability to align her thoughts with my own,-" the Speaker told her and offered up a small concession as he continued, "-the Circle knows that our task has never been easy. In spite of our 'gifts', there is ever danger in the path we've been set – yet this is my point exactly. Right now, I wish for you all to remember that we sit here diminished in number! And why? How? Have you the answer? Guardian Emara? Commander Cahmerhin? Anyone else? No?"

Guardian Cahmerhin jolted at his words – as if physically jabbed in the chest – and he knew her solidly in his court then. In comparison, Guardian Orleara's swarthy face was smooth as death again and yet he saw her study the Maker's markings around the edges of her hands with intensity – a thing he knew her guilty of when seriously considering an issue. A sporadic few nods were offered his way now as he looked around – not enough for him to feel sanguine; not yet, but there was a tone of compromise in the air nevertheless…

That still left Thessilia Emara. His words would have been a harsh reminder of her personal involvement in their fellow Guardian's demise and in spite of his own convictions on the matter, he was not intentionally trying to rile her. She held herself with quiet fury. It tore at him like a physical thing; with one stripping look, she silently scolded him, then looked away, once more deliberately dismissive. *She was not going to let this go. So much for the idea of a compromise…*

Allowing the silence to work its web again, Sinuhé pretended not to see Emara grow stone-faced as he moved again to look directly at the Guardian in charge, *searching…*

Commander Denarlin appeared cloaked in grim thought. Gaze lowered, mind veiled by habit, pale face obscured by a long ream of dark hair, Denarlin could have been made of cold life still, but of course he'd Quickened like the rest of them and he was here now – even if the tilt of his chin found the Speaker questioning whether their leader's thoughts concerned the problems at hand or something else entirely.

With his eyes, Sinuhé Sedjem-Alhath'naar nudged the man. *If he could but glean a hint…*

Their Commander looked up – a clipped shift in the downward slant of his jawline to raise eyes and attention where it had been requested: Denarlin focused on the Speaker in a blink between breaths that made the geometric path of the Maker's runes upon his right temple flash black silver in the diaphanous light as if to herald strange warning.

Of course, it was but a trick of the eye – the First Guardian only offered him a tempered luminous stare and a vague nod. *Carry on…*

At the uncommitted gesture, a need to exhale frustration clawed through the Speaker. With his peripheral vision, he noted Guardian Emara straighten on her seat, resolutely squaring her shoulders as if preparing to do battle whilst seated. It happened a little too fast. He'd barely time to turn his face.

"Guardian Speaker," she began, a little too controlled, "I respect your candour. I hear your conviction and perhaps the reasons are sound. But… but I cannot condone the idea of 'waiting'. Indeed frankly…

"Well frankly, I'd rather arm wrestle Osari'Chi himself and call him brother than opt for your illusion of control!"

Osari'Chi? Brother? The scenario was shocking. Sinuhé covered his aversion, but others did not bother and for a moment Emara seemed cloaked in their open revulsion.

"Madam Guardian, you bend my speech to your own obliterating purpose-" he accused whilst she was still pinned down, "-and your choice of words is as ill-received as they are spoken. Still… I understand.

"However, reveal to me this: would you verily be so quick to walk into our enemy's lair without further knowledge? You would not! You cannot! Guardian, this time there can be no glitches; there can be no avenue left to chance and-"

"Nothing, good Speaker-" Thessilia interrupted, a flash of anger lifting the strands of her vivid hair on new, invisible fingers, "-nothing, I repeat, was left to chance when last, we denied the Mad Ones! We did as we must, yet still-!"

"Well my point in fact!" he shot back.

Thessilia Emara shook her head, curls writhing. For a blink, she looked as feral and cornered as the first time he'd seen her. "Your point in words, Guardian Speaker, is not in sync with mine. You wish for us to question our skills? Our power? For what, when we did nothing wrong?

"We could have prepared then in a hundred different ways; adjusted and procrastinated until the Veils were no more and still the outcome would have been the same: Guardian Envalair would have reacted no differently. He would have been lost regardless!"

Lifting her chin a fraction, Guardian Emara looked around, clearly daring the Circle to argue. No one did.

"We have already talked and deliberated, mulled and deciphered,-" she said with conviction rendered volatile from agitated concern. The Speaker shook his head, but she shrugged, continuing, "-and for what? We spent time on the issue! We sought the council of the Sabén-Heshep and the Watchéran. The Tapestry held no answers, their moss-covered procrastinating council had no insight, and as for the historical record? Guardian, have we not managed to determine that there is nothing more to learn from this by feeble enquiry and dusty records? Have we not managed to determine that now is the time to venture into the field? Surely, if the Long Sleep showed you otherwise, pray enlighten us Guardian Speaker, otherwise...?"

Sinuhé hesitated. Chancing that he might overstep his mark, yet in need of making a salient point, he said, "Guardian Emara, your personal lust for vengeance is rightly justified but so is the Commander's for that matter – and still you don't see him clamouring to draw forth as though the Void is about to be invaded by the Mad Ones themselves.

"Are you truly so desperate to follow in Guardian Envalair's footsteps that you'd throw away the value of your own Oath just to have it your way? Surely you might honour his memory by considering all avenues more clearly before you spit in the eye of Fate and wander blindly amongst the Enemy!”

“Blindly?” For a moment all the Speaker saw was Thessilia’s anger. With a flicker of concern, he realised that he’d nearly said too much but could not dwell as Emara bristled like a burr.

“Now what exactly are you saying here, Guardian Speaker? Are we saying then, that I am not capable of carrying out my Oath just because I do not fear the Mad Ones and their spawn? Is that it?”

Relief engulfed him; the angry frown on his forehead unravelling. *Mercy, she’d come close to making a connection there; for a blink, he’d thought-*

“We fear nothing, but perhaps we should.”

The Speaker startled, his head swivelling along with the assembly to look at Guardian Orleara.

Elbows bent and fingers stippled before her lupine features, the other Guardian was staring at them with ringed citrine eyes made luminous by the truth of her persuasion. There was a candour there that Sinuhé had rarely seen in the trickster Sunerai: something near-tangible.

He hoped she would be able to forward a persuasive point; he hoped she would say something to end this debacle, otherwise…

"What's the matter? Can't get the girl you want?"

Solancei heard the teasing, double-edged words fly forth before she could check herself, but didn't much care anyway. The perfectly-honed New Wood accent helped add slight to every syllable and with her eyes locked upon her sparring partner in casual readiness, her sardonic 'concern' held just the right measure of caustic disdain to make his nostrils flare, if only for a broken heartbeat.

It was precious little to feel encouraged by, but hey... right now she'd take what she could and run with it; the banter was a welcome chance to relieve some of the stress that came with the fact that she'd been stupid enough to almost let a rookie mistake cost her this jackal fight in the very first round. *It was not good enough!* She was uncommonly distracted today; for this, her mentor would have her guts – and worse. The thought made her want to grimace. *She didn't.*

"Oh you may rest assured wench: I always get the 'girl' I want!" her opponent told her with a chilling slow drag of syllables. "It's only ever a question of time – but I like to prolong the chase since it is by far the most enjoyable part."

Smirking just enough to show his words were not meant to be all good-natured, the pale-eyed man faced her with a wolfish smile and flourished his haitu as if to remind her of the threat he posed, but she did not retreat, and he was unfortunately not put off.

"Now clearly," he continued lightly, "you must be of a similar persuasion or we would not still be finding ourselves in filth to our boot laces, now would we?"

Sweeping a creeping unease aside and looking pointedly down her own once-green, now mud-splattered leathers, Solancei kept her feelings under lid.

"Speak for yourself," she warned with a disdain-ripped grin, "As of yet, I can assure you there is no filth upon *my* laces! Nor, might I add, do I intend there to be anytime soon, but hey… chase me for pleasure if you like. It's all you'll get, I fear."

Somewhere, someone in the audience guffawed their appreciation for the remarks, but the individual was lost in amongst the crowd of impersonal, swathed forms that made up the undulating ranks of spectators and neither Solancei nor her opponent gave them a second glance. Instead, he touched her with a hard smile as though to mock the perception of humour, and it occurred to her that he was very good at this game too. *Still*…

As she scrutinized him across the vertical slant of her raised wooden blade, *the haitu,* hoping to gain some kind of insight into his flaws or weaknesses whilst they both caught their breath getting ready for the second round, Solancei drew on her self-discipline not to let her recrimination spread, but her nuisance was steadily brewing. *The spitting rain, the crowd, the foul back-yard stench, the thought of having no choice but to curb her skills, the memory of this morning's statutory argument with Iambre, her continuous problem reaching and linking with the State of Veranto*… yes, it was all a pretty stack-up.

As though in confirmation, water ran from one of her tightly wound plaits down the back of her ear, splitting: one rivulet soon soaked up by her raised leather collar, the other rolling forward along her jaw to drip off her chin. She dragged the back of her simple leather vambrace across her face too late to matter. It was pointless. She wished she'd never come here but Klaas could be so damn persistent. Now she'd probably catch a cold, which might force her to bed for days, possibly leaving Ina and Palea to care for her, and she could already hear their complaints.

But for her present situation, Solancei could've rolled her eyes at the image. Instead, she rolled her neck, hoping to catch an opening; a glitch in her opponent's odd veneer; anything to show her the way to success.

As of yet, she was without luck and the rain was getting heavier. In truth, she wanted to get the fight underway again anyway, but Zanzier seemed to enjoy the interlude of banter and she could still hear the clink of coins exchanged on wagers. She supposed it gave them a stronger sense of participation, but Gods!

In her head, she turned pragmatic. Since there was no choice but to stay here and get soaked, why disappoint?

"So *Simaro* – or whatever you do wish to call yourself whilst slumming it in a jackal fight?"

Focusing her eyes on the man she was fighting, she grinned insolently. "-I guess it's not every day this backward city has the honour of entertaining a queen of my character? Say, what would you wager against the possibility that I will have you on your back within the next quarter turn? We can go both ways on that if you like, though a hot tip would be *not* to bet against the lady."

Winking like a conspirator, she whirled her own haitu twice in a tight circle as to punctuate the words. A few sporadic laughs made it through the downpour and someone shouted out a dare, but if it was to salute her wit or to ridicule her opponent she couldn't tell. Simaro himself looked ever unmoved and Solancei felt like kicking him just to get a different reaction.

"So what d'you say?" she pushed, "Care for an additional gamble?"

"Gamble?" Simaro shot back at her. "Gods grey-eyes, I wasn't even going to lower myself to a reply but you have the sweetest tongue. Say: if it matches an equally sweet furrow, your efforts here seem wasted, no?"

It was almost not worth it, but in response, she raised a dark eyebrow and flashed him a tired, sardonic look.

"If you like, we can make wagers on the likelihood of you ever finding out about that too, but the odds will not be in your favour this time either," she warned him sweetly.

Nodding his head as though with a dawning understanding of something he hadn't previously thought about, Simaro cocked his chin as though better to judge her mettle. In a low voice, he told her, "Well I wouldn't be so sure grey-eyes. Perhaps I will have my men check it out when I land *first-touch*. After I put that shapely ass of yours in the dirt, of course."

Solancei ignored the ensuing heckles rolling off the spectators, some lewd, some telling her what to do to Simaro in turn. *Men! So predictable in most things, and yet…*

For a split beat, her eyes ran towards the three Regulators, charged with keeping the 'lock-down' until this fight was at an end and wagers settled. The men in question looked a formality; little more than cheap mercenary stock, although they had at least been furnished with padded shirts and surcoats, as well as suitably armed with seven-foot, spear-pointed halberds and identical short blades. The latter were currently sheathed at their hips whilst they guarded the temporary, makeshift wood- and wicker-gate erected to shut off the only exit from the brick-enclosed backyard, but as to the extent of their skills with said weapons…?

Seemed the good Simaro had a sense of humour after all. She grinned to herself, then dismissed their presence. *Usually, the Regulators had a bit more 'presence' about them, but hey…*

She glanced at her opponent with a denigrating look for his choice. She was pretty certain that Simaro himself stood surety for the fact that the Town Watch would not bother their gathering here today and in this case, she supposed it showed in his choice of soldiers. *Still… it was not one to pass up.*

"Oh I honestly think my honour quite safe," she told him with a teasing lilt of sympathy to her assumed accent as she dipped her chin towards the three guards, "But when I win, I shall buy them each wine and a whore with my returns, whilst you will have to make do for yourself, uselessly pondering how you could so foolishly have underestimated the sweet speed of my blade. Now, how's that, M'lord?"

Simaro simply tutted. "Grey-eyes, must I spend breath reminding you that sweet things have a tendency to sour? Why string out the inevitable? We both know that words are no substitute for skill. I feel generous, so you may end this now: throw up your haitu this instance and let me deliver *first-touch*. I swear on what God you want that this will be the sum of it."

His tone held a pleasantly persuasive lilt, so at odds with the situation that for a moment Solancei simply stared at him. *Of all the things she'd expected…*

A sudden hush fell over the backyard and his eyes slashed into hers, a light of strange candour building. "You can end this now," he repeated; simply. "A chance to walk away from this with everything you own intact. Consider our spectators now also. Would you have them linger to catch consumption? That hardly seems fair."

People muttered. Whispers of displeasure like waves of confusion and inherent disbelief. *Fair? Really?* Chancing an askance look at the scores of impersonal faces surrounding them in uneven rows of two to three deep along the grimy confines of the tall brick walls, Solancei almost burst out laughing. Without really meaning to, she looked for her mentor through the corner of her eye. Klaas Mehadja was nowhere in sight, of course, but that meant nothing – and she didn't bother entertaining Simaro's offer anyway. It was not in her spirit to back down. It never had been.

Her eyes skipped across the crowd again, and now she did smile. At this rate, the tempestuous weather of this province would render any pleasure of wagers-won a dubious delight indeed. And it served these Zanzierian double-standard pricks just right, she thought. Hunched against the elements and buried deep beneath cowls or wide-brimmed sodden hats, their oft-keen audience looked more than a little uncomfortable. Sure, their enthusiasm might soar or wean with the flow of action and it was of course also what determined her takings – but truthfully, right this very instance – she possessed little capacity to pity their choice.

She did not want to be here – that much was true – but her backside would not be worth a silver fleck if she left this thing unsettled. Klaas had sent her here to train and she was doing this for Iambre, and for her oaths, and for her peace of mind. In hilarious contrast, the audience needn't have come. *But they had.* By now they might have longed to be away from this enclosed courtyard with its damaged gutters, heavy stench of something rotten, and heightened chances of hefty-fines-including-visits-to-the-local-dungeon if caught by the Law – yet ultimately their lust to pocket favourable wagers had nevertheless brought them here. *So what did she care? Let them have the enjoyment – and choke on it!*

Shifting her balance, Solancei flicked her chin towards the nearest spectators.

"Your offer reeks," she told him flatly. "These people here all knew what they let themselves in for. We are all stuck here until this jackal fight is done. You seem so keen to end the game prematurely, but why? The wagers would be rendered void. Are you not equal to the task?"

As expected, people heckled in agreement then, projecting their contemptuous opinions through the rain as though their voices mattered. Her opponent's unusual offer was seriously pushing everyone's patience, she sensed – and she'd be more the fool to accept than to carry on. People wanted a fight, and in the dance of jackals where no rules figured, only one thing remained ever-sacred: *the first-touch*.

"I am not in the habit of fighting women for sport," he informed her, quite as though she was the only one not to realise this, "Or at least not out of the bedchamber, that is; my offer reeks? See, unless you avail yourself of it, you will never know how good. That I guarantee!"

"Oh honey," she flung at him with a peal of laughter, deliberately thickening the 'New Wood' accent, "You win no favours here."

"Then let's pretend I am offering you the opportunity of a graceful retreat because this is a special day. How's that?"

A crooked sense of humour awakening, Solancei's smile widened a notch. *Much one had to hear…*

"A special day?" she quested with badly drawn grace, "How bloody droll!"

"Gods girl, have you no sense?" Simaro sighed – she thought with genuine exasperation. "We all know that you will not be the victor here anyway. Avail yourself of this opportunity whilst you still can; I am rarely this generous, so take the offer. If you lack a place to stay for failure of winning, we can work something out."

"Hah – yep you'd sure like that," Solancei quipped, truly grinning now at his rude arrogance. *Men! Sometimes they were unbelievable, indeed!* "Your platitudes offend me and time goes wasted."

Simaro grimaced once. Then shrugging water-darkened, leather-clad shoulders, he raised his voice to be heard over the spectators' ensuing heckles against her disrespectful behaviour, "Grey-eyes... my rules, my dance. It's simple. Understand now that one way or another I will win. Do you think you can you afford to lose?"

"Oh I can afford a lot of things," Solancei retorted without pause, lips pulling into a wry smile. "But perhaps with all this talk, it is you who deliberately stalls? Do you perchance lack… stamina?"

Muted heckles saluted her crude insult. *Zanzier! Bloody typical!*

Her nose crinkled with distaste. If she carried on, surely she must raise something of use.

From experience she knew most men would have felt a sense of wounded pride gnawing at their temper by now – surely a true-born Zanzierian like Simaro must be feeling just a little disgruntled! *Surely, he must…*

Spinning her blade in another lazy circle, she let the casual sweep serve them all as a lingering reminder of his inability to pass her guard. Even without the State of Veranto to lend her focus and strength she was accomplished, yet he still seemed to believe her inferior. *Perhaps it was that early blunder…*

"What is ailing you, M'lord?" she taunted through catcalls and blunt comments and imagined – if but for a moment – to have spotted his lip curl in the direction of negative. "I would end this and be under roof by nightfall, but if you need to prolong every break…"

To keep herself loose, she spun the haitu yet again. The polished sandy-coloured practice blade winked dully in the rain; inviting. It was no longer the newest, nor the flashiest thing she owned, but it had won her more than a fair few victories, the worn appearances also furthering the promotion of her cover. With just a tad more luck, it would help her win this day as well. *If only she could get behind the man's veneer. If only…*

If only she also still had the use of Veranto, then-

Solancei ripped her mind from the sore subject before it could distract her from the man before her. *Fleck – and she'd done so well not raking up the embers around that problem, but now-*

Something she'd done – or maybe not done – found Simaro suddenly offering her a shaded smile. In a voice that cut in over the general din, he said, "Very well, grey-eyes. I see you will not bend and your words appear to have inspired our spectators' imagination, all right. Would that you knew the mistake you just made, but it can't be helped."

Spinning his own haitu in a provocative circle, the smile on his pale features turned toothy. "Final chance. Fold now. Does my offer not tempt?"

"Fold yourself," she retorted, never the one to let on the state of her fluctuating mind. Returning his insincere smile, she said, "I think you forgot I'm here to win this silly little game, not to culture undesirable liaisons. You are killing the fun and boring me to death, but perhaps that is your intention? Considering that glitch in your stamina and all!"

And with that, ever-ignoring the angry hiss of voices rising all around her, Solancei smiled defiantly, tilting her chin slightly upwards in her usual fashion that she knew to be both disarming and challenging.

"Well…" Simaro breathed the word under a breath that carried the tint of winter. His pale-blue eyes shifted across her features languidly, and she picked up the sense of subtle change.

A new readiness stabbed through her and though she tried to prevent it, her heartbeat sped up. *Finally.* Simaro's patience appeared spent, his expression suddenly lifting the veil of theatrics she hadn't even realised there.

Eyes flat as polished stone, his mouth distorted to expel a glob of spittle with the same virulent show of derision, as someone ridding themselves of a bad taste in the mouth and within blinks the spectators grew still – she sensed with anticipation.

Rolling his shoulder just once, Simaro looked colder than ice. *Perhaps it was the insult on his prowess? Perhaps it was spurning his offer? No matter what, this would soon be done, thank the Gods!*

Every word an icicle boring slowly into her, he said, "Grey-eyes, I pray you remember this later; I pray you recall how I told you that it's only ever a question of time. Only ever time!"

"Yeah honey, promises, whatever." Solancei simpered, hiding behind perfunctory cheek and earning herself a compact sidelong look off her opponent. She shivered; chilled by more than the weather.

Across from her, Simaro nodded without another word, dropping his haitu smoothly into the second ready-position, then began to circle with new purpose, this time a-gauche.

It was a relief. Solancei kept her face neutrally bland, yet retained a lingering light of mockery in her eyes as she sidestepped, gingerly mirroring his moves with the graceful care of a cat caught sneaking along the narrow ledge of a river barge.

Breathing out slowly through her nose, she ignored the cold rain though it had begun to leak past the collar of her worn leather jerkin. *Klaas and the State of Veranto be hanged; she could do this!*

Watching her with a denigrating expression, Simaro slipped a hand down his face, the action a seemingly unconscious effort to clear rain from his eyes but Solancei did not fall for his small show of off-handed casualness. It would have been a gross mistake; an invitation for him to take advantage whilst under the pretence of discomfort.

Submerging her own feelings beneath a feinted veil of indifference, she searched for an opening. She'd been in multiple jackal fights and had lived to push the offender's face in the dirt. She would do so again today. Somewhere amongst the heavily cloaked audience, someone called out a particularly poignant suggestion for the apparently-delicious shape of her 'saddle' – and feeling annoyed, she flicked the idiot an offending gesture without a single glance for his reaction.

It inspired another heckle but though it raised a few mutters, the words were muffled and could have been meant for either of the two combatants. Solancei let it slide. Simaro seemed oblivious.

"Sure you will not yield, bitch?"

She sniffed and gave him a sublime smile. "Go suck your ventail, rat! It'll be the dawn of a new century before I yield to you!"

"We'll see… we'll see, but done then," he concluded with strange lack of rancour, shifting his balance to circle the other way.

"Done indeed." She echoed, rectifying her stance to suit. With the words, a strange feeling of inevitability seemed to steal over her and she drew a breath to absolve it. *The flecking link to the State of Veranto was nowhere to be found within her. Above, the rain kept coming – huge drops like tears of the Gods, spilling down from the thoroughly grey-cloaked sky to soak everything straight to the bone with their misery. She'd known worse…*

With the back of one rain-darkened leather cuff, she allowed herself the luxury of clearing the water from her own eyes with an economic swipe.

"Let's see then, how much time you might steal for yourself, grey-eyes," Simaro invited, silver-veined haitu ready as he glided a step towards her. "Let's dance!"

"By the Hundred Ancestors!"

Guardian Utarion's disbelieving glare matched his dismissive outburst. Across the floor third-in-command Cahmerhin gasped in a most uncommon, daintily manner, and from near the Speaker, Mehand'Arun's caustic spirit flared as he issued a contemptuous snort that clearly mirrored Utarion's – but this…

This could be just what the Speaker needed.

With an expression so steady it might have rivalled a hovering hawk about to swoop down on prey, Guardian Orleara looked beyond the need of justification. "Guardians, what I am saying, is not that we are craven to consider an alternative, only that the Speaker has a point.

"What if we have truly overlooked the simple detail that could tip the scales out of favour once more? We'd be fools not to re-address the matter."

"The only thing that might tip the scale of anything will be found out there! Within the Realms themselves," Guardian Emara refuted, vehemence returning. "It's the only place we haven't searched! We must return to the Realms, go to Aellnaron! We need to corner the monsters in their halls and seize the answers we demand!"

"Guardian Emara, I beseech you! See the danger of your view!" Agonised by her blindness, the Speaker shook his head. "Is it not obvious that my aim is to ensure that none of us perishes like Envalair?! Surely you concur that mine is a reasonable avenue of approach; surely-"

"Envalair?" Thessilia Emara cut in, voice flat, sizzling anger held tight. "So is that what he is reduced to now? Envalair?"

Too late, Sinuhé realised his mistake even without looking at Guardian Denarlin – who'd doubtlessly be frowning now. Several Guardians mirrored the sentiment. Thessilia Emara had gathered her searing anger and held it close, but as though she could not contain it, nor herself, her consternation reared up but a blink later.

Words spilling like heart's blood, she said, "Richarmarlan Envalair was one of us, Guardian Speaker! Our second-in-command, if you are in fact still able to recall such fact?! Do not presume to denote him so easily. It is not your place and don't you forget it! Gods End, call him by his due title or do not mention his name at all!"

"But of course." Consternation flashed through Sinuhé. "Please, accept my apology. Dear Maker, it was not my intention, but it seems that in my haste to find your approval, I am in fact achieving just the opposite. Guardian Envalair will not be dishonoured, nor forgotten – and let me be the first to acknowledge that for the affront of his killing, our path will lead to war! I simply stand here to dispute the timing, nothing else!"

Thessilia flung him a suspicious stare and Sinuhé knew she'd be wondering what he was doing but it was suddenly simple. It hadn't been his motive to mention 'war' with the apology, but as though he'd weaved a little magic, the others appeared unexpectedly a sliver sharper; a sliver more honed by interest.

He nodded grimly, but at least he was telling them no lie. *There would be war. Eventually...*

Only Emara was not impressed and her stare deepened when Guardian Utarion mumbled to himself with a glint of magma in the eye, that if such be the case, the Speaker had won his support after all.

Ever-used to hot-headed Utarion's need to fight 'something', Sinuhé did not comment, but the change he'd been looking for was in the air, and indeed even Commander Denarlin had flexed a raven eyebrow in interest. *Good...*

Emara's scowl deepened. She sensed it too. Sinuhé had no doubt that she would've loved to box his ears right then. *It didn't matter.* The cold air no longer seemed chilling with 'loss', but with promise. *Seemed even the caretaking Elementals approved...*

"Guardians of the Upper Circle..." The Speaker drew himself up with new purpose. "War we will have – but how will we honour Guardian Envalair if our retaliation is not backed by adequate intelligence?

"Let us not bring the Mad Ones fair warning of our Quickening! Let us discover first how they brought one of the Maker's own to know death again; let us discover how a Drehstragian was permitted and able to enter our sanctuary, and how the Magic ripped; how we lost control of the Venzoians!"

A few heads nodded sagely to concur, so he quickly carried on, "Fellows, Guardian Emara would see prudence as a weakness; she believes the enemy will see it thus also, but in counter, I say: let us prepare in the right way so that when our return is revealed, it will be too late for them to rise against it. Tell me: is such strategy not of sound and worthy merit? Indeed, is it not worth a little restraint to face the coming battle armed to erase past failures as we should? I believe that if Guardian Envalair had still been amongst us, he would have been the first to stand in accord with this. Guardians you must assuredly also see this clearly?"

"I find myself wondering,-" Guardian Emara sounded the essence of reason, "-how it is that the Guardian Speaker believes himself entitled to form decisions on the basis of what he imagines Guardian Envalair might or might not have wanted. Indeed, I personally rather suspect that Richarmarlan Envalair would have agreed with little else but the need to rain down fury –

unless of course, Guardian Sedjem-Alhath'naar has indeed had confirmation from the highest place that this is not the case?"

"My fellows, are those the words of reason you wish to follow?" the Speaker retorted with an overbearing expression that would have suited better, had he stood before a group of bickering children. It appeared to raise Thessilia's hackles as per subtle design to make her appear brash, and as he yet held the other Guardians' attention as he continued, "Well, the Maker defend, I cannot condone it! And, as Guardian Emara well-knows, I need not explain my reasoning! Mark my words, though: ignore the past at your peril; understand your present to improve opportunities, but plan your future to live another day! That is the core my goal!"

"I am not usually in favour of the word 'caution', but I cannot deny Guardian Sedjem-Alhath'naar,-" Giant Guardian Cahmerhin injected before Thessilia could draw breath to speak, "-so on this day, *the Destiny of Ice and Blood* will officially stand in accord with the Guardian Speaker. Let it be known."

"As will *the Song of Perish,"* came the melodic, oddly-hypnotic voice of Guardian Arachk'thea. "There is little need for further explanation. On this day, I too will stand for caution. Let it be known."

Sinuhé lowered his bright blue gaze in gracious thanks, the path to his success marred only by the hairline cracks below the surface of the symmetrical beauty of the perfect central floor.

He'd almost achieved what he must, but Thessilia Emara's consternation at this turn of events did not feel good. To her like none others, the loss of Richarmarlan Envalair was particularly painful and in her lingering grief and outrage, she did not seem able to acknowledge the actual enormity of the Upper Circle's next step. She had already argued nigh on a millennium back now, that there'd been nothing foul at play to twist the events in this dreadful manner. In her view, the Venzoians had just been down-right lucky on that fateful eve that 'took' Envalair. The Twins had been young – barely more than children: the Veils had swayed on the cusp of failing and the Mad Ones had managed to pass some of their spawn through the Boundaries as a result. *'It must be so,' she'd maintained, 'it had to be so!'* Clearly, in spite of everything, her views had not changed.

"Guardian Speaker, if I may?"

Sinuhé righted his gaze to settle on Guardian Utarion, simultaneously shifting a notion of mild surprise from his face; for a moment he had no tongue for words because the other Guardian's civilised manner instilled confusion. However, feeling inspired by the Guardian's unusually agreeable conduct, and thus hoping that the Dayle would bring forth some valid point of consideration rather than just the dross of a battle-seeking crusader, Sinuhé inclined his chin to permit the man his say.

"So you wish us to entertain your little side-step for how long, exactly?" Guardian Utarion enquired after a blink, unconsciously fingering his ancestral ring as he continued to display a bewildering amount of composure in comparison to his normally hot-blooded attitude. "Also, whilst on the topic of adding up, tell me again: what do we gain for the time we lose, Speaker Guardian?"

"Yes, honourable Speaker, what do we gain?" Thessilia echoed tersely – as for a moment – Sinuhé and Utarion looked each other in the eye with an understanding they'd rarely shared over the millennia.

"Much! We gain much!" Sinuhé never blinked. "Now, think upon it! Each one of you considers himself indestructible, but so did Guardian Envalair! Dear Alérathnar, don't you see? I only wish to spend a little more time researching the Library again. Regardless of Guardian Emara's persuasions, consulting with the Story-Makers first will prove the most logical step. There were many avenues left unexplored when we were forced to return to the Oratorio; many an issue still too confused to make sense, and that be even with the aid of the Council, but you see, now…

"Well, now we can go back: get to the crux of the matter!"

"Aye, you may have a right point there, Guardian Speaker," Utarion allowed in a voice as though confessing and with a frown on his wide forehead that made the normally-assured Dayle seem uncharacteristically torn by his own words.

"Time lends perspective, aye," the Speaker reiterated, mirroring the other Guardian's choice of expression to create an illusion of solidarity, "And so I say we may begin to understand how the Mad Ones were capable of doing the impossible by returning to our first point of reference! It has never failed us in the past and that way I might learn how that Venzoian filth was capable of slaying-"

"Guardian-" Isavelia Cahmerhin interrupted with a touch of discomfort, "-that will suffice, I think! Now, who else in the Circle will stand with the Guardian Speaker?"

"The Path of Twilight will join your council," arose the steady voice of the swarthy-faced Guardian Orleara, though her sharp Sunerai features strained with reluctance, as she added, "Let it be known."

"As will *the Wisdom of Knowledge,-*" the golden-eyed Guardian Lucareo hastily echoed, "-for now, let it be known."

Isavelia Cahmerhin's silvery eyes looked across the assembly, for a moment longer lingering markedly upon Emara, but the reluctant woman refuted the other Guardian's scrutiny with a simple, curt shake of her head.

"Any others?" Isavelia Cahmerhin enquired at length, turning a questioning glance to the First Guardian, "Commander Denarlin?"

Sinuhé allowed himself to drift sideways to trail Cahmerhin's gaze. He noted Thessilia following her example, as did the others. In Emara's eyes, he spied a sliver of doubt, but also hope. *She did not think Guardian Denarlin would stand for this.*

The Speaker exhaled softly, distilling rising disquiet. *It was a possibility.*

Throughout Sinuhé's talk, their leader had never said a word of disagreement or encouragement, though. As Speaker, Sinuhé had risked using the notion of Envalair's preferences as a touch of propaganda, yet in this moment he was very much aware that no one – *including Thessilia Emara, with her very prolific sentiments* – would stand even half as qualified to speak on behalf of their lost fellow, as was Malandaar'Vahran Denarlin Cor'Esardan. *The argument was not yet won…*

Of course, Emara knew this much too and he sensed her lean forward on the edge of her cathedra as if she might impress upon their general her present state of persuasion to help sway him, but she could not reach for his mind within the circle without incurring condemnation. It would be considered a slight by their fellow Guardians and he didn't think she'd risk the offence. *He hoped she would not.*

For luck, it appeared he was right. As though appeased by the idea of imminent settlement, Emara's curls even alighted across her shoulders to rest once more as she waited with what might have been baited breath for the First Guardian to speak – yet for a curious handful of heartbeats, Guardian Denarlin looked set to ignore them all, when he gave no indication that he'd honour Cahmerhin any kind of intelligible answer. Then, just as Sinuhé began to ponder whether Denarlin had in fact been listening in the first place, their Commander looked up, fixing his gaze directly on their third-in-command with all of his usual, all-too-familiar, lack of compromise.

"I am... as of yet... not of any singular persuasion," he informed in a musing voice that carried overtones of preoccupation, "Still, I suspect it will not be long."

Bemused, the Speaker drew himself tall, "But First Guardian, I-"

Though seemingly of a hazy disposition, Denarlin raised his gaze to the Speaker with an expression of cool neutrality that somehow still had the power to silence the roar of argument through cutting candour. At a loss, for he did not know how to interpret their Commander's behaviour, the Speaker swallowed words and action in favour of patience. *The First Guardian was never pre-occupied. Whatever would be next?*

Solancei's Memoirs

The Province of Tarléon.
Ocean's End.
Autumn of 780 P. C. W.

You think me little more than a morbid girl who selfishly jammers on now? Perhaps you think me a terrible adult of double standards? Well perhaps I am – I lose perspective sometimes these days – but for this, I will not apologise.

So what if I bemoan the misery I felt? I have to write this, so I aim to ensure I do so with a certain flair and in a way that might enlighten you to a few things when others may take a different view. For one, I am not done telling you about that day of my parents' funeral because it was a turning point of a sorts.

See, I re-live the occasion now with the understanding that fairness held no bearing, neither upon my age nor feelings – but no one ever told me that, so I would tell you this truth of life now, both to prepare you and to spare you the illusion others might paint to the contrary. The sum of this? Well, I suppose that will be yours to fight later. At that funeral though, I was ignorant and uneducated in the ways of the world, and hence everything felt all so very unfair to the seven-autumns-old me. *Unfair and worse...*

I was stood there quivering with equal parts cold and regret – and with the threat of the sudden onset of tears that were bound to spill no matter how I blinked, everything seemed to grow. *I hated the abject feeling of weakness it brought on. I was not weak. I had everything I'd ever needed... but that was before, wasn't it? Before...*

The tears were so close at one point that I reverted to a bad habit and bit down hard on my bottom lip – something I'd ever been wont to do to distract myself from things that might hurt! Despite efforts, how could I ignore that my chin still wobbled as the memory of the stout, red-haired Taliana sallied past my defences, determined to cut me open? How could I ignore the chill in my heart?

Feelings grew: like beasts of horror, I couldn't stop them. *I couldn't stand the sorrow; couldn't bear the pressure of questions and darkness in my head, couldn't breathe past the ice in my heart... I felt suddenly scared, though I needn't have... if I didn't cry, I might pass out instead, my head felt very strange; not my own...*

Yup, it was as unpleasant as it sounds, but already things were afoot to save me. See, I say this day was a turning point – not because of my loss, but because of what happened to me as a result. The terrible event had put me in perfect alignment, and now I needed but to 'embrace and accept', so I did.

I imagine that's why this next thing suddenly happened; I believe this was why I was able to create my first true link with the State of Veranto; I believe that's why my head and spirit and body suddenly managed to align into something... *something beyond 'thought of the physical'. And there...*

For lack of a better word, it felt like 'peace'. Such deep, floating peace, unlike anything I'd ever vaguely managed to achieve before this point – and you will not know this, but I'd known moments, where in childish desperation, I had tried for something similar because I did not want to be what I was, or rather: what I was not.

Now you understand, I hope, that at this particular point, I did not consciously make the decision that I should 'rise' to the occasion and 'make it so' because at that point it was far from a realised thing in my head. In actual fact, the State of Veranto registered as little more than a tiny inkling to move in a certain direction because it felt right: like staring at a step that once mentally climbed, would lead me to the next, and then the next, and so on and so forth – but yet again I did not know this at the time. Soon, however, I would – but that's for later.

So... the State of Veranto...

Such a strange abstract thing; such a peculiar talent. Most do not understand it. I had never even considered that I might have that gift, for it is a rare affinity to possess, but nevertheless, that was it: the 'thing', the 'notion' rising to help me conquer my grief – and later so much more. Of course, moments before I experienced this wonder for the first time, I was standing there on the ice, about to blubber like a scorned maiden on her wedding day – and all I knew was that such behaviour would not do. The Tarléonin people are hard. Tears waste energy and fluids. I lamented how my former nurse and maid would have told me to be brave, and not to cry for such a minute thing as death, and so – seemingly out of nowhere, another thought came to me.

Taliana would always test me: in how many bites can you eat an apple? How long can you hop on one leg? How fast can you skate?

Not crying seemed a final test of sorts – or rather, it occurred to me that I should treat it as one, at least. And so I let a part of me dissolve; float deep – or high, depending on which theory you take to hold true – and there was suddenly that freedom from tattered emotions! Yes even from the cold! I remember that I vaguely recognised it as some kind of deviant from something that felt mildly familiar because in my ever on-going efforts to fight against – *what they'd called* – my own personal 'Demonai': my 'obstinate' nature, I had probably been nurturing this ability for Gods only knew how long, only never to understand what was brewing within because I had never achieved such an enlightened effect before.

In hindsight, I knew it was just the case though – because I'd always failed to please my parents and most of those surrounding them, and there were consequences – worst of all my own personal disappointment that I was seemingly incapable of applying myself as they wished me to do. I didn't like me either, so I would go into myself to seek an escape: to seek out 'distance'. *It happened a lot; I guess I'd had practise because they'd all sought to 'cure' me of my chronic flaws.*

Don't bring the chickens inside: my mother locked me in a cupboard. *Seek the distance.* You will not get any supper: my father wanted me out of breeches. *Seek the distance.* My mother gave me red welts across the fingers for helping out a stable boy. *Seek the distance.* I fell off the south gable end, sliding from the slanted roof because I'd lost my footing on the vertical. *Seek the distance – oh, and the hedge doctor for a broken wrist.* Next time you will go to the Tower: you will never be a lady. *Seek the Distance.* The Gods are not amused by ugly things. *Seek the Distance.* Yup… as I said: plenty of practice had come before this day!

Still… the State of Veranto… who'd have thought… so I'd finally found the distance and what lay beyond, but did my new-found peace bring happiness? But of course not – not even a drop's worth – but Taliana would've been proud that I did not cry. I chose to believe this – *what did I know?* - but I rose to Taliana's final challenge, regardless, and…

And so it was at that point I was able to pull back my shoulders beneath the white fur of mourning, the would-be tears now freezing in my eyelashes before they could chill the cheeks. Untrained that I was, the effect was of course not foolproof. In fact, it lasted on and off – more about that soon – and so I must have blinked a thousand times that morning. I blinked, then blinked again: for shame my ever-long lashes – an only feature to receive regular compliments by my late mother – now fluttering like ice-wrought feathers against my skin in a way she might just have deemed 'endearing' in one of her good moments. Such a shame for everyone, but at that funeral, for the first time I appeared to do everything just right, and here was my idea of irony born.

Now to be sure: that was a stray thought to have, an unrealised self-directed distraction perhaps, but as I blinked it brought to mind the strange image of the snow moth's serrated wings – oh and I tell you: I very much liked that idea! You see, snow moths are beautifully mottled black and silver, with white tufts on the apex of each twenty-inch wingspan and I could see myself as a moth then… floating away, dissolving on the snow and returning when it suited.

Still, I did not float away of course – and as I sit here thinking back, I confess it seems an odd detail to recall. I have no explanation for the fact. Perhaps it was the pressure of the events? But then again, maybe not. The State of Veranto is a wondrous thing. At my parent's funeral, I learnt this for the first time.

Solancei

First Touch

A surge reaped all emotion from her body.

Opening her grip to flex weather-beaten fingers, Solancei gave Simaro no further insight into her state of mind as she curled both her hands around the long, leather-bound hilt yet again and brought it up at a new angle before her chest. *Already he was a pace closer.*

Swinging his practice blade towards her head, Simaro grinned and pounced, closing the gap between them. One, two, three: rapid siding steps to eat up the ground, his attack was alarmingly fast, but Solancei recognized his intent and was already moving to evade and counter. Spinning, bending slightly to avoid contact with nought but a calculated hairs breath to spare, she whirled her own blade in a blur, altering the grip to bring up the wooden sword straight before her torso to deflect a second lightning pass.

The dull clatter of wood shattered the air but only briefly as she flexed and twisted to let the blades slide apart. Wheeling in synchronicity, they cleared each other, yet Simaro almost immediately changed leg, turning to pursue.

She ducked.

Complimented by a bit of fancy footwork, she finally managed to produce a well-timed counter-offence to force her opponent into defence. *Good... yet not good enough.* Still... she'd moved within the perimeter of Klaas' brief. Nothing too flashy, she'd been told; she understood the precaution. And Gods, it grated!

Haitu only, girl!' Chief Eso's warning echoed yet again as she shifted balance mid-move to evade the stab he aimed towards her. *'The man knows combat like the weight of his own blade. He is not just your average mercenary, who does not understand one form from another – he will know, and he will see the pedigree of your training! You do one thing to indicate that you are not simply 'Cheska from New Wood' and we could be in deep – understand?'*

Yes, she understood very well but begrudged it. With her attempts to reach the State of Veranto constantly failing and half her vicious abilities curbed, she felt as though her mentor had asked her to fight with one arm tied behind her back.

Solancei resented the pretence; she also resented not being able to finish this before Iambre's summon arrived, and she'd already made too many mistakes!

Haitu cracked. She spun and slashed, forcing him backwards. *Yes, she wanted to be back at the main Keep in good time to soak away her aches in a bath laced with milk of lavender and in time to change her clothes and become a lady so that she might face 'Iambre the intolerable' with a little dignity and weight, rather than looking the stinking vagabond with mud-caked boots and tangled hair that would not conform in the time she'd have left to get both herself and her mistress ready for banquet! This was so distracting...*

Like a cornered thief in the night, Simaro rounded on her. *Rats no!*

Habit saw her sidestep his attempt and she flowed into a turn to coincide with her sword arm extending to risk a rapid backhand swipe towards the sudden exposure of his neck. It was a tiny opening, but…

Very audible exclamations of shocked surprise emanated like an accompanying rush of sound from their rat-tackle spectators but she had no time to spare for their petty concerns of wagers nearly lost or won. All her attention remained with Simaro.

He managed to evade her bold manoeuvre with an uncouth blocking that made him falter with a slight stumble – and for a moment Solancei read a glimmer of real emotion from the man, as utter surprise flared hot across his otherwise steely features.

It was gone before she could felicitate her own deed, the momentum carrying her clear with a couple of tight spins, yet still she sensed in her core that he'd been rankled. *Maybe she was getting somewhere then…*

Haitu already on guard, she faced him anew, her blade a notch higher in the third ready-position now. There was no triumph in her near-success and she felt hemmed in. Sure, for a beat, victory could have been hers but the world was full of *'near-almost'* and *'if-only'* and neither sentiment had ever won her a thing!

Expelling a puff of pent-up exasperation, she cursed her mentor. *It felt wrong to hold back, curse it! For a moment Simaro had been off-balance and yet-*

Klaas insistence that she must cling to prudence seemed a jest and she could feel her frustration building. Such a lack of discipline was a danger of its own though and yet she still fought an internal urge to yell out loud at the world, as – feinting high but sweeping his blade low – Simaro shoved forward with cunning and speed to catch her short. It had the crowd calling out in renewed support of him then, but Solancei wasn't impressed. This old trick was well-known to her and she instantly came back at him, twisting her weapon, using little but a blink to turn defence into offence and the two swords collided low, then high, grinding…

Pushing her, Simaro flung her back. She cussed. Unable to whip her own blade up and around to defend or deflect, she didn't think as she dropped nimbly to one knee…

For what seemed one long thunderous heartbeat, the point of Simaro's haitu looked sure to strike true regardless but she was still reacting: twisting to deny the contact and Simaro's wooden blade sailed past her chest, like a tempest across Lake Etruia... *overextending... missing the mark... creating another opening...*

Solancei saw the chance and took it: forcing her protesting body into action, moving to follow in union, synchronising her timing to fit. It made the spectators scream loudly in alarm and protest as they saw her spin on her knees to extend one leg, but the rain seemed to buffer the sound weirdly.

'Thud!'

Re-emerging her into the world of time and sound, she completed the move to send him floundering. It was not perfect – *the ground was too slippery to control the outcome* – but it worked in her favour regardless; Simaro wavered, flailing almost comically to stay upright, then proceeded to half-fall, half-collide into the nearest line of spectators. It was not what she'd hoped for but she still sprang to pursue, only the audience's rough-shod attempt at keeping Simaro on his feet nearly undid her then.

It seemed sheer bad luck, but they saved him, their steadying hands on his arms and back enough support to fling him directly towards her with near reckless disregard for the outcome!

This Jackal was turning into a shambles but with movement made faster by the sleek wetness of the worn paving underfoot, she slid from the imminent collision with an unrefined stumble of her own, sucking down a rapid breath for what had nearly been.

Gods' curses, but her progress stank worse than a midden at the height of summer! And Simaro was too flecking lucky, or else the Goddess Ruhmista'Cha the Foul simply hated her today! Either way, it hardly mattered, of course – soon, she'd lose this Jackal to Simaro's superior strength, unless-

Ignoring the sweat of her heated exercise as it mingled with the fat droplets of cool rain to trickle down her face, she calmed her breathing and faced the man she could not quite seem to get the better of. He hadn't expected this however, she realised with a sudden sliver of insight as she found his eyes. Out of the two, she'd just come out on top and Solancei almost smiled. *A Zanzierian. Bested by a woman... Oh, imagine...*

Simaro's eyes narrowed. *As if he saw her for the first time, suddenly.* This time she did smile.

By the rise and fall of his chest, he was labouring to stay in control and she'd be willing to bet that he'd not readily pursued an attack because he was perchance not quite as certain as before. *Also, imagine...*

"You tread the steps of this dance well after all," he told her unexpectedly, though with a hint of darkness rather than felicitation.

"I know," she replied without modesty, "you should see me at a banquet when there's music: I'm quite exquisite!"

And at that it was his turn to smirk at her. She offered him a small rapid curtsy that unexpectedly provoked a glitch of elegant sinister assurance when his hitherto stony features dropped with the foreboding promise of chilling things to come. *And there it was!* Persistent skill had done what grating comments had failed to deliver on, and she suddenly had to fight an almost irresistible urge to laugh out loud. There was absolutely nothing funny about any of this; nothing whatsoever, and yet, this very moment was ever a delight! *The 'moment', when her opponents invariably discovered that she had actually survived their dance through more than plain good luck; that 'moment' where they realised that she was intent on winning and were forced to concede she might even succeed!* Simaro, she saw, was realising this now; realising and resenting!

"So shall we finish this, then?" she enquired, squaring her shoulders. "I don't have all day even if you should feel the need for another break."

Not biting, her opponent shook his head.

"You have some skilled moves, and you have such spirit too," he commented in a voice that made her blood go oddly cold, "But moves will not save you ever-more, and a spirit can be broken when it suffers. I think I shall endeavour to poison yours!"

The uncanny promise found an odd feeling stealing over her. Absurdly, he reminded her of the giant icicles she'd known to watch out for whilst growing up within Ivanor Fortress. *Yes, an icicle made flesh,* she thought: *sharp, cold and similarly void of feelings.* And those three-foot spears of ice had been things to remain ever-watchful of, lest one should suddenly drop without warning from the eaves of the main hall to kill passers-by without discrimination or recourse, just for being in the wrong place at the wrong time. She'd once seen a worker killed-

'Focus on the dance!' Klaas' caution rang out in her mind, overlapping. *'All else is of no consequence and yet of all importance. Be mindful of everything but not to the point of distraction. Distraction will undo you!'*

And Klaas was right. Of course. She could not let memories, nor words, touch her. She would take this man down and claim the win. *When she viewed it thus, nothing in the world seemed easier. That was how it should be. Easy...*

Blade swiping high, Solancei feinted right, adjusted – and nearly scored 'first-touch' again, as they stepped together like a pair of rushed dancers synchronising their steps to match each other's flow. However,

Simaro caught the would-be defeat with the tip of his blade, skilfully flicking his wrist to then chase her.

She cussed the Gods and ducked, a swivelling turn to ride under a soaring cut to evade. Then, using the fluidic speed of her momentum to fly from his next spearing thrust, she twisted her body sharply, flowing into *trailing-ferns-on-the-beck* to buy time and extricate herself from danger. It got her out of the tight spot, but-

'Borderline, girl!' Klaas' voice seemed to grate in her head and she knew by the gasping audience that Klaas would've been right. *Fleck!*

Angry with her own breech but unwilling to let it rule, she swivelled like an angry snake, launching forward with a slicing upper-cut, the haitu striking Simaro's mid-air with a resounding clash vibrating energy up her arm. It had Simaro push to lock her down, but Solancei dropped her shoulder, twisting to separate.

Around them the pinched faces of their spectators became a blur – their verbal excitement now reborn to the full, and yet it was mere background noise to accompany the conflict of swords and the hush of unrelenting rain that seemed to whisper promises of disaster, should she not commandeer a favourable outcome. Like the icicle thing, she shook it off.

Hooking his haitu to slice under a sweep, Solancei cleared Simaro's reach, gasping for breath, dearly missing her link with Veranto and the ability it would've given her to push harder, move faster and endure longer. *How Klaas had ever believed her capable of winning a jackal fight against a man like this?!*

Cross with the self-doubt, she aborted the question in a blink. *Klaas hadn't known about her little problem with the State of Veranto, so by default, the Chief would be expecting her to win.*

Without the Veranto though, and with the 'sanctions' Klaas had placed against her in regards to the Art of Kizano…

The rap of Simaro's haitu against the edge of hers made her teeth jar and her odds steadily decline. There was no shame in it, of course; just sheer fact! *However, can you not do this small thing today, then what about next time? What about Iambre? T'lexara Corunan Vitalioni! For your Oaths and the clandestine title alone, you cannot relent! You must not!*

With a grimace to match the effort, she threw back an attack and let the ancient title anchor her in the present. *She had to win!* Not for any misplaced notions of glory, and not for the winnings that would flow into Klaas' pockets either, but for her own peace of mind and for the real protection that her skills would afford the Crown Princess – should reality ever breech theory!

Gods, if you begin to contemplate the possibility of defeat now, you might as well offer up your sword as well as Iambre's neck, for then you will never again be worthy of your sworn duty! And such a notion is absurd and utterly unthinkable!

With a grunt, she threw her haitu around to slap away a triple unit of smart stabs aimed at her ribs, one after another; Simaro sidled left, risking exposure, and she might have done something about it, but her mentor's explicit demands prevented the required finesse.

It was ridiculous! Klaas was being unreasonable! If judging by the angle of light in the sky, Iambre would soon be expecting her; she was beginning to lament the way Simaro heaved at her: without any expression upon his face and yet with a near-visible touch of eviscerating guarantee his crystal-hard eyes. *Somehow she mustn't let it matter, but perhaps…*

Striking hard left, flowing into a backward swipe and spinning with the inertia of her blade to come at him, this time with a frontal assault,

Solancei didn't have pause to leisurely dissect and interpret her own feelings further. The rain made the fight seem gruelling and his strength was grinding her down now as surely as any words she might have spewed to get at him.

'Efficiency is the key to success', Klaas' proverb echoed in her mind, *'Economic efficiency and skill that is, girl!'*

Gasping, for a brief glitch in her concentration made her momentarily sloppy, Solancei saw his blade descend. *Like bright steel, nuisance flared!* Angered with her lack of progress and Klaas' shackling, ridiculous demands, Solancei felt her nature push against the narrow perimeters placed upon her. *This was indeed ridiculous! She'd had enough! Let Klaas and the rest of them jump into the Void with rage, but Gods take them! Enough was enough! She wanted to finish this and get the fleck back to that big ugly Keep; she-*

With a grimace for the scream of her ligaments, she changed footwork, turning a would-be retreat back into an immediate assault and as their haitu crashed together in angry rapport, Solancei swayed, then spun – *smooth as ribbon sliding off a naked arm* – to direct a sideways kick at her opponent.

It was a moment too late to regret the display as he staggered; a moment too late to recall that she'd just grossly overstepped Klaas' command in regards to the use of Kizano; a moment too late not to feel the flow of vicious certainty in her bones. As it must, her assault hit true and as Simaro gasped in surprise, so her personal accountability went straight to the Void along with any care she might have had in regards to Klaas' feelings on her oversight. In less than a rapid blink of an eye, she'd sent Simaro staggering, this time winded from a boot in the guts, and she was already shifting to complete her move, fluidly switching her grip on the haitu to bring it into position. *Three...*

The spectators were howling like feral wolves; Simaro cursed the Gods without restraint, but she was too tired to gloat. Striking out physically felt good. It was a weakness she did not often permit herself, but flowing into the final step, she gloried in the pleasure. *Two...*

Wielding her haitu like a dancer with a prop; like an extension of her own arm – the outcome was inevitable. Simaro laboured to re-assert his footing, but it was done. *One...*

A herald of defeat, her haitu flowed in a tight circle towards his arm. Simaro saw, but she'd won past his defence and with the knowledge of certain victory in hand, she brought her dull sword up a notch to punctuate their fight – landing *first-touch* to the corner of his shoulder with a perceptibly sharp rap.

And there! Another one bites the dust. Well fleck, if that hadn't been about time! Fleck indeed!

Weakness Will Out

A pause followed Denarlin's cryptic words, but Thessilia's heart was already plummeting.

Sinuhé Sedjem-Alhath'naar sang a good tune, but he'd be wasting their time if allowed to rummage through the evidence and facts yet again. *What did Denarlin not see?* The Circle had been through this a hundred times or more, and still the present found them empty-handed: no closer to understanding what had truly happened on the night Richarmarlan Envalair died; no nearer to discovering where the shards of the astrolabe might be, or indeed if the Artefact of Time could even be mended! Pride shaken and minds brimming with fury denied – and yet they could but sit here, whilst the unknown writhed like poisonous tendrils of Elvern magic within their Circle. *The Veils had failed. For an impossible count of heartbeats, the Veils had weakened and it had been Chaos, it had almost been the beginning of the end – and from there-*

Guardian Emara steered clear of that possibility in a wink, glancing instead at their general.

Bizarrely, Denarlin looked distracted – a strange concept to consider – and for a blink, the Speaker looked old, the ageless quality of his heritage somehow shining through to add the tally of millennia to the furrows on his brow and the depths of his Human, Elvern-blue eyes. *Was he as puzzled as she about Guardian Denarlin's lack of commitment, or did he know the First Guardian about to refute his oh-so-sensible reasoning?*

To Thessilia, Sinuhé's persistence bordered on obsessive though. *Yes, they faced obstacles, but...?* A Guardian preaching for caution was like someone saying that the Mad Ones were not really insane, but merely misunderstood. It was plain and simply wrong – and mercy, the Speaker was a Guardian of the Circle no less than any of the others, perhaps even more so than their Commander. *So what could suddenly make one of their oldest go arguing so heatedly against everything that was in their nature to do?*

"Lord Denarlin, I..." the Speaker sounded a paler version of himself, then seemed to regain some of his moral fibre, "I... forgive me, Guardian, but I do not understand."

"You do not understand?" Malandaar'Vahran Denarlin questioned mildly, the softly accented baritone communicating a hint of slewed acerbic surprise, "Or you do not wish to understand?"

Thessilia sent the Speaker a surreptitious glance. For a moment the Commander's question appeared to have stunned the older Guardian, but in truth, he did not appear the only one.

Guardian Cahmerhin sat straight, her wide shoulders thrown back, her robust bucket-like chin dipping low as though confounded by their general.

Mystified, Thessilia frowned, the pencil line between her brows drawing deeper a moment later, as she noted Guardian Rhindarhlar Mehand'Arun's feelings on the matter filter through the Oratorio like a cloying smoke that stuck like acid in the back of her throat.

"I have yet to know the Speaker disoriented by lack of understanding," Guardian Mehand'Arun announced, not towards Denarlin or Sinuhé, but catching Thessilia with an unlikely ray of support in his dark-ringed teal gaze. "Yet be this the day of firsts to leave our good Speaker numb, then maybe we should allow Guardian Emara her say?"

Sinuhé raised his chin – Thessilia knew to gainsay the other Guardian – but something in Mehand'Arun's bearing seemed to stop the old Guardian. Looking from Denarlin's unreadable face, to Sinuhé's uncertain bearing, Thessilia swallowed surprise as Mehand'Arun glanced her way with a fey smile.

In perpetual contempt of most things, the Elvern Guardian's chiselled features held just the prescribed amount of strident derision and sardonic arrogance – something she'd normally decry and distance herself from. Yet because she had long since been broken off the illusion that his impossibly handsome perfection could somehow make it up to the world, something had to make his presence worth her while and perhaps this was it?

Weary of Mehand'Arun's antics and reluctant to humour his Elvern deprecating manners, Thessilia sent him a flat questioning glare. *Would she be able to allow his abrasive antics if it meant him backing her views?*

As expected, he spared her any premature felicitations, though he did deign to return her gaze with a hint of calculated candour. *Was he promoting a hidden design? Could she afford to care?*

Thessilia knew she must – but now was not the time. The Speaker appeared mildly troubled still – a fact he involuntarily revealed as he ran a hand along the already pristine pleats of his robes as though to smooth the fabric.

She noticed Mehand'Arun's gaze take in the small tell as well, an almost eager energy flowing off him. *What are you hiding in that clever mind of yours, Sinuhé,* she mused with sudden insight. *What are you truly protecting?*

Lowering her eyes to think, for a moment Thessilia shut out the assembly. The silence was pitiful, almost bordering on something that felt like airborne reluctance. Denarlin felt aloof to her – like a shade of presence only; if there was ever a time to push-

Mind brewing with unfounded possibilities, her right index finger slowly tracing the well-known route of carved petals and roses where they wound across the armrest of her old seat, Thessilia turned aside Mehand'Arun's weighted pressure on her, then realised that she could not shut it out. *If she made an outright call for arms, Mehand'Arun would follow, but would the Commander oblige?*

Not willing to test the bond of her and Denarlin's former relations, Thessilia elected instead to lift her eyes directly to the Speaker.

Sinuhé Sedjem-Alhath'naar returned the look with an air of personal unease. Yet, like a charioteer holding the reins of a crazed team of Eikyr on the verge of erupting from a steady trot into a full-on tilt, the cunning Sedjem-Alhath'naar was not letting go of his advantage!

By the nine chained-levels of the Venzoian Castes – but she could allow him to keep it! Not while some members of the Upper Circle had still not declared for his designs. She must push.

Emara permitted her polished features to mirror her heart, and though the Speaker obviously tried to calm her with one of his looks, she would not relent to the power he possessed.

With Guardian Mehand'Arun's pleasure like a dagger at her neck, collecting harshness to armour each syllable, she held Sinuhé's clouded eyes as she glided upright from her seat declaring, "*The Mercy of Steel* denies the validity of the Speaker's case and condemns his logic. May I request the floor?"

The behest was a formality. However, out of respect, she waited just the prescribed blink for the Guardian Speaker to silently acknowledge her bidding. He did so of course with the practised grace of a man skilled at his task and as he withdrew to the edge of his seat, Thessilia glanced once at Richarmarlan Envalair's empty Cathedra, allowing the Circle to follow the direction of her stare, and understand. Vaguely, she sensed Sinuhé's abrupt incredulity at her sudden ability to look at the reminder of their loss, but she could not play these shadow games now. *For Guardian Envalair she would look at it forever if that be what it took. For him…*

"I am astounded,-" she began, pinching a hold of her flower-embroidered skirts to lift the heavy brocade clear of the steps as she left the dais, descending the concentric, shallow stairs to enter the central circle, "-but here we stand: Guardians of the Realms; Alérathnar's chosen… and you decide to do what?!"

Staring at each Guardian in turn, Thessilia let the question flay their conscience and whilst studying their expressions, her earlier suspicions deepened. *She was indeed missing something. But what?* With snake-like precision, she whipped her attention towards the willowy Jonaeus Lucareo.

"You Guardian!" She forced his gaze to hers with charm and demand. "You are *the Wisdom of Knowledge.* Why would you condone this madness? Why would you support it? Surely you must see the folly of procrastinating?"

"Guardian Emara, alas I cannot…" Guardian Lucareo trailed off as though unable to finish the sentence. Faster than a heartbeat his large golden eyes sought support from the Speaker but his gaze shifted so rapidly that as Thessilia blinked, she couldn't be quite sure why she felt a sudden unease steal over the Maker's runes on her body.

"So you would ride to outright war then, Guardian Emara?" The Speaker injected, stepping forward once more as though unable to contain himself. "We have oft been of opposing opinions old friend, but surely you know that we cannot afford such brazen action. Not presently."

"Oh, I am well aware of what we can afford,-" Thessilia gambled, countering his questioning frown, "-and perhaps you should listen!"

"Guardian Emara," the Speaker ventured with acerbic scorn as he squared his shoulders. "I am the Historian; I am the Keeper of Chronicles! Why do my words incite such pause in you when we have an unprecedented threat to our existence to consider? Guardian Lucareo understands the prudence of discovering the truth of our unsavoury experience. He understands the need for us to go armour ourselves against future demise. Sure as the Quickening, that is worth a little of your time Guardian?"

"No!" Thessilia's answer was cutting-blunt, without remorse. "If I must finally End, then who am I to complain? I did not Ascend only to slink from duty when times turn against us! Guardian, if my voice is to be of any worth then I'd rather perish in defence of the Realms: with the roar of magic in my ears and the steel-edge of *Oblivion* delivering the tormented! Indeed, that is why we accepted the Maker's pact, why we still breathe rather than rot and fertilise farmer's crops now thriving in ancient battlefields! Wrath, as I stand before you, how can any of you think of honouring your vows with anything less than All? How-"

"Oh but they can't-," injected Commander Denarlin, strange rue stalking his tempered voice as he killed her momentum, "-because something new stirs them from the original path. In truth, I was hoping the Guardian Speaker would mention it, but evidently... not."

Leaning slightly forward as though in anticipation of some kind of pre-perceived answer, their general spun the silence against Sedjem-Alhath'naar, regarding the older man with eyes of green stars and intractable equanimity for a moment longer than most might deem comfortable. Then he calmly stated, "Death is a stranger to our existence and yet it has ever stalked our presence: that it touched someone in our midst is ultimately of no consequence for this debate."

Thessilia felt her face drop. For a beat the Speaker looked astounded too – but including Thessilia with a glance, the Commander remained matter-of-fact as he added, "Circumstances are what they are. At best Guardian Envalair presumed to ignore his orders, and in result Death claimed first prize in the chaos that ensued. Now, I have listened to your words, felt the weight of your concerns, and I dare say the Guardian Speaker has a right to call for caution, yet I am also forced to wonder at his prudence. Tell me Guardian Sedjem-Alhath'naar: is this truly how you wish to leave it?"

"I-" the Speaker began but was silenced by a sapient look from their Commander.

It left a once-more flummoxed Sedjem-Alhath'naar working to gather his aplomb. Thessilia righted her face, folding away her own frown with effort.

Apparently satisfied, Denarlin reclined in his seat. With an economic gesture of unrealised habit, he pushed an errant length of long sable hair back over one shoulder and quirked an equally sable eyebrow at the Speaker, "Well…?"

Thessilia held her breath but this was too good an opportunity for her to ignore. *Rule or ruin, she had to try this…*

"Guardian Speaker, I will stand with you if you can guarantee that I know all the surrounding circumstances that have prompted your current stance and conduct." Thessilia smiled pleasantly, but the look of alarm flashing across the Speaker's mature, now-pasty-brown face, made the smile seem frozen.

Bothered by the sense of reoccurring unease, she offered their Commander a sidelong glance of inquiry. He returned her a veiled look but she knew him well enough to interpret the presence of guarded candour in his delicately-slanted eyes and her guts turned in slow recognition. *Something was indeed wrong – and the Void defend them… Denarlin already knew exactly what!*

The Speaker drew a harsh breath and exhaled. With a sardonic smile of capitulation, he acknowledged the Commander. "How long…?"

"Guardian Speaker, amongst our ranks you might have been the one fortunate enough to hold the highest mortal age before the Oath made its claim, but I was still the first…" – and here Guardian Denarlin offered the Speaker a tempered smile of his own as though to take the sting from his words – "…let's just say that I have known long enough."

"Commander?" Guardian Cahmerhin began with a hint of alarm, "Commander, I don't think that-"

"Ah but I think that we should!" Denarlin shot back at the Ermaron Guardian before she could finish.

"But Commander,-" the Speaker pleaded, "-mine is really not the place to reveal-"

"No Guardian Speaker,-" Denarlin curtly agreed, "-but mine is! And I would have all the facts laid before the Circle before we make stands to change our course!"

Thessilia killed a slow smile. *Malandaar'Vahran Denarlin Cor'Esardan did not sit on his honourable title out of pure luck and in his voice was the well-known tone of silvery demand, sharper than the edge of her blade, Oblivion, and twice as deadly.*

"Commander, so be it." Guardian Cahmerhin surrendered and inclined her wide chin in deference to his will though she remained tense like a boar sensing hunters gathering close.

The electrifying attention that ensued would have unnerved most men but the Speaker simply took a moment. As if to ward off the demand still standing between them, he pinched the ridge of his hooked nose between thumb and forefinger – and, as the old Guardian Chronicler stared at his feet in a most uncommon parody of reflection, Thessilia had an uncomfortable feeling that she knew what was coming.

To waylay concern, she drew a deep breath to match the old Guardian. *Should she perchance be right in her suspicions, then she'd probably have no choice but to heed the Speaker even if it was not what she wanted, but Gods rot!*

"Honoured Speaker, you toy with our time now," warned Paimar Utarion with an irritated scowl of features that made his already narrow lips seem like bloodless slashes in a face of scarred hardness. Leaving his solid ring well-alone now in favour of flexing one large hand into a hammer-like fist that Thessilia knew capable of crushing the reinforced skull of a Venzoian Mashraah Dah, Utarion's eyes narrowed on the Speaker in demand.

"Well, perhaps I am at that-" Evidently undaunted, Sinuhé offered the impatient Guardian an acetous smile. "-but if I do, then it is only because I find it hard to determine an agreeable way by which to approach my subject even if it does stand to underscore my convictions."

"My fellow Guardian?" Guardian Arachk'thea injected, flowing to her feet with the strange grace of liquid-contained. "Please? Please, would you allow me to ease this for you? Please, would you allow me to unburden?"

For a moment the Speaker seemed stunned. Then he nodded heavily.

Thessilia withdrew slowly to her seat. *Suddenly she felt very little like speaking.*

"I would have you know that the Sight is no longer with me," Guardian Arachk'thea stated in such a wearisome tone, that something seemed to shift within the Oratorio, courtesy of her power. Arachk'thea's luminous complexion had been strangely tinny since they'd reclaimed their Seats of Heritage and Thessilia grew colder still as understanding dawned. *She'd hoped her instincts were wrong; she'd hoped she'd been the only one, but…*

"How long?" she heard herself say.

"My fellow Guardians,-" Arachk'thea seemed to shrink, her light-sensitive pupils contracting, "-you should know that mine has been a darkness not measured by the deepest ocean! Indeed-"

For a moment the other Guardian couldn't seem to force out the next words, but then she concluded, "Indeed, I had to consider if Alérathnar's Power was no more!"

From watching her demeanour, Thessilia knew those words had not come easily to the Guardian of the Fhearan people.

"How long Guardian?" Cahmerhin repeated with wooden features, her brown skin paling to the colour of dry mud, almost in twin-resemblance to Sinuhé's unhealthy pallor.

Arachk'thea drew a soft breath, "I… I fear… I believe I lost the Sight around the passing of Domina Ily'ran the 5th. After then… after then I have seen nothing of the Realms; nothing of the enemy."

Ignoring Lucareo's subtle intake of air and Utarion's outright curse, Arachk'thea smiled winningly as her race was wont, but her pupils were still mere slits of pain.

"So there…" With the floating grace of her heritage, accentuated now by the trailing skirts of her coat and the flash of golden-red scales across cheeks and shoulders, the Fhearan Guardian swayed just once in courtesy as if to assure them that in spite of her affliction, she was not prepared to forget her place amongst them.

To Thessilia the ensuing silence seemed to whisper like forgotten ghosts scratching at window panes to get in, yet the Fhearan Guardian appeared not to notice as she shrank back like a crouching shadow to fold her long body into her cushioned chair.

Curling long fine fingers bedecked with scales, rings and arcane symbols, the stricken Fhearan clenched the arm-rests of her seat and seemed to rediscover a little of her usual flamboyance, but Thessilia quenched a shudder. *Domina Ily'ran the 5th had given her spirit to the oceans near seven centuries ago! In the dark, that was a very long time indeed. Even for one of them…*

It made her weary but in a rush of insight, she knew that the Fhearan warrior was right. Things could not remain hidden. *Seemed this was a day for unexpected revelations…*

"I am uncertain of the time, but-" She paused as her colleagues swivelled, their attention descending.

Thessilia thrust her sense of weakness to the back of her mind. "What I mean to say, Guardians, is that for some time now, I too have found it impossible to see clearly. My senses seem laced with fog, the dreamscape of the Long Sleep has been hazy, and…

"And whilst I had hoped it was but an erratic defect brought on by Guardian Envalair's actions, I see now that it was not the case. The Quickening came and… and still nothing!"

Unable to carry on, Thessilia Emara killed a deeper shudder. She wanted to look at Denarlin to gauge his reaction but just then she couldn't bring herself to meet his gaze.

"You… you are blind too?" Arachk'thea enquired, so quietly that the flutter of butterfly wings could have drowned out the sound.

Thessilia grimaced. It was an uncomfortable debility to admit, but…

"Blind as a worm," she confirmed and saw the cracks in her fellow Guardians' veneer begin to split arrogant poises. *Gods rot indeed…*

Lucareo went next then, his normally warm voice rendered reedy as he accounted for the blindness that had severed him from the Sight – and, as others followed, Thessilia extended a sliver of forgiveness towards the Speaker. *His knowledge of this had turned him craven, but only out of pure need.* She understood this now for his nature was to 'mediate' and 'document'. *The Void defend them all, but without the Sight, was he even able to reach the Maker?*

The idea disturbed her, but she daren't ask. *Sweet mercy, well now it was she who was craven!*

In the end though, even Sedjem-Alhath'naar revealed himself afflicted – and for several centuries no less. Then Guardian Mehand'Arun – whose conceited Elvern heritage would normally force him to deny any flaws – unexpectedly added his voice to the others, finishing the disastrous tally by announcing a simple: "Ninety-two years of silence and counting!"

"But it's not possible!" Guardian Cahmerhin exclaimed with the look of a bewildered good-wife somehow not comprehending that her cook had run away with the maid. Glaring towards the Speaker as though he should rectify the situation, her voice rose a notch in outrage. "Poisoned pips, I thought I was the only one! How? How?!"

Her words were like a spell releasing. The third-in-command's outburst saw the other members of the Upper Circle cut in to throw a firework of questions at the Speaker in an uproar of activity that seemed unprecedented.

They wanted answers, and they thought he would have them. Sweet mercy indeed!

Thessilia Emara watched with flaring consternation, as some of her fellow Guardians shot to their feet whilst others simply spoke loudly to be heard whilst gesturing emphatically. *Dear Maker... it was like watching Chaos descending, but the Sight was everything – their link to the Maker's power, to the Realms, to the Circle, to their awareness of the Mad Ones' monsters and agents... to... to...*

"Please, please... calm yourselves," the Speaker urged without success, his voice drowning in the storm of others so that he had to raise it substantially, "Order! I call for order! The Circle is not a circus! Guardians, please!"

It seemed he spoke to deaf ears. Stunned by the impossible development, Thessilia simply occupied her seat, undone by the enormity of it all. *Was she alone unable to conjure up any words to join the verbal fray surrounding her?*

Buried under the echo of loud voices, she stared across the priceless splendour of the main floor.

Richarmarlan's absence crawling yet deeper into her, the vast circular oratorio felt suddenly as cold and empty as the hearts of the Mad Ones. The accompanying ruckus of echoing voices cutting across stone and glass was an uncanny development, mocking the ever-unchanging light of the Void that soared down on them as though all was well. *Mercy, but it wasn't.*

Staring blindly ahead, Thessilia found Marlan Envalair's empty seat and her gaze slid onto Denarlin. As the only other person here, the First Guardian had remained quiet; she watched him frown, and-

A sudden thunderbolt hammering through her, staggered hope filled her. *So far Denarlin had never said a word. Never a-*

Thessilia's breath hitched – then relief soared.

The Commander had said nothing?! Please, dear Maker: could it be that maybe… Just maybe…? Could this still be well?

A Change of Rules

The sound of falling rain prevailed. Nothing else.

Flowing away from and out of his immediate reach, Solancei came to a halt then, sucking-in a couple of hard breaths to recover. She'd won but as ever she remained just a tad wary until she'd witnessed the last fight go out of her opponents as well. *You never knew; sometimes people were 'fired-up' – unable to acknowledge defeat – and until she sensed herself safe, she kept a tight rein on her emotions.*

Apparently gob-clobbered, but finally subdued, the spectators looked on in what she interpreted as 'stupendous incredulity' and despite her care, she allowed herself the pleasure of a narrow grin. *Whoever had been brave enough to wager their money on her, had just won a small fortune. Klaas would be pleased. Well… perhaps. All considering…*

The earlier sense of strange foreboding returning, her moment of wry amusement was soon replaced by a measure of her former unease as Simaro turned towards her with a deliberate care she did not like the look of. *The man was smarting from more than the contact of her wooden blade…*

With his haitu in one hand, he regarded her for a moment, still as a silent wraith through the hazy rain, poignant reluctance and measured comprehension rolling off his gaze. Then he finally seemed to relax a fraction to give her a smile of narrow lips and displeasure.

"Well-well then, grey-eyes," he allowed in musing tones, "Here we are then."

"Indeed." She agreed, somewhat drily, fighting the urge to grin.

Rolling her head sideways instead to smooth out a stressed tendon in her neck, she waited semi-patiently for him to unfold whatever repertoire he thought useful. Some people needed to vent some steam at this point, others took their defeat in good spirit, whilst others still, simply left in silence to lick bruised egos. When unfortunate, Solancei usually belonged to the latter group, but for now it didn't matter. She'd won and she commonly bore the loser's boorish behaviour with stoic calm. *As the winner, she could afford to. Usually…*

Simaro scrutinised her for a moment longer, then he grimaced, a mere shadow of a smile twitching at the corners of his mouth before fading.

Casting a furtive glance towards the sagging veil of leaden clouds above, he looked back towards her, head at a slight angle so as to keep his vision uncompromised by the persistent deluge.

"You should've taken my offer," he told her without preamble; the statement simple.

"You what?" Solancei straightened, bemused now but willing to humour him, "And have denied myself the pleasure of *this*?" She raised an eyebrow with droll sagacity. "Perhaps we'd better not pretend now that I had ever any choice in the matter."

Simaro's narrow mouth quivered as though he found her candid insight amusing but the sentiment never reached his pale eyes and she quickly killed a shudder before that obscure unease could reveal her mindset. *Don't be foolish! It is just the rain; just the rain… and yet…*

How she dearly wished she'd had Veranto to keep the essence of his cold ire at bay. His hostility hit her like a wave, smothering, and suddenly she couldn't have felt more isolated from her ability if it had been locked away in one of Iambre's pretty glass baubles. There was nothing she could do about it though, so she shrugged off the notion.

"I believe you owe me?" she questioned bluntly, jumping straight to the ritual part of the jackal fight, wishing for nothing else now but to be gone from there.

Simaro grimaced again, then looked at her with a scornful expression as he began to move towards her with measured purpose.

"Clever bitch!' he scolded, completely ignoring the reference to her dues, "Tell me now blade-whore: why the long wait to surprise me?"

For a moment Solancei simply stared at him, uncomprehending. *To what was he referring? Was he denying her the win?* Then she realised that he was relating to the way she'd managed to score *first-touch,* and met his intensity with a faint smile.

"I guess I tired of the game." She shrugged. "Always save the best for last. That's what they say, is it not? Now, I believe you need to speak-"

"Do you really think we're through yet?" he cut in with such a curious lilt that it inadvertently made her take a step backwards in sudden alarm. For a few heartbeats, she was wholly undecided as to which action to take or what answer to give. Then determined to hold her ground, she stuck her chin out.

"Yes, we're through," she argued, glaring down her nose in firm warning. "You are required to offer me the ritual words of surrender as per agreement to close the challenge and render the Jackal completed. Nothing more."

"But we are not finished,-" he refuted, trailing ever-nearer, the crystal coldness in his eyes now cutting, "-and, I therefore owe you nothing."

"Nothing?" she questioned, the quick tendrils of 'wrong' digging their barbs into her core. "You must be jesting, right?"

Heart suddenly beating a little more rapidly against her ribs, Solancei resisted the urge to retreat a step further as he drew nearer still, pausing right in front of her. There was a different sentiment in his near-colourless eyes now – a *knowing* almost – and the chill of the rainy day slithered along her bones like the caress of an unwanted friend.

Casually shifting his weight slightly from one leg to the other, he leaned forward, settling into a comfortable stance.

"You…-" he whispered, tilting his face slightly as if to look at something behind her before continuing with a contemptuous twist of his mouth, "-you do not come here and insult me like this! I assume you know who I am?"

Tensing, but nodding her head fraction, she gave her silent assent. *Yes… I know.*

"Very good," he carried on, "Now know this also: I owe you nothing because as of yet, we are not finished!"

Not finished?

For a beat, her head scrambled up and she almost conceded her ground then but aware that he was toying with her, she killed the urge. People had tried to make her cower before – *it shouldn't matter* – but suddenly she felt as raw as the very first time Klaas had thrust her into one of these mad fights, not knowing what to expect. For shame, the sudden shouts of definite support for Simaro began to pour out of the audience: crude catcalls and remarks better suited for a brothel. For shame, she'd heard worse too – and none of the voices seemed even half as unnerving as the solid presence directly in front of her. She wasn't short for a woman, but he stood more than a good head taller than she – and he pushed this to foul advantage now, sidling even closer: violating her personal space, clearly seeking to bully with his physical presence.

It almost worked. Almost…

A cold gust of wind, perhaps a spirit of bad premonition, seemed to sweep over her then and she scrambled her defences. *She could deal with this. She had to.*

With a dark creak of moist leather, Simaro drew his face uncomfortably close to hers and for a split heartbeat they seemed locked in place, motionless in time and space, both staring at each other: her wanting to move but seemingly couldn't, and he…?

Taking in a multitude of tiny details in that infinite bit of time, Solancei sensed she was hovering on the edge of a crumbling ledge. This close, she could smell the wetness of his clothes clearly; could easily determine the underlying scents of clean sweat, herbs, horse and dank leather as well. In fact, this close the day's-worth of blond brush covering his chin was clearly noticeable, as was an old scar, barely more than a nick above his left eye – and as more facets spun to fracture into form, her perception of Simaro deepened…

Unsure how she could have missed the detail earlier, she became weirdly aware then. *The silver flecks in his already pale-blue eyes were what seemed to lend them this lighter frosty quality, so wholly at odds with nature!* She didn't understand it but it put her off-kilter and with an unexpected pang of realisation, she suddenly knew exactly why this unusual unease had been gnawing at her since the moment she'd laid eyes on him; knew exactly why this was all about to split four-ways bad!

Because the jackal fight itself did not matter to him – winning did! Winning and something else too… something…

She tried to assimilate this new insight, but something seemed to hitch. Their agendas here did not exactly run on dissimilar courses and yet nothing made them similar in any other outlook. For one, quite unlike herself, Simaro's ambition had absolutely nothing to do with training and testing or learning. It did not even have anything to do with money or wagers or maybe even the law – *his was to do with control!* – the truth was revealed to her in a flash as the hitch smoothed out like a stubborn knot in Iambre's hair suddenly conforming to the demands of her steady ministrations. *Control…*

Had she been alone she might have allowed the unexpected feeling of dread to pull at her face with a tremble of her mouth to balance the shadow of concern she feared might have momentarily coloured her gaze, but now she buried the revealing twitch, knowing it might be too detrimental if she did not.

In place of the serenity usually offered her through a link with the now-uncooperative State of Veranto, and in then postponement of simmering fright, she relaxed her face, allowing a bland expression of aloof calm to ride over all else. Pointedly, she fixed upon a spot of broken mortar on a far-off wall.

So let him have his fun; it didn't matter. All she had to do was ignore every screaming nerve in her body, telling her to react when the actual reality had made it impossible for her to move a single muscle.

"Huh!" he grunted to himself, perusing her for a beat longer. Raising a wet kid-skin leather-clad hand, he made as though to touch her face, but habit kicked in – *a writhing sort of derision combining aversion with affront that started deep down to rush like clenching fire through her mind.*

In a blink she reacted, swiping away the attempted familiarity with a low hiss of warning. It was just what she'd needed, and where fear had crawled, icy disdain flowed forth from the inferno to kill the remainder of unease and indignant anxiety.

"Don't!" she advised in a tepid voice of narrow patience.

Simaro only grinned, raising his hand for a second attempt. She avoided it easily for the pass was clearly insincere, his aim directed to stir offence rather than true harm. *But curses...*

Solancei tensed and ducked sideways when he made to catch her a third time. He was riling her and succeeding, but she was keen to extricate herself from this before the situation could escalate; the fight was over; her win had been witnessed! *If he did not speak the usual words, then what did she care?*

For one a maddening heartbeat foolish enough to think it over, she made herself turn from him…

A hand shot out, seemingly from nowhere, seizing her like a vice by the throat; the violence was rapid, his choking hold instant. It buckled her for a blink; for an eternity; for long enough that he succeeded to force her backwards – the strength of muscle and resolve combining to manoeuvre her as designed.

Too many feelings and half a dozen stumbling paces followed, bleeding into one as she clawed and fought for breath. His hand on her neck was like a metal cuff, bereaving; a part of her knew she could resist with half a dozen clever moves, but it was a truth belonging to a foreign part of her; a part she presently seemed unable to connect with.

He is mad! The thought zig-zagged through her mind. *This is pure lunacy! Pure-*

A violent shove released her, but she lacked breath to yelp as the brief notion of the hooded spectators swept the periphery of her vision as they scattered from contact like dark roaches from daylight. To the left Solancei caught a brief impression of one man's face frozen in-between grim pleasure and dismay, then she slammed back-first into a gritty wall she hadn't even realised would be there. *It shattered the notion of shadowy insects…*

As the last air rushed from her chest on a wheeze, her knees buckled like they'd been wrenched out of joint by a giant, but it became wildly secondary in comparison with the need to alleviate her screaming lungs. Amidst the chaos there was little thought for retaliation – the world seemed to flip upside down as she met the ground, sucked in a mouthful of air on a caustic cough, then clawed down another…

Something flashed past the top of her head where her body had been, the butt of a haitu striking the wall with a dull crack. *Mercy!*

Struck by a minor deluge of chipped brick and gritty shots of old, crumbled mortar that had been dislodged on impact, she cowered for a blink; belatedly understanding, the near-hit send a wave of energy through her. *Gods' wrath! Had she not faltered…!*

Jolted, she looked up just as he adjusted and swung again.

Led by simple instinct Solancei ducked and flung herself sideways, physically feeling how the haitu narrowly missed her head this time and she was instantly sprinkled by a second eruption of flaking red stone and grey mortar as the already-brittle wall sustained the injury in her place.

Heart about to jump through her chest, she gasped. *Had he hit her true, it would have knocked her senseless! Gods be good, was he trying to kill her?!*

She needed to do something, but coughing for air, the strange development seemed to have robbed her of skill. She couldn't seem to fix her ailing wits nor get her body to comply with the need to defend. *He is mad* – the thought penetrated her the semi-daze of her mind like a spear – *the man is a lunatic and I need space!*

Alarm spurring her on, she sought and scrambled what faculties she could. The audience seemed to caper like mad spirits all around, but they did not interfere, so she scurried forward on hands and knees, dragging her own practice sword like a broken wing behind her. *Not fast enough,* her mind yelled, *not fast as you should be!*

Just a few heartbeats were all she needed though. *Just a few, to gain her feet...*

The ground failed to co-operate. Covered in wet dirt, slippery to fault with sporadic, uneven flagstones, the saturated sludge seemed to wobble as her weight came down on cracks, spilling out watery cold mud and a stomach-churning stench of stale liquid rot to match.

She cared not. Liquefied filth painting her hands and legs as she scampered to escape, she regretted not that she was hobbled by the disgraceful setting – *though it certainly didn't help* – but cursed more the ignoble feeling of panic she experienced. *And, so much for no dirt on her laces...*

Heartbeat cantering, then bolting, when her hand slipped across a large bit of loose rock, slicing her palm, she tried not to imagine where Simaro was. *The sting was nothing. She needed space!*

As if to taunt her efforts, she heard Simaro laugh with mean delight. She tried to gauge his position, but her breath seemed like a raging river in her ears as she regained her footing, slipped, sued for purchase – only to fail yet again as haste made her blunder like one of the motley fools skating for entertainment on the frozen sea of Ocean's End. *Damn Klaas! Damn!*

"Hey, we're not finished yet!" Simaro roared behind her as though to enlighten the crowd, the scuff of his boots on the concoction of rugged pebbles, mud and ancient flagstones offering her warning of his approach.

She did not pause to look; she could not, but apparently seeing his chance to halt her, the mad opponent launched his haitu leisurely. Sensing him move, she ducked with cringe-worthy cowardice to keep going whilst the intended blow yet again connected with only the wall to provoke an explosion of flaking brick-work that mixed with the rain to become a shower of pitted hailstone.

Solancei sucked down a hard breath, shaking her head to dislodge a few red flakes. *If she'd ever know Veranto, it felt in another life. Flecking curses! Go! Just go! Gain space to regroup your assets! Just-*

"Run then, grey-eyes!" He encouraged with a hint of scorn as he swiped at her again but managed to land nothing more than a glancing blow on her shin, "Oh run as you like blade-whore, but I already told you: we are not done!"

Barely listening, Solancei gritted her teeth around the incidental pain that flared. It was too brief for her to care about; another swipe followed, herding her onwards, narrowly missing as she kicked out to deflect the intended trajectory with a heel. *Acutely, she felt trapped in a bad dream.* All around them, the spectators roared at this bizarre turn of events, and though her quick thinking had saved her from another smarting bruise, it also cost her the already-tenuous forward momentum. *With a sinking feeling for the sensation, she slipped...*

Issuing a wordless exclamation of triumph, Simaro swooped down to pull her towards him by the scuff of her rain-tawny doublet. It was like being dragged backwards by a team of mastiffs but fuelled by sudden heat Solancei curled her fist, using the contact to turn with the inertia and punch.

It caught him in the ribs. She had not the room for better, but he faltered slightly – gasping a curse under his breath – and the world jolted anew. *It bought her precious moments...*

Not enough space to manoeuvre, she couldn't bring finesse of the sort that would create the impact needed, yet she hit him a second time – even as he solidified the grip, spinning her face-first into the wall he'd just abused. It threw her intended punch off and the impact made her grunt – yet she pushed hard against him, using the wall for leverage as he hitched a tighter hold, wrestling for control.

She thought she felt him falter as she kicked back, elbows connecting with his guts, but-

Thoughts scattered in a kaleidoscope of pain as her head hit the wall. *A crisp yelp reverberated through the rain, yet surely not hers?*

Senses floating, for a beat her body felt weightless as all sound ceased to be, the blistering, spinning stars that blossomed inside her mind, somehow creating a universe of their own. Then her body regained feeling and a roaring sound returned to her ears. *Stars and pain made her vision swim. She was reeling, yet didn't fall… it… it made no sense…*

She blinked, trying not to blank out as her stomach rolled to match the echoing throb in her head. She wavered, expecting to fall, then came round to hazy reality.

Simaro was holding her in a vice-grip that ground her left cheek against the wall so tight she could begin to feel its coarse grittiness engrave itself upon her skin like an unwanted tattoo. An onset of numbness followed. Not the Veranto kind of numb. Just numb. *You have to fight. You have to…*

She struggled weakly but the world was still reeling. Blistering sparkles burst before her eyes, sending her vision strange. *This was not the time to push against impossible odds – without the State of Veranto, his strength had her at a disadvantage; trapped…*

Senses fighting uproar and shock as if she were a mere novice, it flickered through her mind that this should not have happened. Somehow he nullified her skills, yet with the Veranto she could've conquered this-

'Choose your battleground as carefully as you would an item of jewellery for a state banquet,' Klaas would warn. *'And choose wisely! You alone must decide when to bide your time and when to fight. Know patience. You can kill the ox, but not if it sits on you. Know when to fold and when to bluff, lest haste or pride becomes your undoing!'*

'Yield!' her schooling screamed at her as she fought against the onslaught of useless apathy until her training finally won out. Slowly her head cleared of stars, leaving behind a soft lingering thump; belatedly she got a sense of the crowd as people cheered in seemingly unreserved appreciation for this turn of events. *It left a reek of chaos in the air. It was ludicrous! Sheer madness!*

Aware of her own stunted breath; aware of her opponent's breath hissing in her ear, Solancei pulled to gather some composure. *She could fight later, but not like this; now was a time to 'fold'.*

Ceasing her last weak struggles, she made herself go slack. *Pick your ground. Indeed...*

"Fine!" she relented through clenched teeth. She was squashed against the wall. It made speech difficult but not impossible and trying to ignore the pulse in her head, she pushed all detrimental thoughts to one side as she grated, "You've made your point. Now what?"

Simaro snorted as though amused, then bent closely into her shoulder as if he intended to confide a juicy secret. "Well if I finally have your attention now, do try your best to please me, yes?"

"Please you?" she repeated; dumbstruck. *Could she hear his smile widening?!*

"Yes, please me." He breathed lightly in her ear, his exhale like a warm breeze on her cheek.

Steadying her will, she clenched her fingers around the hilt of her momentarily useless haitu in an effort to divert the strain of her discomfort, but still her heart jumped when his fingers dug a hold of her shoulder to suddenly spin them face-to-face.

Her vision clouded. She fought it in the manner she fought all else.

He offered her a biting smile. "Now… why don't we try this again, shall we? After all, it's only ever a question of time, grey-eyes! Did I not say?"

Solancei stiffened and narrowed her eyes. Anyone who knew her would've recognized it a sure sign of warning but for once it was more than that as a few stars burst across the periphery of her vision. She blinked repeatedly. *Not helpful…*

With a bemused look for her discomfort, Simaro bent closer, experimentally curling his fingers around her neck in a proprietary fashion.

"So tell me, grey-eyes: do you feel weighted by ripening regret yet?" His nose was a mere inch from hers, and his voice tainted by the sense of discernible superiority streaming off his person.

With an effort, she stopped her eyes from flickering to serve him all her attention. In a strange way, she was pleased that his smile was an insulting curve for it ignited in her a simmering, stinging anger. *The pounding in her head was lessening…*

"Regret?" she mocked, tone cloaked by a wheeze, "Flecking rat, the only thing I regret is the existence of liars and cheats!"

Amazingly, Simaro simply laughed out loud then. *It was all too weird. Like she'd been thrust into the Void by accident and was now forced to weave herself a way back out, only the living did not belong there, and…*

She killed a shudder. *The Void? Then rather here!*

Simaro smirked with a new glimmer of steely purpose drawing into his eyes. "Oh come now… liars and cheaters?"

The smirk stretched. "Don't look at me with those flashing eyes of scorn. This is what it is. What would you do next? Pout those sultry lips? By Inkar'Chi the lewd, I pray you don't or I might just be persuaded to test if this feisty spirit of yours would prove equally troublesome when flipped face down on a pallet."

Simaro smiled to engage her imagination, his stare a lingering challenge, and for a heartbeat Solancei was rankled to the core. *His hand on her throat was only mildly restraining and his guard was down.* Indeed, she could win free, she thought, but… *but not without serious repercussions to her own health.* Gods, but he was in the perfect position to pay back even the most 'courteous' punch in the groin – and he would! For sure, the way this was heading, he'd be on her in a beat and she couldn't afford to take a 'hit' just to prove a point; couldn't afford to be laid up whilst her duties were left unattended. Gods, no matter what, she just could not afford to listen to Iambre's endless list of complaints-born-out-of-concerns that would inevitably engulf her life for the duration of any subsequent recovery. *'Choose your ground…'*

"So grey-eyes," he prompted, thumb flashing softly across her bottom lip, dragging her mouth slightly open, "Where might you feel we're at?"

Solancei stayed motionless. Derision burned her sense of pride and yet the choice was an easy one, after all, so rather than following her heart, she calmed her ruffled equilibrium and gave him a nonchalant shrug as she returned his gaze.

"Well for one there will be no 'flipping' onto any pallets, I assure you!" she promised, "You deign to touch me again and it will be the last thing you do in a while. That's where we're at."

For a blink Simaro's eyes enlarged with surprise, then he snorted as though he couldn't quite believe her brazen stance.

"Gods, you banter with your betters like a twirl for an extra quarter-coin of bronze when already the price has been agreed," he commented, pulling back from her immediate personal space with a long look for her expression. "But it's no matter – some things are not worth buying anyway."

"Indeed." She mouthed in a whisper, leaning into his hand just a hair deeper to level him with a cool stare.

A harsh speculative frown momentarily sawing across his forehead, Simaro briefly looked ready to test her determination, then he smoothed away the evidence of temptation, a slight gesture of indecision last to chase the corners of his lips down to neutral. Then, without further insight, he clenched his fingers round her neck to spin her fluidly free of the wall with one last sharp jolt of pain to the soft column of her neck.

It bruised, but she'd lingered on alert for just such an unpredictable change and kept upright this time to quickly reclaim her balance. It was a shady relief to be rid of his touch – backing away from him, a hundred different thoughts flew through her mind, all in contradictory, un-coordinated confusion. Just as she'd warned herself earlier, this wasn't good enough either, but then again, nothing seemed to be at the moment!

You're acting like a novice, she scolded herself, *just get yourself out of this now! Just back away!*

And with a mental note to practise Veranto more stridently to overcome this newly-found, disturbing inability to control her seemingly wandering thoughts, she vowed to let Klaas work her harder and longer without argument. *Soon. First thing after this. First thing after…*

Clearing her mind of random matters as best she was able, her gaze turned flinty and direct. Simaro's glittering satisfaction cut notches in her assumed calm, the rift of unease ever-ripening as she crept backwards, but anger rolled in her too, and if she knew it was never a good thing to let it rule, she was still thankful for its presence. *It bolstered her. What next? She simply could not read him.*

"Good people of Zanzier,-" he spun away from her scrutiny, raising attention as he strolled back to occupy the middle tread of the narrow courtyard, "-my apologies to you all for this delay! You see, it would seem that my challenger had not been accurately appraised of the rules and was in need of educating – however, after our brief misunderstanding, she now assures me that she's more than eager to carry on."

At the announcement, the spectators whooped. Solancei knew her eyebrows guilty of treason as they travelled high in independent consternation whilst her spirit drooped with incredulity. *Continue? Had she just heard him right?*

For a moment it felt as if the pounding in her head was set to return, but she stilled herself, letting her gaze fly to measure the mob.

It looked as though they were privy to some undisclosed bit of information, for Simaro's words were well-met and overall she spied only a few who seemed upset to have their outdoor experience prolonged. It churned her stomach but whilst she was not willing to play whatever game he was up to, she feared she'd have little choice in the matter! *Curses on Klaas! This oaf left her no choice! Fleck!*

Eyeing up the make-shift palisade still guarded by the hired men, she spent just a few blinks contemplating the odds. Again, the timing was poor and she rejected the notion. With the feel of the crowd the way it was, she was not even sure she'd make it half-way there. At least not... *not without a diversion...* and it left her only one option.

Almost she sighed. She was tired but she tried to adjust her spirit. *Good and well then. Good and well, but first...*

Turning towards him, Solancei squared her shoulders, making her movements deliberate and slow so as to convey her peaceful intentions without any margin for error. Simaro cocked an eyebrow in interest, but when she made to lower her practice sword in outright surrender, he flashed her a look of spurious disappointment.

"Don't even think about it, grey-eyes! Not if you value your health." Somewhere between chilling contempt and prayer, the low-pitched warning forestalled her action, and as though someone had just wound up the twine of an already tightly-cocked ballista just one notch further, she felt the tension quiver all around them. The ache in her jaw where his fingers had dug-in to push her against the wall hard enough to bruise, seemed to throb in line with the returning-ache in her head; a sudden icy weariness penetrated her bones, tightly followed by a sense of resignation that couldn't be soothed.

What was it he'd said earlier? His game, his rules? Well indeed!

She was no soothsayer but there was no way in the Void this was going to stay low profile. *Klaas be damned: no way!*

Old Friction... And New

"First Guardian?!" Projecting her words sharply to be heard over the buzz, Thessilia raised her voice to seize Malandaar'Vahran Denarlin's attention, "Please, Commander Denarlin, please...? How do you-

"Well, what I mean to inquire, is how…? How do you fare in this?"

It was highly irregular behaviour, but with the madness surrounding them, she thought it necessary and as voices dwindled and gestures stilled, the assembly seemed to pause, observing her with curiously vague expressions ripened by bewildered silence.

"The Commander?" Guardian Lucareo repeated with just a hint of surprise. Then Thessilia saw him blink owlishly, understanding brightening his face. She smiled, and without another word, he settled carefully into his seat. As might have been predicted, others quickly followed suit.

It was like reaching the eye of the storm, she thought. Ever-quick to catch on, even Mehand'Arun looked piqued, his attention shifting from her, to the First Guardian and back, in less than a breath.

"Why I do believe Guardian Emara is right," the Elvern Guardian agreed then, in his tone a trickle of droll wonder as his attention shifted once again from Thessilia to Denarlin.

"Well? First Guardian?" Mehand'Arun pushed a fraction later, never blinking as he pinned Denarlin with a luminous intensity that could have dissected the heart of a fly, "Verily, what about it?"

Rather than respond to Mehand'Arun, their first-in-command tilted his head a fraction so as to give Thessilia an inscrutable look.

'Really,' she seemed to read him thinking with a blade-edge of caustic resignation and she offered him a near-imperceptive shrug of

apology but did not back down. Arching her brows, she challenged him to own up. *Had he not been the one demanding the floodgates be opened?*

"Well, what have you to say, Guardian?" Mehand'Arun pushed again, narrow-eyed, cat-soft.

Leaning forward just a few inches as if in fey anticipation of some delicious detail he might tamper with, the subtle move set the long plaits of his silken hair swaying with a metallic clatter as the Dragon Silver chips scattered within their weaves softly collided against the russet panels of his Spell-Weaver coat. *It seemed a sound from another world...*

"Guardian Mehand'Arun." Commander Denarlin finally acknowledged the other Guardian, effortlessly composed, but with an edge of disapproval as he looked at the faces turned towards him, to include Rhindarhlar. "You all know, of course, that I stand ready to answer – if you but stand ready to listen."

Guardian Sedjem-Alhath'naar shot everyone a disapproving frown then, clearly furious with their earlier conduct now. It found most of them instantly a little less self-serving than before, but Thessilia ignored their rekindled serenity as well as the Speaker's reprimand in favour of scrutinising Denarlin with the same inquiring Human look, she would have conveyed him back before the Words of Power took them into Alérathnar's eternal embrace. What she needed was insight! *Malandar, old friend, forgive my imprudence, but what hope might you offer?*

Piqued, she held her ground, yet for a moment, as Denarlin met her eyes, he seemed almost...? *Almost amused?*

Wholly certain that she'd read him wrong, Thessilia tracked the absolute unalloyed perfection of his unlined face with her gaze, only to receive a now-carefully bland look. *What was he doing?*

"Well, First Guardian, what would you tell us?" Guardian Mehand'Arun demanded – once more impatiently – his insolent smile ruffling the Speaker, who all but spluttered at the lack of proper discipline since the Elvern's use of the supposed-honorific sounded closer to insult than an esteemed title.

"Respectfully, Guardian Mehand'Arun!" the Speaker admonished, though with little sting since he could seemingly not hide his own interest much longer either.

Allowing his attention to swerve from the offender so that he might also study their general, from the poorly veiled look of speculative assessment the Speaker threw Denarlin, it seemed as though he was just really 'seeing' the other Guardian for the first time since the Quickening, but at least – *unlike some* – he managed to retain a measure of propriety.

"Oh yes, yes! Of course!" Mehand'Arun belatedly flung out of hand as though to wave aside some trifling bit of incidence. "With respect then, Guardian Denarlin: what we're all aching to learn, is whether you – in all of your seemingly life-long *courtship* of Kira'Cha – might now also claim freedom from this *blindness* that seems to have afflicted us all?"

Thessilia saw the First Guardian's mouth open, then close again. It was all he gave away, yet the others were less polished. In the wake of the words, something heavy seemed to descend over the Oratorio, dampening the flow of air.

Kira'Cha? Courtship?

Stunned for a blink by Mehand'Arun's open offence, Thessilia almost shot from her seat in anger. *That Guardian's behaviour was too crude, and as for the repeated lack of respect…!*

It was an assessment shared, she knew. All around the Circle, she saw jaws clench and spines stiffen as her fellow Guardians hissed in displeasure to hear *that name* spoken so carelessly within the Circle. *Yes, she might have thrown about Osari'Chi's name earlier but that had been different; here and now, Mehand'Arun was once again deliberately trying to rankle the First Guardian, but he'd do so over her flaying tongue!*

Thessilia gripped the arm-rests of her seat and sucked in a breath. Bracing for verbal conflict, yet reassuring herself with a flash look from the corner of her eyes that her blade Oblivion was still within good reach, she raced her eyes to the First Guardian.

Denarlin, however, having somehow anticipating her intentions, warned her off with an instant, a near-imperceptible twitch of his chin in her direction.

'It's nothing,' she heard him thinking, as he raised a placating hand in synchronicity to the remainder of the Circle, likewise ordering their moods to settle.

Nothing? Guts, but it wasn't!

And yet she still sank back into her seat whilst the First Guardian directed his attention onto Mehand'Arun with the adroit care of someone willing to spend a blink or two humouring an inferior creature, but only because he must.

"Guardian, it seems a sad detour, but if you wish to go to the past at this crucial point in our debate, I really must urge you to get your facts right." Denarlin sounded civil, his voice pleasantly level as it cut across the Circle, yet the smile that accompanied remained quite the *unpleasant* reminder that the First Guardian's grace of patience was already eroding.

"Indeed, might I help you recall for just one moment-" the pleasant voice took on a dangerous velvety edge, "-that I did most assuredly not court anyone but your sister, where in fact it was you who was repeatedly driven and spellbound to go seeking out alliances with the Lady of Luck in exchange for certain promises."

Denarlin smiled with a raptor's lack of compromise, the would-be affable gesture rendering his pale face hard as smooth granite. "Now shall I go on about the futility of wasting time? Would you like to dredge up the tally of offences caused in the name of obsession? Indeed, shall we re-visit this time of chaos like good friends reminiscing? Or, would you say we are done scraping through your questionable past in favour of addressing the issues that matter to all?"

Mehand'Arun curled his lip as though to speak, but seemed to rein it back. It might have been an effort though. The man's star-shaped pupils grew large with ire and black with the essence of his Affinity as his eyes flashed long-held promises of teal fire and reckonings to come.

It caused Thessilia an edge of dread. Denarlin simply shrugged. *Untouched.*

"It was a long time ago, of course,-" Malandaar'Vahran allowed after a blink, emotions unruffled, "-and yet it is somewhat hard to forget just how much grief your ill-advised alliances cost everyone whilst you wreaked chaos across the continent in your ridiculous quest to rectify perceived slights and mete out independent 'justice'."

Fuelled by the First Guardian's word, Mehand'Arun's dark anger seemed to grow a notch. With repressed scathing undertones, he whispered, "You dare-"

"Oh, I dare, Guardian!" Denarlin overruled, harsh promise, yet void of rancour. "But strange is it not? Strange how we must always return to that one amusing fact? Still… I suppose we all retain a glimmer of our former perversions, don't we?"

Rhindarhlar Mehand'Arun snorted as though contemptuously amused then and a little of Denarlin's frosty blood seemed to warm as heat floated into his gaze suddenly – yet it did not last, for he quenched it.

As though to convey apology, the First Guardian's attention flickered briefly to encompass the other members of the Circle before settling back on Mehand'Arun's tight frame.

"We have pressing problems at hand,-" Denarlin proceeded in a tone laced with a detached coldness that could have frozen them all, "-and so I will have to insist now that we worry less about what I dare and forget entirely about your prior 'affiliations' with Kira'Cha. That way, we might all settle our minds on the subject that actually merits interest. Shall we?!"

The corners of Thessilia Emara's mouth twitch. *More than a hint of personal reprimand in that one! Very smooth! If it had been possible, Mehand'Arun's porcelain white complexion would've turned even whiter; still, he could turn to fine powder for all she cared – his conduct merited little else!* For one, the antagonistic Guardian should've known better than to try and provoke a scene in front of the Circle, but he recovered with a dignified shrug and a mien of aloof disregard – as though the choice to end discord had been his and not their Commander's.

Thessilia was not fooled, however, and she watched him with a frown of concern. Beneath that pale, unlined skin Mehand'Arun would be seething and the last flash of pointy double canines, embellished by a hooded flicker of animosity in the depths of his slanted Elvern eyes, told her more than words.

Guardian Denarlin ignored him though and Thessilia had to follow suit. Experience had taught them it was usually the best way of dealing with Mehand'Arun's *foibles*. Yet sometimes…

"So?" Denarlin enquired, almost too-eerily calm as he turned to face the Speaker, "I believe you have a question? Please proceed."

With a gracious nod Sinuhé Sedjem-Alhath'naar hesitated but a heartbeat, then plunged ahead, "Yes, very well. So… so now respectfully then, Commander: you see how it is with the Circle but as of yet you do not reveal to us the details of your own status? Does this mean that you are still hale and sound? Have you retained full use of the Sight?"

Denarlin paused a blink, then said simply, "Regrettably no, Guardian Speaker, unfortunately, I have not."

The Speaker shifted as if aggrieved, but seemingly not ill-touched, their commander looked to weigh something in his own mind, then continued, "Everything said however, I think it fair to judge that I am perhaps not as severely afflicted as everyone else. For one, I have retained a lingering connection to the Tarvia of this age. It is not as clear-cut as I should have liked it; furthermore, I have no inkling as to the location of the Alscara, but… well, perhaps we might be arrogant enough to assume that the Twins will be found within close proximity of one another?"

Commander Denarlin looked from the Speaker, who seemed semi-relieved, to the Circle, pinning everyone with a cool, analytical stare before stating, "Now, be that the case, we will secure them soon enough. Indeed, mercifully my instincts appear untainted in certain other aspects too and what remains of my Sight still allows me to feel the enemy, so in that respect, the Maker's Power is still strong."

"Alérathnar smiles upon us then: the news is not quite as dire as I had feared!" The Speaker breathed with open relief now, even as Arachk'thea's scales drew new colour from the revelation, earning her a nod of regard from Denarlin.

Few things knocked the old Guardian Speaker for long, however, and Thessilia saw that the former diplomat was already past many previous concerns as he rubbed his hands pensively. She expected he'd waste little time to capitalise, and indeed it was only a few heartbeats, then he suddenly imparted, "Commander, with your candour it has become apparent to me now that there are several options for us to pursue! It's a-"

"And yet you know that I can condone only one!" the First Guardian cut in with flat disregard, his attention drawing away from the recovering Fhearan Guardian in favour of the entire Upper Circle.

Offering the assembly a steady look, he continued bluntly, "What we must do is track down the Twins and re-assemble the Artefact! That is where our work must start. I am as aware as any just how badly our strength remains compromised – but neither the loss of fellow Guardian Envalair, nor our diminished ability to draw upon the Sight, nor the destruction wrought upon the realms, can prevent us from upholding our sacred Oaths. You feel this already."

Thessilia hid a slow smile but Guardian Denarlin quenched her triumph with a sideways glance before she might perform her small show of righteous jubilation. *Denarlin knew her too well and still... I win!*

"Very well Commander." The Speaker looked weary now, yet also a little relieved. "Your word is law, but... but what about-"

"But what about the magic then?!" Guardian Mehand'Arun called out bluntly, interrupting yet again without reservation, "What if the flows are as 'shredded' as we fear? Tell us Cor'Esardan: what are your recommendations in that regard?!"

Silence fell.

Despite her reluctance to support the Speaker, Thessilia felt her mood spike once more. They all had a right to speak their mind as equals; to pose questions and disagree, but at Guardian Mehand'Arun's spiteful tone and lack of courtesy, she understood why the Speaker nearly choked for what must surely be the tenth time since this Quickening.

As a matter of fact, she was not far behind – only this time, she was just about ready to reach for *Oblivion* rather than waste breath on posturing! *Richarmarlan Envalair was gone and that one wanted to discuss the magic?* It was another important issue, but right now it didn't seem proper to think about this before the problem of the Twins... or the Astral Aide... or even the circumstances of Guardian Envalair's demise! *In fact, it seemed downright disrespectful!*

Blind to the reactions of others, Thessilia was on the edge of her seat again before remembering herself and the Bond of Peace she was sworn to observe. From his cathedra next to second-in-command Envalair's empty one, Mehand'Arun's moon-pale plaits gleamed in concert with his luminous skin as he shifted to recline in arrogant grace, seemingly content to have cut the discussion like a flare splitting the heavens on a starless night. *Sometimes she just wished Arbar'Chi's Quills would take the man! Oh, and she wished-*

Though soured by his display, Thessilia held the peace but did not dare take her eye off the contentious Guardian's deceptively handsome face as he appeared to revel in their attention. Indeed, as she might have expected Rhindarhlar Mehand'Arun looked without remorse as he centred his stare, not on the Speaker, but squarely on the First Guardian. *As if he expected an actual answer!*

It aggrieved her – guts, but she should have known he wasn't done! As it had happened ever so frequently before, Mehand'Arun's barely stemmed contempt for their Commander seemed to issue like waves of physical wrath off his hunter's-hard frame – and as it seemed to be happening just as frequently, eyes of teal fire crashed with those of emerald ice, as his and Denarlin's gazes met and locked.

Thessilia bit her tongue. Hard.

Rhindarhlar Mehand'Arun was like a badly healed injury: ever so often it would flare up and cause trouble! Ever so often...

Her eyes flashed across the First Guardian. Denarlin still appeared composed but she recognised the deception; the colour of his eyes was growing too deep and his star-pupils too wide. *Gods rot but in that respect, he was too much like Mehand'Arun and could not deny that part of his heritage even though he might still have wanted to, but-*

Thessilia shook her head. *But this was the Circle! What in the Void was Mehand'Arun trying to do? Usually, he was far more subtle than this! Without the Sight, did he think the Maker would not see? Did he think he could stir up old ways?*

A heartbeat passed, then...

"We are waiting." Rhindarhlar Mehand'Arun challenged with corrupt patience and Thessilia felt like giving him a piece of her mind. It wasn't necessary, of course. Denarlin looked still as a predator, his demeanour subtly changing to match the eyes.

"The magic, Guardian Rhindarhlar Mehand'Arun,-" Denarlin bit out then with coolly arched derision, "-needn't concern you! You should trust that Alérathnar will not leave this matter unaddressed. You should rest assured it will be taken care of!"

"Oh but Cor'Esardan, such faith you have," Guardian Mehand'Arun shot back with a touch of sarcastic fatalism, offering the breathless Circle a lazy, insolent shrug. "You claim the magic will be 'taken care of'? Well, perhaps it will – who knows what will transpire now? We, of course, all know that the Maker is... well... *busy*... so who would he pick to set the matter straight in his place? The Watchéran of the Sabén-Heshep? Our honoured Speaker? One of the Towers?"

Denarlin blinked and Mehand'Arun managed a smirk of creeping affront. "Or perhaps… perhaps you believe yourself qualified to pursue the task? Could that be so? Oh well, wrath eat me, Cor'Esardan – one might almost agree with such a charge, yet after Old Verranor even you should be so blessed to be called on to undo a disaster of-"

The First Guardian rose so smoothly from his seat then that the action was a blur. With some effort, he appeared to halt himself from rounding on his fellow Guardian, but something that threatened to shrivel life and plunge the Oratorio into sub-zero temperatures seemed to shift in his gaze as he held Rhindarhlar Mehand'Arun's gaudy stare as though nothing else existed.

The unabashed display of aggression, found some members of the Circle shrink away as though physically repelled; as though in effort to disassociate themselves from Mehand'Arun and his arguments. Thessilia's gaze flashed to Malandar's hands, she couldn't stop herself. *The gift of his denied heritage had bled through his skin to coat the tips of his fingers as though he'd dipped them in ink, the fine spidery filigree lines already drawing up towards the first joint of each digit as if gifted independent life…*

It was not much, but it was a warning that he stood ready. Thessilia hated that she understood. Denarlin was not fond of the name Cor'Esardan; Rhindarhlar Mehand'Arun seemed to get some ghastly enjoyment out of throwing it in their Commander's face whenever he got the chance, but this was about more than insolent tones or lacking respect for rank within the Upper Circle. *This was… this was twisted on too many levels. In spite this lasting lack of goodwill between the two, this was not the place!*

Thessilia's gaze flew to Guardian Mehand'Arun and her consternation deepened when she saw him poised on the verge of conflict, half-way out of his Seat of Heritage in open response to Malandaar'Vahran Denarlin's unveiled challenge. It shouldn't have been so, but Mehand'Arun carried about him such a look of pure pleasure, that Thessilia felt a pang of alarm spread through her core. *This was not right – earlier she'd threatened to break the peace, but it had been a bluff: she would never do such a thing, even for Marlan's memory, but this…!*

Malandar don't do this, she silently begged their commander. *Malandar old friend, just don't!*

"Please Guardians," Sinuhé whispered as though worried that speaking any louder might bring down further chaos, "Remember our location… remember…"

But the Circle was stunned, and no one listened as they bore witness to the escalating argument – Emara included.

It had been such a very long time since she had even given a thought to their origins – *belonging to another time, it had no meaning anymore –* yet in this very moment, Rhindarhlar and Malandaar'Vahran looked so alarmingly similar that they could've been of one blood!

Abhorring the thought, the concept chilled and for one overwhelming moment, memories assailed…

Angrily, she pushed the unwanted past to one side but it did nothing to detract from the fact that as the two Guardians continued to eye each other like a pair of winged K'Pahr squaring up to fight, only the conflicting colours of hair and eye attested to the fact that kinship had never been part of their heritage.

"Please, Guardians recall your place," Sinuhé Sedjem-Alhath'naar beseeched again, louder now as he chanced a hesitant step forward as though to intercept, "Please, desist! Do not break the Peace of Alérathnar! This is not why we are here!"

No reaction! The Speaker made a strangled sound of frustration as his warning fell unheeded.

Though not cold, Emara shivered, old times unearthing. Out of nowhere, ominous thunder rumbled somewhere in the distance. Denarlin looked unforgiving and for one long moment of uncertainty, she thought the Commander might actually break the Bond of Peace…

A furious slash of lightning bearing Mehand'Arun's Weave stabbed across the Void beyond, only to be sundered by another as Denarlin eradicated the poorly-veiled threat without blinking. *And still Power continued to gather…*

"Guardians desist!" the Speaker barked in such angry disbelief that his sentiment must have finally carried physically to the Commander for though he still appeared grim, he visibly checked himself then and let the gathering flows of Power blink back into the Void. For half a heartbeat longer, his gaze continued to linger on Mehand'Arun's though, yet then he shifted —with some apparent reluctance breaking the contact with a withering expression of contempt.

In response to the Commander's abrupt return to sanity, Mehand'Arun's nostrils flared once in open disbelief. For one shocking moment he bared double canines in a silent hiss at Denarlin's back: a true old-fashioned feral Elvern challenge, yet just the same the pale-haired Guardian stopped shy of leaping forward, and Thessilia knew a glimmer of relief as he finally released his own flows of Power. *So… even he would not dare pursue the conflict any further then. Even he…*

Whispers of shared relief issued from the Circle like a near physical breath.

The dark tendrils retreating to leave their Commander's fingers unblemished once more, Thessilia slowly exhaled. *Spell-Weavers! Always too much trouble!* Every one of the Upper Circle possessed a measure of Affinity but to step between two 7th Tiers loaded with all of the Maker's glorious Power…?!

Emara shrugged with displeasure for what had nearly come to be and unlaced her clenched fingers with a soft sigh. She was glad that Malandar had seen sense; glad the incident was over and the peace unbroken, but why did it feel to her as though some very real, but hitherto-undefined limit, had just been hacked to pieces by the two Guardians' behaviour?

Sensing the touch of golden eyes, she shared a moment of lingering concern with Jonaeus Lucareo and their eyes floated in tandem to the pale-haired Elvern.

One look upon Guardian Mehand'Arun's form as he slinked back into his ornate seat, challenge rescinded, was enough to assure her that he remained utterly furious, but grouches carried no weight here. *He'd have to shake it off!*

She smoothed down her curls and refuted Lucareo's lingering gaze with a reassuring gesture that feigned more personal faith in the Circle than she actually felt. *There was nothing they could do, anyway.* They both knew the Guardian Speaker would take careful mental note of these proceedings, but that was that. For sure, Mehand'Arun might be foolish enough to challenge their Commander; might even be arrogant enough to break the Peace within the Circle, but when all was said and done, Guardian Denarlin still wasn't. *Mehand'Arun would not win; he never had!*

"Good then." Punctuating and sealing the subject, Guardian Denarlin's words called her back to the Circle just as he reclaimed his Seat of Heritage with a soft swish of dark robes and subtle leather.

"So with the risk of sounding condescending, I will assume that this settles us all in agreement on the question of magic," the First Guardian stated with a clear hint that his patience needed no other challenge and the complying silence was telling.

With a quiver of a new wry smile the First Guardian inclined his chin vaguely towards his would-be challenger. "Well and good then. Now, since the 'esteemed' Guardian Mehand'Arun appears to be his usual, charming-self yet again, I suggest that we do not offend our allegiance with any more randomly-pointless subjects! Already, we procrastinate while the Veils draw apart! Time waits for no one; nor do the Veils! Try and remember that – or they will surely fall for good this time!"

For mercy, Guardian Mehand'Arun had the grace to look penitent then. It was not much but Thessilia saw their general unclench his jaw, a touch of the carefully-hidden, but still pent-up ferocity leaving him in response.

"The Circle already understands that everything has changed and yet – essentially – it has not." Leaning slightly forward, Guardian Denarlin made a brief gesture of conciliation towards Sinuhé. "Of course the Guardian Speaker makes an appealing case; one that we must certainly honour…"

The Speaker looked immensely relieved, if only for a blink. Then, with a sidelong glance towards Richarmarlan's seat, the Commander said, "And so honour it we will – but not to the exclusion of all else! You know, that we could never placate our instincts as completely as the Guardian Speaker would have us do! It is not in our nature – even with stunted Sight and a diminished number, we would not be allowed the peace, the Oath is too strong, too commanding. Still, permit me now to suggest a compromise? Something we can all endure?"

As supportive as they'd just been of the Speaker, several of her fellow Guardians were nevertheless already offering the Commander sage nods of approval and Thessilia Emara gave in to her ever-present Human-nature, and grinned. *If Denarlin had cast a spell in their midst to persuade them, he could not have done a better job to win attention – and just like that, everyone got what they wanted. Just like that. Well… more or less, of course.*

Her smile widened.

But let the Speaker gather dust in the folds of his voluminous toga! Let him drag Rhindarhlar-pestilence-Mehand'Arun by the scruff of his black-embroidered collar to see the Story-Spinners and pick at the stitches of the Tapestry and old History! Meanwhile, she'd be applying her assets where she was supposed to and unlike Sedjem-Alhath'naar she would not be cowed by the past. *Not even if Richarmarlan Envalair's absence grated upon her state of mind! Not even if it felt like a dull hatchet retching across her heart as though her right to name him Husband had not long since faded!*

Guts no – not even then!

Solancei's Memoirs

The Province of Tarléon.
Ocean's End.
Autumn of 780 P. C. W.

So you recall, I trust, what I told you about discovering at my parents' funeral that I had the affinity to reach and link with a peculiar concept, named the State of Veranto? You recall how it benefitted my disposition?

Well, now I have to talk to you a bit about the flip side.

Have you ever felt what it's like when people whisper at you, about you, all around you? And you can hear everything, yet you're not supposed to?

In case you by some miraculous stroke of fortune can still shrug and stand ignorant, then count your blessings – but allow me to enlighten. You see, it creates a certain kind of pressure on you. *In you.*

A pressure to ignore the things said, yet to hear them; a pressure to listen, but not to listen; a pressure to rise above it, and yet an urge to defend and respond! It digs into you, burrowing deeper and deeper until something's got to give and on that note, let me confess something to you before I get to the real point.

See I'd already known plenty of pressure by the time I reached seven, so the concept was not foreign to me: I was never an easy child; I had been known to rebel against authority – apparently because I was many a thing I wasn't supposed to be – and as a result, I was familiar with the pressure of expectations and the pressure of others to instil upon me their values of imagined perfection.

The pressure of expectations drew up the worst in me though. *Why?* I told you already: what do I know? Perhaps I feared the rush of heady anxiety that rides upon people's notion of what 'good breeding' should entail? Perhaps I do not fare well under restraints? Or perhaps it's something else, slithering within my core like an illness?

In any event, it so happened that people had expectations of me; so many expectations. And I might not have minded, but the way they conveyed the need for me to conform and curb myself into their narrow moulds called 'tradition' and 'nobility'…?

The pressure would grow within me, and within the people surrounding me, I suppose. It would grow and grow until finally something would give, be it me or my parents and their staff. *It made me few friends.* No wait, let me rephrase that. *It made me no friends.* I was perceived of as 'trouble' first and foremost; people would recall my due title as a secondary inconvenience, but was I concerned?

Yes and no. By the time I found myself on the ice watching my parents' coffins slide from sight, I was not, but there had been a time. *Before…*

I say 'before' since I'd known plenty of attempts to help me learn restraint and control so that I might understand the need to curb my own behaviour, and one such lesson was the re-occurring 'visit' to the battlements of Fjeldarah's tower.

The Tower was supposedly to help me ponder my wayward ways and what might happen if I yet again played trivia with mother's word and father's repulsive ideas of how my time should be spent in itchy woollen skirts too long to climb without them snagging at my ankles, preferably-with-my-nose-turned-in-worship-and-prayer-that-the-Gods-might-send-us-even-temperatures-to-better-culture-the-pure-see-through-ice-so-coveted-by-the-rich-western-provinces. *Yeah, I know…*

But nonetheless, there I would shiver and freeze for undisclosed lengths of time, exposed to the elements and my own thoughts, for as long as deemed necessary – grateful beyond measure when Taliana would finally be permitted to fetch me inside to stand before my parents with the renewed hope in their eyes that I'd learned. And for a while, I thought I had, and things would even out, but then…

It was a 'treatment' that should have worked. I hated the hard feelings that grew within me whenever I perceived I'd somehow disappointed or failed to achieve a required merit, but with time it meant less. I wanted to conform, but somehow it was just not in me. I did not know I had an affinity to link with the State of Veranto, but it was manifesting – aspects of its uses slowly trickling into my core – though I was yet not conscious of the fact.

Still, the more they 'punished' the less I cared – and then I slowly learned to rise above it, which in turn brought more pressure: the curse of unguided talent,

I believe; the curse of me reaching for some unformed, yet-undisciplined glimmer of Veranto, whilst on the cusp discovering a 'back-door' into working it in a semi-unconscious manner.

So why did no one grow smart enough to realise my abuse? Why did I not grow smart enough to embrace sanity?

Well, no one registered my affinity. If they had, things might have panned out differently, but Tarléon is a frontier province that perhaps lacks certain 'refined information', or dare I say it: 'care'? You cannot get further east before the endless ice takes hold. People are busy surviving. A lot goes into that; a lot of skill and attention. Taliana might or might not have realised the root of my problem, but if she did, chose to ignore it. Yet in her own way, she repeatedly saved me: whispering seemingly magic words in my parents' ears to bring lenience where harsher methods might have been applied to help me comply. *Gods, she'd been one of my only allies – and now, next to the graves, there was nothing left for me but the 'new deep distance' which promised another kind of protection even though my eyes burned.*

And now, if you would allow me, I would return to my original point, please. See, the State of Veranto is marvellous when you can shape it; when you can control how it moves within you. However, when or if you cannot, it might just break you, or worse. Because what the State of Veranto does to you in the most brutal, most basic stage of learning, is to – for lack of a better description – take away your ability to care: an example of which I have tried to convey to you with my story above. Of course what happens is that the Novice is guided through this in a safe environment where they may learn to build on this to overcome the extreme urges and develop an inner map of strength and resilience to coax forth the additional benefits that matter: like heightened vision, pinpoint focus, peripheral wherewithal – all of which might eventually bring to form a true Master.

In turn, as a Master, one might use these now well-developed skills and abilities to push past pain and illness of the body, to promote heightened stamina and lower the need for rest, to make you harder, faster, to create a more accomplished scholar, a Kizano dancer of martial arts beyond normal expectations, et cetera. Of course, building upon this, a true 1st Grade Master can do more, but that is a side-note for later, and the point, for now, is to make you ponder how an untrained child can possibly differentiate between the sublime extremes offered by Veranto and the sublime danger of taking any small blessing too far?

I need not say it, but I will. Without a mentor, a child will of course not know at all – and so I later learned, neither did I! *And I was lucky. So, so lucky…*

I was no self-taught prodigy – or maybe I was, but I could argue the validity of this point for a century, the more humble side of me ever winning. Still, as it were I could not just do any and all of the above. *Not yet, at least.* However, what I had done, and could do, was to dabble on my unconscious level just enough to abuse this yet-unquantified, unqualified, budding ability all hundred ways of the holy script, to set myself above the pressure of parents and title – and it came through on the day of the funeral – my tight needs and emerging ability clicking yet again, but deeper, stronger, better defined, than ever before.

The flip-side of Veranto is the tightness that comes after the calm and the peace. To the untrained, it can be overwhelming to the point where the very power it will give you over mind and body, does not seem a blessing but a frightening ordeal to shatter your understanding of what's real and imagined.

I was at peace, the grief and fear of shaming myself and the dead gone as if evaporated, and that's probably where a novice under guidance would have been told to halt and ponder the event, yet I did not have a mentor to tell me 'halt' – and I guess I had embraced the link a little too eagerly, but in any event – next came along the 'blessings' of enhanced senses to knock me off my perch as everything expanded and grew crystal.

It stunned me. It made me lose the connection, but as I struggled to stay linked to the peace, so came back the unfurling of my senses, and Gods…

Had I indeed cried, or ranted against the Gods, or stomped around like a certain spoiled Heiress I can think of, perhaps people might not have watched me with strange thoughts that day, but I didn't – and so they did. A whole outside world of mourners and retainers, priests and nobles, pressing against my newly perfectly-detached – but still-developing – awareness, rendering me both numb and subjected to a strand of pressure I had never before experienced.

It was an unpleasant realisation, banked by my new serenity – but behind raised hands and veils they whispered. *Whispered about this young Duchess' remarkable composure, so beyond and above her years, and if only the girl knew the truth of her parents' demise…*

I warn you: the State of Veranto is a double-edged blade of purest Kaisor steel. Abuse it and you will suffer! Walk the line within the perimeter of your ability, and it'll be your most arduous friend and weapon. The second thing I experienced for the first time at that funeral, was this dual-sided phenomenon of my ability – for the detachment: this bizarrely perfect 'entity' that helped numb me, was just as easily broken by the pressure of new, unexpected feelings of deepening dismay and anxiety.

You see, the Veranto allowed me to hear the comments otherwise too obscure for the common ear, and that threatened to fell me, even as the detachment grew enormous! I think I must have pushed hard at Taliana's image then, for it became brittle and shattered – just what I'd needed – though maddeningly the whispers soon allowed the cold back in again till I could no longer have said if the Veranto or the weather were to blame for the glitching, stretching numbness within me.

Had Taliana and my parents really been murdered?

Gods' mercy, it seemed that all the mourners thought it so! Oh… and that I alone, knew nothing!

Solancei

Heiress of the Realm

Crown Princess Iambre del'Dulac Isthalani Actarione paced circles around the central table.

A sweet-smelling, colourful arrangement of fresh flowers adorned the middle of the costly piece of furniture, but she remained oblivious to its presence for the same reason she also utterly failed to enjoy the opulent grandeur of what was supposedly one Castle Zanzier's finest suites.

Instead, and not for the first time, the same thought kept echoing through her mind raising excruciating, visceral disappointment. *Typical – by the hanged rat and bone – this was just typical!*

Iambre frowned, then smoothed her face recalling her mother's words about lines, only to frown again – and Gods' hate! She'd been left waiting before – *one could often pretend it were of no matter* – but this fig was too hard to swallow and she was done chewing; done glossing over her misgivings.

Rats, and what was the point of such stupid pretence anyway? There was no one watching but Palea – and if she was hardly putting on the best regal display for the girl, at least it was not the first time her youngest handmaiden had been subjected to this lack of decorum either.

Iambre twirled the usual strand of hair around her middle finger till it throbbed, eyes glaring at the lofty ceiling rising in several arches to form a series of five domes all painted with swirling designs of midnight blue around each central rosette layered with bronze and gold leaf. *If she'd had a tail it would have swished...*

It was a ridiculous thought; she didn't know where it had come from but that seemed to be the case with many of her notions these days, and for a moment she wondered if Lance-Captain Bilandro Metavo would have liked her more – *or less* – had she had a tail. Biting her lip, she released her poor finger, but the damage had been wrought, and there… *Bam! Just when you thought yourself beyond capacity to think up more rubbish… 'Bam', it caught you by the roots! Rats, but for all she knew, Bilan might not even like her at all anymore!*

"My Lady, perhaps we should-"

The Princess rounded on her handmaiden with an expression that must have conveyed her nuisance just perfectly, because Palea cut herself off and shut her *pretty* rose-bud mouth with a very audible click of teeth.

It was unfair; *she* was being unfair – *rats, obscene even* – and Palea did not deserve the ire owed someone else, but death and daffodils…!

Iambre sighed with a shimmer of regret. Trouble was that she'd had a lot of practice with 'obscene' recently and she was getting very flipping good at it. Too good, perchance – given the fact that Solancei was definitely late beyond late, and apparently prepared to accept whatever consequences Iambre might mete out, in favour of ignoring her summons. *It had happened before – it would happen again, but-*

Spinning sharply on her heel to stalk towards the grand fireplace with the carved doves and soaring Zanzierian eagles, Iambre dug another round hollow in the expensive carpet she was abusing beyond reason. She had no intention caring whether she ruined the costly Alahbrodai rug, nor could she currently summon enough compassion for the poor cleaning maid who'd have to comb the weave for several hours before realising it might be a lost cause. *Once she might have. Later she definitely would. But not now. Not yet! Yes, obscene indeed…*

Eyes drawing to the large water clock above the fireplace's centrally positioned eagle, she wished that she could slow it down and tried not to flinch as each drop of water trickled with the certainty of time across the twelve hollow lily pads. *Time… never enough; always searching for more; always wishing…*

She swallowed a hint of unexpected unease and tried to rekindle her suddenly-fading streak of anger. There was something obscene about that clock too, she thought with a sour mien. Something she disliked almost as much as the daunting tapestries hung side-by-side in gilt frames across the long back wall; something that made her want to turn her eyes from the sight, yet it also repeatedly prompted her to return for another look.

Her eyes fluttered back to the clock.

Maybe she should have the ugly thing brought to Lancei's chambers for the duration of their stay so that the woman would have no excuse for poor timekeeping – but she supposed the clock could not be moved, just as she rather suspected that Lancei would be taking no heed regardless.

Iambre sucked in a deep breath. *Had she really been that unreasonable, that she warranted this kind of treatment from her best friend? Had she really been that horrible and was she really such a bad person that she'd lost track of the very answer to those questions?*

Exhaling, she felt the answers should make no difference. At least not in respect to people attending their duties. It wasn't like she herself was particularly ecstatic about ten days of pomp and prattle, but she'd endure and she'd tend to *her* duty regardless of petty arguments and differing opinions.

Or… at least she would do. Providing her pesky handmaiden could only get over herself and come help her ready before the arrival of her escort! Sure it wasn't as if she feared that Bilan would mind if he arrived at her door to find her still dressed in a short frilly shift, but-

Cheeks colouring, heart skipping, Iambre tried to steer her imagination away from such a scenario. A look down the front of her lilac silks didn't help her dispel the notion though and she could jammer on about Lancei's tardiness and her obstinate absence, but it didn't change the fact that it was without a doubt the issue of Lance-Captain Bilan Metavo that kept her childhood friend from making a tidy appearance as requested.

Bilan... Lancei. It was so complicated and yet it was roaring simple. If she didn't exactly need Lancei's blessing to pursue her feelings for the Captain, she also didn't need the endless nagging, nor the righteous lectures on right and wrong! *Yes, she might be wandering slightly 'sideways' with her affections, but she'd never forget about her duty to the realm; never forget about what was right! Why did Lancei fail to comprehend?!*

For a moment the spike of anger came back, burrowing deeper into her core, and Iambre lengthened her prowling stride.

Fine! So lately she might have been somewhat unreasonable, but was she not going to make amends for her shortcomings tonight? Did she not intend to do some very un-royal grovelling in private to the very two people she truly cared about?

Reaching the end of her salon, Iambre kicked at a helpless tassel and heard Palea issue an almost inaudible sign. She ignored the handmaiden and wondered if she could also ignore the urge to rip those ghastly tapestries from the walls.

The gory cross-stitch scenes seemed to haunt her, the renditions of the particularly important events of the Chaos Wars hardly something she would have chosen for herself – and in her heightened mood, she had to wonder how these Zanzierians had deemed it suitable for a lady of any stature and name? The priceless Iddian carpet with its beautiful shimmering colours of purple, red and gold were certainly the prettier choice – shame they lay beneath her feet and not the hideous antique wall hangings – but such was her existence it seemed: full of things she'd rather have spun sideways and upside down to suit her dreams and wishes.

Iambre scowled but try as she might not divert her mind from the real source of her misfit anger. *Which was idiotic! She was the Princess! The future Queen of Ostravah! And yet she was subjected to this… this waiting game! As though she were the handmaiden…*

Kicking at the row of tassels as she staked back down her salon, past Palea in her pretty state of patient concern and pink organza layers; past the seating arrangement of imported Iddian settees of heavily-carved wood and brocade layered to match the rugs; past the heavy table with the flowers; past the pale cream sofas by the fire…

"My Lady?" Palea tried again, her tone coloured by light anxiety, "I mean only to say that the afternoon is waning, and perhaps…"

Iambre paused her gait. Turning around, she capitulated with a heavy sigh and flopped into a pale-green love-seat to offer her young handmaiden a gesture of resigned compliance.

"Palea dear, I know the afternoon is shrinking," she forestalled the other woman, "Drat, I also know I have a banquet to attend and that I have a duty to preen my feathers for all of Zanzier's best and most worthy to inspect and inspire, but Gods…"

Palea nodded like a sage twice her age. "My Lady, I understand but if you would but permit me to make a start, perhaps My Lady would feel better armoured to wait out Solancei's arrival in a manner less strenuous to her health and…"

Palea paused. As if embarrassed, she licked her lips, then smoothed her skirts with neatly-gloved hands, before saying, "Well… it's only… that is to say… it is only to remind My Lady, though she is of course well-aware, that the Zanzierians are avid sticklers for-"

"For stuffy, old-fashioned hankerings for what once were?" Iambre cut in with a grim twist to convey the truth of her persuasion. "For pompous lords so far up their own ancestry that it's a wonder they've managed to crawl into town in favour of an event so insignificant as my wonderful little visit?"

"My Lady…" Palea sighed with sustained goodwill and shrugged helplessly as she shifted as if to come forward.

"Palea I don't need your comfort," Iambre forestalled – a little, suppressed guilt seeping into the tone, though she could still not help the nuisance either. "In fact, what I need is Solancei to come as requested, nothing more."

Sitting forward, she rubbed her eyes. *Was she getting a headache? It wasn't like her.* Gaze wandering briefly to the golden wall-sconces where lit tapers burnt in smokeless elegance to illuminate the salon, Iambre wondered if this was the culprit rather than Lancei? There were certainly enough straight candles in sight to supply a large temple for a month and they'd all been lit to compensate for the dreary afternoon light.

She sniffed, fingers going to her temples. One could not argue that the light did serve to spread a warm soft glow throughout, but if it served to displace any discomfort one might otherwise have felt with the bleak day progressing, it was also making the air somewhat stuffy.

The rustle of Palea's skirts brought her head up. The handmaiden wore a tiny frown, her eyebrows arching with concern, and whether Iambre had wanted it or not, this time the woman did not back off.

Flowing to her knees, Palea said, "My Lady should not make herself ill. Please, I know we did not get a good welcome here but all the more reason not to build on that grief now. You can win these people over, I know this in my heart, but…"

Iambre paused her fingers' circular movement and snorted with mock derision as she looked at her lady with a first real quiver of mirth. "Oh Palea, you are sweet. Tell me again: how many summons has Solancei Calverhana had now?"

Palea lowered her lashes. "Three, My Lady."

"Hmm, yes I thought so," Iambre mused, hard-pushed to stop her mood from deteriorating again.

Solancei. Three times. What was the matter with her stubborn daffodil? It had been days and days since she'd fallen off that stupid horse of hers and last Iambre had seen, there'd been nothing wrong with Lancei's legs either! *This had to be about Metavo…*

The notion knocked a hole through her defences, allowing a new wave of disappointment. *How could Solancei simply treat her like some casual acquaintance rather than her liege lady? How?* Here she was: prepared to offer her friend many an honest concession this afternoon, but now? The planned heart-to-heart was rapidly becoming less likely with every drop of that blinking clock; respect went both ways. She guessed she'd been warned, but if Lancei wanted to take their issues over Bilan Metavo to new levels, then Iambre could play that game too. *Now see if she'd stand for this!*

"Palea?" She smiled at the younger woman although that spike of anger was returning. "I think we may not have a choice but to make the best of this… *this unexpected situation.* Kindly, might you begin preparations?"

Palea blinked in surprise but recovered from her loss of composure in a beat. "My Lady, I would be honoured. What would-

"I mean, how flows your preference today?"

Iambre pursed her lips. "Palea dear, my plan was simply to somehow glide through this evening without causing further offence. Gods, you good as said it yourself: Knights Commander Zulavi is already looking down his refined nose at my inability to get my own people to stick to the schedule and arrive at his gates on time. I needn't give him other reasons to question my qualifications, that's all."

Palea's lips bent in a perfect moue of understanding. "Indeed. Just leave it with me, Princess."

Gliding off towards the gilt bedroom doors, Palea began humming to herself, and Iambre's humdrum tension made one final attempt at undoing her. *She didn't let it, but the thought of allowing Palea to take sole charge of this…*

She quenched a sigh. Palea was a neat scribe and a brilliant secretary, but she was still the youngest of them all by a whole six years, and having come into her service directly from the temple of Zulari'Chi, she was still usually more involved in parchments and inks than with dresses and facial paints. Of course, it was no lie that Palea's skills looked very promising in the latter area – indeed, she'd seemingly adopted the Etruian style with the passion of a true native, but she did not yet have the attention to detail that Iambre would demand tonight. The hair alone might take Palea several hours even if Iambre remained intent on toning down complexity in respect of the more austere Zanzierian preferences. It didn't mean she wanted to look 'Zanzierian drab', however. *Death and daffodils, no not tonight! Not when Bilan was going to be her escort. Not when he-*

She killed another grimace and just about stopped herself from wringing her hands. Of course, her third lady, Ina Uttorian, would've have done nicely, but she was currently still at the local shrines bearing crown offerings.

It was rotten luck; impeccably stupid timing! Had she not sent Ina, Solancei's presence – *or infuriating lack thereof* – would have seemed less an offence, but well… some things were ever beyond irrelevant, were they not?

Iambre shot to her feet. "Palea?!"

The handmaiden rustled back into the salon, a questioning expression lighting up her doll-like features, enlarging the woman's already-enormous summer-sky eyes.

"Palea, see that you keep your selection plain for the purpose of appeasing Zanzierian sensitivities but please allow me to retain a hint of sophistication too, or I might just shrivel and die."

Palea curtsied. "But of course My Lady. I have read the briefs. I can do this."

Iambre nodded, relieving herself of the urge to stalk after the handmaiden to supervise like an eager matron, as Palea retreated into the dressing room once more. Again, she was being unkind. Palea was not all hopeless. She would take pains to do well since all her 'efforts' were set to influence people's perceptions of her rights and capabilities to serve within the Princess' inner circle. *Trouble was: Palea thought this was just about another state banquet, yet it was so much more…*

Toying with the long strand of hair again, Iambre indulged in a smile as her mind spun with equal measures joy and anxiety that Captain Metavo would soon be turning up at her apartment doors. *Captain Metavo… Bilan… here…*

Even if it was not proper, her heart seemed to not care one whit for duty and future as it twisted with a sweet sort of anticipation she'd only ever known when thinking of *him.* It was an impossible match, of course: one that would never be sanctioned, but Gods…

As she tried to picture the Captain's familiar face and somehow failed, her mind still breathed the name with an ease that stirred excitement and more than a little panic to be seeing him again. *Would he be able to understand that she was trying to amend for her terrible behaviour? Would he be able to understand and forgive? Or had she lost him before he was ever really hers?*

Iambre swallowed nervously. For Bilan, she had a reason to look beautiful. In fact, she amended, for him she wanted to look breathtaking, because-

Because he deserves the effort? Because you want to remind him of what he's been missing? Because you are too fickle for your own good? Because…

She sighed hard. Was it wrong that she wanted to distract him with looks in order to twist his disposition? Probably. But if he was still determined to refuse her; if he should remain unsusceptible to her apology, she'd need every help she could get, and if that still wasn't enough?

Iambre chewed her bottom lip. *Would Lancei just show already!*

Solancei swallowed feelings of irony.

She'd tried to oblige Klaas; really she had, but now there was only one way she could possibly stop this mad Zanzierian from laying a hand on her again – and it was not going to involve a diplomatic exchange of sealed parchments and signed charters! Instead, *'Cheska from New Wood'* had just been given a promotion in skills and motivation – the haitu alone would no longer be enough – and in turn, she wondered what Simaro would choose to throw at her.

With the thought, a surge of apprehension bound her feet to the ground as she considered the limited options. Why he'd not availed himself of more tricks earlier, she didn't know – didn't understand – for she knew him highly trained and consequently imagined him surely able to claim Master of Kizano, 3rd Grade.

So why had he held back? It was a worrying question she did not have an immediate answer to and she'd have to assume that he wouldn't prove as 'courteous' a second time. Indeed, since he'd proven unwilling to accept her first win, there was absolutely nothing to indicate that matters would differ now, and this… *well, this was tricky!*

Lowering her lashes as if to centre herself in preparation of resuming the fight, Solancei kept half her attention on Simaro, simultaneously chancing another surreptitious glance at the guards by the makeshift gate. *He* was in the way but that needn't stop her – and in a blink, she'd made her decision. She'd come here to partake in a jackal fight, not to see it escalate into some imbecile situation where her mad opponent – *Gods curse him to the Beyond* – called the shots!

Watching Simaro slash the air experimentally with his blue haitu, she shook her head, cursing under her breath. Right now, the Gods might as well take her for the idiot she'd been for allowing herself to be trapped in this situation. And whilst they were at it, let them take Chief Eso Mehadja's flecking, persuasive tongue as well.

'Just a light bit of exercise before the call of duty.' She could recall the Chief's smoothly-persuasive words without fail. *'A new challenger has stepped forth – no duel – only sport. It'll be tricky but a win is not impossible and I expect you'll do quite well. It should be naught, if not a nice bit of practise.'*

Practise? Hah! Solancei knew she'd have to curb her overpowering need to ram those very words right down Klaas' throat when next they lay eye on each other! *That. And more!*

Pushing all ideas of strangling Klaas from her mind, she drew a clenching breath and mumbled a small prayer for Kira'Cha to lend her a sliver of good luck. She usually preferred to make her own luck rather than trust in favours bestowed by the capricious Goddess, but right now she'd need as much as she could get, and if only the 'Empress of Games' would extend her a fraction of goodwill, she should be able to see this through. *Should...*

As it tallied, the light in her opponent's eyes could have melted the hoar frost from the walls of her keep back at Ocean's End but she looked him blandly in the eye.

Someone's crude comments gripped Simaro's attention for the briefest of time and in that split moment, where his eye drew towards the joker and his mouth curled up, simulating appreciation, Solancei steeled herself and attacked.

Keeping the dull practice-blade close to her body as the air suddenly seemed to explode with echoes of warning calls for Simaro to '*beware the witch*' and '*foul play*', Solancei feinted, swerving hard left.

Up and away – her haitu moved his with perfect intent as she dropped below his defence to ride a tight spin into a crouch that became *pebbles-in-the-surf.*

Just as she'd hoped, the speed and voracity of her attack saw him briefly disadvantaged and with compliments for perfect timing, the sweeping drop-kick hit the back of his shins, upending his balance, spilling him onto the ground. *The notion was breezy, but she hoped he bruised!*

Completing the elegant form with the flickering speed of a once-faulty compass-needle unexpectedly locating true north, she bounced upright, leaping clear. At this moment she'd have but fractions to act if her plan was to work; Simaro might be on the ground, but he was by no means decommissioned – a true fact indeed, as he spun, disregarding the additional ruin of his leathers, to rapidly twist his bulk and perform a counter-strike with a hasty *rushing-dog-slashing-fern.*

Flickering her haitu sideways, she repelled his angry attempt to hamstring her plans and launched directly over another of his swipes, a flash bounce easily negotiating her past blunt retaliations without mishap.

Yet as she'd known, he was fast too: slipping slightly to gain a knee it took him only one sinuous move to recover purchase, then he was back. *Back in her way...*

Solancei shifted her haitu without breath. *She could not allow him a blink of respite or-*

Barely touching the ground, she bounced off on her left foot, pirouetting on her right to flick her body like an acrobat at a banquet feast.

A glimmer of his surprise registered; she used the advantage, uncoiling her leg, aiming for his jaw…

Simaro seemed to shift before her eyes – or maybe it was but a trick of the rain, she'd never know: *snake-retreating–past-the-waterfall* struck him high on the shoulder – *not where intended* – yet she almost didn't mind. *The inertia spun him sideways, killing his balance, sending him to the ground once more, and that-*

Haitu clattering against a broken flagstone, Simaro landed face down with an escaping grunt. Her technique had not a whiff of elegance, she'd be going home with dirt on the wrong side of her boots, and her attack hadn't even knocked him out as it might have done in more favourable circumstances – but because this was Zanzier where women did not do combat, and because she was no longer holding back, the attack had still worked an effect. His demise melted the collected enthusiasm of entire backyard between breaths, as for moments, all stilled bar the deluge: no one moving; no one speaking.

Solancei allowed herself an insolent grin. She could've jumped him, wrapped her legs around his neck and torso to take him down by the aid of his own bulk and her speed combined, twisting limbs from sockets, or worse – the effect would have been similar – but something had warned her against the risk of close combat. She could've followed through to keep him down as well, but-

The day was growing old. Don't play all your cards. Keep a little tucked away…

She backed up. Half-way on his front, half-way on his side, Simaro was labouring to roll onto his back but he looked stunned, *dumbstruck,* and she briefly wondered if he'd cracked his head when he went down. The grin widened. *Well... no matter the time of day, the-bitch-in-her-thirsty-for-more-payback flecking well hoped so!*

Combating a heady sense of unbalanced urges, she made herself back up further from his cloudy, incredulous expression. It was foolhardy, of course – she knew she should be making a break for it – but her actions appeared to have frozen the entire assembly of spectators into a broad backdrop of grey sculptures; her own tension still coiled within her like a spring, and...

Solancei couldn't help herself.

"Well then..." she drawled in her New Wood accent, eyes deliberately boring into his as she kept retreating. "It's been fun of course, but I really must get going. Please... oh please don't make it too hard on yourself that I got you. After all, you nearly got me too, so..."

On a sudden whim, she twirled her haitu in the mock parody of a young recruit saluting a superior officer: the smart economic flourish to bring the blade up vertically before her torso, often witnessed but never taught to her. Still looking him in the eye, she dipped her forehead briefly to the wet wood, the would-be gesture of respect nothing more than a teasing, disrespectful bob of the chin. *It would have to do.*

With a lopsided grin for the situation she ripped her eyes from his, spun and tore directly towards the gate without further delay.

Elation soared. Speed was hers: all pains were gone and the nervous energy that still burned like acid within every fibre of her body helped lend her flight wings. She was taking a chance: Gods, let it work...

"His rules!" she shouted boldly, "His rules! This is it! The Jackal is done! Your concerns lie with him now!"

In peculiar contrast to her urgency, everyone assembled remained stunned just a moment longer: round eyes and slack jaws working where bodies failed. It was enough; in truth, the comical aspect more than she'd hoped for – then time re-synchronised itself and suddenly the entire back-yard disintegrated into noisy chaos as the spectators began to shout and argue, simultaneously jostling and pushing as they sought to be seen and heard.

"He will pay you!" she shouted loudly, sidling past two men who'd abuse her on the terms of wagers, successfully redirecting a few others too, as their attention swung in the balance, "He will see this right! His rules, not mine! His rules!"

Shouldering around the stunned men, she flung her hood up, pushed past a surge of wet cloaks, ducking around a small group in open argument with a *number-runner* who'd lost his hat and now clasped his satchel close whilst backing up from the demanding hands clamouring like octopus arms to catch and bring him to them.

Pushing into the rapidly deteriorating lines of people, Solancei ignored their calls for compensation or the demands for answers. Ahead, alerted to trouble, the hired guards stood a little straighter than before, but to a man, they too appeared uncertain how to handle this.

"See Simaro!" she shouted one last time, bending her chin low to hide her face, shoving one short, plump fella into the path she'd been weaving, "His rules! Everyone gets ten percent! High wagers are nulled! See the number-runners! His rules!"

"Stop her! Someone stop the blade-whore!" Somewhere behind her, Simaro must have re-gained his aplomb, for the shout bellowed forth and hit her where his hands couldn't.

A cold surge rushed through her.

"Stop her!" His demand rang louder, "She's a criminal! By Anchan'Chi, stop her! You filthy trench! I will flay you!"

Solancei killed the perplexing grin that threatened to split her face and shoved hard to pass past a group of men avidly gesturing at another bookie. She past them before they comprehended she was present, yet from the corner of her eye, she caught a glimpse of a tall burly man, throwing back his oilskins to draw a short sword.

Consternation bit her like flees though she could not pretend at surprise. *So much for the Regulators searching people then! Fleck!*

Upping her pace Solancei skipped forward, forcing power into her muscles to close upon the first guard. Given the fact that they were busy keeping half an eye on the rising revolt, as of yet, the three hired men didn't appear to have realised the exact danger of her inherent approach, but to her it mattered not if they prepared.

On her left, someone brave, but foolish, loomed forth to make a misguided attempt at stalling her progress, but she reacted without missing a step, downing the hooded figure with a single, twisting elbow to his chin.

It seemed to open something. Behind her, someone else reached out, snatching at the fabric of her hood and Solancei – flowing sideways a little – sent two swathed offenders back into the arms of those surrounding them with a harsh rap of her wooden blade for one and a fast sideways lick of her boot for the other.

For mercy, after, there was no one else she needed to 'persuade'. Some people wanted their dues, while it was abundantly clear that others just wished to be away before trouble came calling.

It left only the last obstacle – and knowing that once she'd made it past the makeshift gate, the backwaters of Zanzier would provide ample cover to make good her escape, she aimed for the drooping arch of the only exit, elbowing past a handful of nervously careful spectators and a yellow-cloaked, back-peddling number-runner.

Daft fool! Yellow was a bad colour for blending in. High odds were he wouldn't get far.

She wondered if he might take the bet, then shook herself and focused on the Regulators. She deemed them none too keen to 'tangle', yet with an urgent bit of shuffling, they readied their halberds nevertheless to make a passing attempt at protecting the palisade from breach. *Half-wits! Did they think she'd go through it?*

She grinned. The nearest guard stepped forward, his squashed expression one of determination. *His mistake…*

Feinting, slashing out with her haitu to whip aside the halberd, she fluttered past him, leaping right towards the brick and mortar to let the momentum whisk her into a one-hand-touch wall spin. Kicking out with her heel as she moved forward, twisting one-eighty, the guard almost managed to wipe away a blossoming look of pure indignant horror before her foot hit his face. *Easy…*

Vaulting clear of his prone body, haitu descending, she engaged the second guard in a flash whilst mid-jump, striking him a direct blow across the front of his face. *Also easy…*

Landing with grace and balance, she ignored the guard as he crumbled before her with a yell of pain and a fountain of blood surging from a broken nose; already she'd whipped her haitu into the third-ready position and was advancing on the final guard when she realised he wasn't going to be game.

With his weapon still in hand, the man appeared to have forgotten its presence altogether as he matched her every advancing step with a retreating pace of his own. *Oh well…*

Twirling the haitu in a tight circle, she abandoned the attack and turned to the make-shift gate. The Regulators would be no trouble now. Her ruthless display had seen to that and without another glance at the last man standing, she tucked the haitu safely under one arm and leapt up, clasping at the gate's thick network of uneven planks and willow-weaves to heave herself further upwards, half-scrambling, half-climbing when she found the foothold to allow it.

At around nine feet tall, it didn't cause much of a problem for her, and though the construct nearly reached the top of the brickwork arch, she was nimble and would have enough space to twist her body over. *If only she wasn't stopped, of course – pray Gods that man with the sword had been caught up in the uproar she'd created, otherwise…*

But perhaps Kira'Cha was with her in the yard after all, for people directly below had engaged in loud disputes, now utterly waylaying the only guard still unharmed as he struggled to contain their ire, and – perhaps ironically – attempted to find answers to many a rising question about procedures.

For a blink, their eyes collided as she looked back and she almost winced in sympathy, for it seemed to her he perhaps rather regretted still being conscious, but it couldn't be helped now. *Maybe a helpful spectator might punch the man? If so, that couldn't be helped either.*

Now amplified by the tall walls, the noise had reached a deafening crescendo by the time she had one leg safely over the gate.

She paid the furore no mind as she dropped her haitu to the deserted alleyway beyond, then curled her arm tightly over the top of the raw trellis in readiness of descent. She did not feel guilty to have caused the upheaval. Simaro was just as much to blame for that one and just to alleviate her sense of justice, she chanced one final look before she made the leap.

A crazed kind of mayhem met her eyes, the spectators' naked urgency catching her short as it filtered into her, the buffer of Veranto still not there to make a difference. *This had all gone too far! This was never how these things went; never! This was so much madness!*

Like second nature, she scouted briefly for the man with the sword but failed to spot him in amongst the undulating bedlam as men hustled and pulled, growing more anxious by the beat.

The Regulators would not be able to stand against that sort of mob. Gods help them: from her vantage, the crowd looked like a nest of vipers about to boil, and-

A sharp jolt nearly upended her from her precarious perch. Several irate people had reached the gate - now purposely colliding with the structure in anger of proceedings. Spectators pushed from several directions. Directly below, someone yelled a profanity as he was pulled backwards whilst another spectator got punched in the face. Wish granted, the Regulator got hit in the eye and went down, just as a round of fisticuffs sparked to life.

In spite herself she cringed. High time to leave, she started wriggling free.

"Regulators! Attend! Now!"

The harsh shout echoed from within the human pen, striking her dead mid-move. *Regulators? Mercy, what the fleck!?*

Solancei raised her eyes, easily locating her former opponent.

Now back on his feet and evidently untouched by the mini-riots, Simaro had nevertheless not been left unchallenged for he stood besieged by a narrow ring of crazed, capering spectators. *Was it respect, or fear, or both, which prevented them from physical contact with the man, and for how long?*

He appeared to be refuting their persistence with what looked like cold fury rimmed by stern impatience, yet his near-colourless eyes locked onto hers now, the reality of his animosity grew thick on the face of angular lines and callous excellence.

It made her feel wrong. *Gods… they both knew exactly who the winner was, and still…! For this, he might just kill her!*

Shifting her gaze, Solancei felt a burst of panic well up. Almost randomly she spotted the man with the oil coat – he'd been hemmed in by a ring of angry men that clearly demanded to know where the sword had come from. However, as if he'd felt her scrutiny, the armed man caught her watching and snarled, instantly dispelling with whatever courtesy that had bound him, to saddle a punch in the nose of his closest 'complaint'.

The brown-cloaked, hook-nosed victim went down as though hit by a sledgehammer, scattering the remainder of the small group as 'oilskins' began wading through the masses, stepping carelessly over those who had fallen and persuading the others to shift back with random threats of the disputed weapon. *It rallied two other men to his side. Not fighting. Joining.*

As she saw the new-comers shoulder yet more spectators aside to draw short blades, Solancei realised the true extent of her troubles. The three 'oilskins' were weaving a path straight for her; she needn't look at Simaro to guess his complicity. *Fleck… fleck… fleck!*

A hard jolt went through the gate again, nearly upending her a second time. In a beat, her gaze flew between Simaro and the three men. He smiled across the distance like a raptor, a slim silver whistle appearing in his hand now. It shifted the ice in her, unhitching her limbs.

Head pounding for a blink, Solancei experienced a rush of crazed urgency and pushed herself sideways until her hand found the wanted cross-beam on the external side much as she'd hoped. Clasping it lightly, she swung herself off to land feet first in the rain-soaked mire below, whilst from within the yard, the word 'Regulators' continued to echo amidst the raised clamour of voices. *Her mind was dazed by question and concerns. What the fleck was going on?*

Then came the high-pitched thrill note of the metal whistle, just as someone banged into the gate again, giving the thing a sizable 'thump' that made her jump from fear. *Mother of all crap!*

Another thrill of the whistle propelled her into action. The entire mob was about to stampede and when the gate fell, they'd descend upon her shoulders like a herd of buffalo if she did not move! *Mercy!*

Rattled, she jacked herself forward, snatching up her haitu in passing as she ran towards the first narrow alley. Somewhere within the yard, Simaro hollered something else but the sound seemed muted now and she was glad.

There was a strange sort of fluffy fright brewing within her. Behind her, she could hear the makeshift defences crack under the sustained pressure from within, but for a moment the wicker-trellis remained strong enough to hold back the mob. It might aid her escape. *She hoped it would.* Even if it meant that people would be spilling out like an upended barrel of rotten fish.

I don't care, she told herself, though for once not feeling the truth of it.

Emerging through a narrow gap between careworn, four-story 'bricks' on either side, she careened into a second, smaller courtyard that she recalled crossing when she'd arrived for the jackal fight. Verily, it could barely be named 'backyard' – it was indeed really no bigger than a large chicken run, but from the next passage she'd have three possible exits and then again three: plenty of routes through which to get lost, as well as to lose Simaro! *Just a few more alleyways, and then-*

She was in the middle of the 'chicken run' when the shadow appeared to block her path. It surprised her and she baulked her run, skidding across the muddy slosh to a dead-pan stop.

Facing her was a man in an outfit of worn, yet serviceable character: boots, breeches, faded grey shirt and a dark-brown boiled-leather brigantine. The look was finished by a plain sash of Zanzier blue cinching his waist and he was armed with a pair of long knives, curved in the style of the Nomads of Yellow Snake.

It briefly puzzled, however with his plain shorn hair and long stubbles, the man was clearly no nomad, a fact that was backed by his light Zanzierian complexion below a smear of grime on either cheek.

Eyeing her with too much knowledge, he sauntered a casual step forward, hands moving to close around each of the carved-bone hilts protruding from his sash.

In turn, Solancei took a step back, reacting instantly, but a subtle sound stopped her from further retreat. Awareness stretching, she turned her head a slight fraction, never daring to take her eyes entirely from the form in front – yet she didn't have to in order to know trouble.

From the corner of her eye, she spied a glimpse of the same whisper of blue against plain, drab clothes and knew without a doubt that the slight lisp cutting past the rain, must equal the appearance of naked grey steel in someone's hands…

She swivelled lightly a little more left, chancing a glance towards the undulating, slightly wider path she'd just come down but she was already too far into the 'chicken run': the two men were behind her now.

It took no genius to understand that they were not there to escort her home. This she could've done without…

Weighing sparse options, her mind stalled. A low trellis door was opening on the right, allowing a further three men to join the odd posse and it halted her dead on the spot. They were as plainly dressed, but adorned with similar sashes and armed – and without a sound, Solancei found herself suddenly backing up that one step toward the first man again.

Swiping strands of wet hair from her face, she hated the conclusion of her superficial assessment. *The Gods hated her! Surely they must!*

"I have no money or valuables," she informed them, feeling slightly light-headed. "I did not collect any winnings."

"Winnings?" A man at her back sounded amused. "Who said we're here for any money, petal?"

Solancei resisted the urge to swivel towards the voice but did not drop the man from her peripheral sight as a sudden uncanny thought flowed into her mind. *It sent her head blank as for a moment everything connected. Then her stomach turned.*

"You're his real Regulators," she whispered, trying not to pale at the implications. "You are here in case of…? In case of this?"

None of the soldiers offered her a reply, but as the first man exiting the door drew a standard sword bearing the Zanzierian bird-of-prey stamped into the blade beneath its curved quillions, she needn't ask again. *It seemed… unreal.*

She fought her weak head as her vision seemed to spin, if only for a blink. These men were no random renegades. Indeed, the two men to exit last were armed with hooked, half-moon spears and curved swords, the latter still in their sheaths, the former held at the ready and perfect for tripping you up!

She swallowed nuisance, then the notion of biting fear. *Curse the Gods! And curse Klaas!* One hard-faced man raised an odd metal whistle to his mouth to blow one sharp trill note that seemed doomed to echo forlornly against the walls, and yet…

Tricky bastard Simaro, indeed! Fleck… and then double that!

Tense with apprehension, Solancei swivelled slowly, feeling her senses explode as she sought to keep them honed enough to respond to any threat from whichever side it might come. In spite of the narrow corridors and limited space, she was willing to bet the sound of that whistle would have carried sufficiently to reach Simaro, and her mind kicked back into action with an alacrity she usually only enjoyed through the State of Veranto.

"Now little lady, easy there." The one with the whistle drawled, the words a Zanzierian-laden hush as though he were approaching a wild horse about to rear up. "Just nice and easy, now. Put down your haitu and all will go well."

Well for whom? These men might look like riff-raff, but they were decently armed, which made them more than mercenaries yet less than soldiers. *Somehow she feared they had not come cheap – just as she feared they'd know how to cut with the sharp edge. So what were the choices?*

Watching them askance as they circled nearer, she swallowed tension and unconsciously bit her bottom lip. Fear and anger and surprise momentarily swelled one more time, then condensed to become of puny insignificance as she breathed deeply, inhaling and exhaling slowly as taught by Klaas to cleanse her mind.

Over the years there'd been many a trick, many a wise teaching to go with the simple breathing, and as the cumbersome emotions lifted, so reasserted itself every hour of Klaas' hard physical training within her core.

Calm followed. In a strange way, it felt almost as if she'd suddenly managed to re-connect with the State of Veranto. *She hadn't, of course – Gods curse it!* But as her perspective deepened it just didn't seem to matter now. *This was what it was all about – always! Assassins would strike whenever; they would not care if you were heart-sore or tired. Always, it would narrow down to one exact moment in time, and then the next, and the next again. That Simaro was a flecking cheat was already abundantly clear – now she just had to deal with the scummy by-product…*

"Oi… lady! I will not ask you again. This is Zanzier business! Put up your stick or we will make you, do you hear!" Harder tones now from the man with the whistle, but ignoring the warning Solancei shrank back, aware that she'd be getting no more space no matter what she did, yet flashing the man to her hard left a crooked, mirthless smile of apology. *He'd be the first to come at her.* She saw it; knew it from his stance and from the way he was moving. *And so, he'd be the first to kiss the ground, and she'd be gone…*

As though in understanding, the man cocked his near-shaven head towards her in greeting, then offered her a candid look of black, close-set eyes and a lewd shrug of insincere apology that saw Solancei's smile deepen. *He was underestimating her. Good…*

Slowly her fingers curled around the hilt in her hand. *No*, she thought, as she checked the men at her back with a furtive glance, *that flecking cheat Simaro was not like the others all right! Not at all! Yet at least…*

Well at least… if this was all just staged for her, then Klaas would surely get all money's worth today!

She bit her lip again.

And as for herself? Well, a real sword would've been nice… for this…

Visit from the Chief

Iambre released her trapped finger, the hair un-twirling with springy cheer. Tonight she was going to ensure that Captain Bilan Metavo understood just exactly how badly she felt about the whole 'Wilderness incident', and she was going to eat her pride and apologise because until she could be sure of his affections once more, she was just a shell anyway. *She only hoped he would forgive her; she hoped-*

She sighed, feeling suddenly very alone. Only Lancei knew of her illicit feelings for the Captain of their retinue – only Lancei and no one else – and her cursed cousin was right of course: Iambre's mad feelings were polluting their lives and Lancei wanted her friend to bury them deep and start concentrating on Tuxama and things that were actually important, but dang it!

Lancei should've been there. When you looked at it, this needn't be about herself and Captain Metavo; Iambre was a representative, a diplomat. The borders of Tuxama would soon enough be greeting them all and Iambre did not want to think about that yet. *Not yet.*

She drew in a tight sharp breath and expelled it through her nose with a hiss of resignation. *She and Solancei were still friends. If the woman stepped through those doors in the next few moments, then she might just still forgive her if she made an effort to catch up on time lost, but Bilan was going to come...*

With a sparkle of arched humour that could've belonged to Lancei, Iambre forced herself to look at the bright side. If Lancei was not here, then at least she wouldn't be able to interfere either, and when Bilan came, Iambre could make good on her wish to manoeuvre herself some much-coveted alone-time with the man. *It didn't happen often – if ever.* Solancei had an infuriating need to chaperone every waking moment Bilan came near, and it was…

Well, it was hardly romantic!

Feelings mixing: something bitter co-mingling with affectionate pride, Iambre thought of all the times she'd tried to dismiss her friend, but with Lancei also operating as her life-shield it was an impossible command. Iambre had lost count of the times her futile anger had been left unsatisfied whilst her foul cousin had quoted infuriating snippets of the very oaths that forbade her to leave the Princess' side without due reason or just need.

Just need? Did the danger of a Shield's charge standing all but ready to kill her own protector perhaps not count?

Perhaps it might have done, but when Bilan had begun to wonder why Solancei appeared to be more in charge of Iambre than vice versa, she'd let the matter rest and since then allowed Solancei to hang around. It was less hassle and some things about certain secrets were just not worth thinking about, yet sometimes…

Well, sometimes she wished it would have been possible for her to tell her Captain the truth. Sometimes…

Iambre ground her teeth.

'Either the Captain goes, or I will.' Those were the words Solancei had spat at her not long ago during their trials to reach Zanzier. Iambre had simply figured her friend riled up as badly as she, but now?

Stiff concern wrestled down her brimming anger at the thought. *Could Lancei really have made good on her threat? She'd sworn oaths and signed covenants: if she had left she'd be in breach, yet…*

The Princess got off her seat to resume the impatient pacing, this time for slightly differing reasons. It seemed unlikely that Lancei would risk an offence of such magnitude just to thwart Iambre's need for a pretty hairdo or just the right amount of rouge on the cheeks, but where did that leave them? *With a petty show of obstinacy? With a first brick torn from their now-dangerously precarious foundation of friendship?*

She hoped not. She really, truly, hoped not!

With a pang it occurred to her that Lancei might actually be really mad at her this time, to so vehemently thwart a summoning. Their arguments had been so frequent that any small word or look had sparked disagreement and discord recently; indeed, she was only too painfully aware of their less than agreeable parting this morning – but…

…but had she really abused her friend's goodwill that badly that it should come to this? Had she?

Casually, her gaze went to one of the vast tapestries. The scene was ugly – but it was a distraction for sure.

Iambre snorted softly; Fabrano Icolor – *a once famous Knights Commander of the Realm's Legions* – might just have triumphed and won the terrible war that had torn the lands apart for nigh-on a full quarter of a century; he might just have beheaded Thain Phudor, the long-hated leader of the revolts and the foul man responsible for starting the Chaos Wars in the first place, but Iambre saw no victory in the gory details. The event lay hundreds of years in the past, yet everyone knew the stories that by the time the Chaos Wars had ended, the entire realm had been brought to its knees. All but three of the old families had perished and the lands had been rent; broken; the people suffering; starving.

And for what? A sheer misunderstanding?

Iambre was pleased for her ancestors that the wars had ended, of course, but the peace had been hard won and because of the declarations signed back then, her entire future now lay before her: planned and sealed. *Huzzah!*

Like always, she caught herself warring the flesh of her bottom lip to stop the splinter of desperation she normally felt at that particular thought. *She'd never bit her lip until she'd met Lancei; it was such a bad habit, curse it!*

She swallowed the sad self-pity that she hated to admit existed. *She did not like that tapestry and she certainly didn't like Lancei's deliberate absence.* She prayed the latter wasn't rooted in betrayal; prayed that she had not alienated Lancei enough to find her willing to take that one step too far beyond forgiveness, which-

No! No, it wasn't so at all. She knew it in her bones. Her wayward cousin might have pushed the limits of her welcome in Servangar well-past reasonable breaking point several times, but the Oaths – *the clandestine title of Royal Life-Shield* – that very duty meant the same to Lancei, as the duty of Crown Princess meant to Iambre. It always had done and would continue to do so – *something she also felt with certainty in her bones!*

She looked back at the tapestry, marrow cooling. *Had Thain Phudor felt just as betrayed by his friend or had there been no goodwill left in the end?* The idea made her shiver and she turned sharply from the feature, but the life-sized cross-stitch with the severed head and Phudor's slumped body at the Knights Commander's feet seemed to burn in her mind. Solancei was not well-loved either and Iambre was suddenly freakishly inspired to wonder if people would cheer similarly: with bloody swords and pikes held high, were she to cut off Solancei's head one day?

Angered with her friend or not, the freak notion sickened. The leering look on Fabrano Icolor's face was repulsive, even more so than the severed head at his feet, and to her mind, the artist must have been of limited imagination if this was the look she had considered best suitable to display Icolor's triumph. *Could she perchance demand the horror removed from her chambers? Or would the ruddy Zanzierians think her twice the weak-bellied milk-sop then?*

Sadly she imagined she knew the answer to that one alright. *Knights Commander Zulavi of the West could doubtlessly find some kind of offence in such a request too and she'd already done quite enough to raise his ill-will. Quite... enough.*

Iambre drummed her nails against her chin in pensive chagrin. *Zulavi...* yes here was another problem, she feared.

Cutting out a wince before her reflection in the two oval-framed mirrors by the double main doors might reveal more than just a haunted expression, she was taken aback by the woman peering back at her like a caricature of her usual self. Her complexion was still golden Etruian tan, but the colour appeared superimposed over paste – her cheeks slightly sunken, her orbital skin too sallow for health. It both surprised and alarmed. She did not feel in ill-health and this was the day Bilan was to see her up close for the first time in weeks. *Would he notice? Would it matter? If he was still of a certain mind to conduct himself infuriatingly proper, her unflattering colour would do cursed little to steer his heart sideways, and...*

Now she did wince. Outside the light was changing; the weather was as abysmal as her temper, yet she went to the seven tall panes of yellowed window glass anyway, feeling only slightly beset by vertigo to stand before the floor to ceiling feature. It was perhaps her borrowed apartment's best feature, she allowed: serving the occupant a magnificent view of the most sympathetic half of Zanzier Town. Still, the darkening day beyond ruined the effect: steely-grey nimbus clouds drooping low between black-tinted rain clouds and the downpour now resuming with more than a touch of its earlier ferocity to obscure like a mystical fog.

She stepped back, chilled by hidden draughts. The loaded drops harrowing glass and visibility as the wind flung the rain against the entire town with tempestuous design, instilled a sense of weariness for the days to come. It was too late in the day and the weather did not seem in the slightest interested in letting up, and…

…and neither – it would seem – did Solancei.

Lost for a moment, an unexpected knock on the tall outer doors of her salon caused her to jump in her skin. A spike of sudden apprehension nailed her to the spot with fear that it was her escort arriving already, but recalling the hour, new hope replaced the apprehension. *Solancei…?*

Swivelling towards the doors in readiness to face her friend with a dignified expression, Iambre calmed herself just as Palea appeared from the inner chambers to cross the wide central runner in a rush.

Another decisive knock assaulted, and Iambre calmed her beating heart as Palea drew open one of the tall panels with an official mien that spoke of royal composure marred by only a sliver of displeasure for the interruption.

Iambre stilled. Licking her lips only to berate herself when she realised that she was chewing on her bottom lip in anticipation of seeing Lancei slink forth in sheepish silence, she worked hard to cultivate a coolly distant expression, except she heard Palea's soft intake of air and realised she could have saved herself the trouble. Surprise marred her handmaiden's bearing just a moment, then she recovered admirably and drew the door wider, simultaneously dropping into a deep courtesy that would not have been necessary, had she been greeting Lancei.

Brow twitching, Iambre masked a small intake of air too.

Rather than a penitent Lancei, it was the ascetic figure of Elite Combat Trainer and Chief of Security, Klaasinah Eso Mehadja, who stepped past the threshold of her salon and Iambre quenched another gasp at the sight of the older woman. *Gods, but she looked a vagabond!*

"Your Grace is not yet dressed? My apologies, I intrude." Ignoring Palea, the Chief's eyes found and took stock of the Princess in a blink, her clipped words succinct. Looking less than apologetic, however, the other woman marched towards the princess with typical purpose, utterly disregarding the trail of water and filth dripping of her sodden dark uniform and tall functional boots. *Odd...*

With a gentle stab of concern, Iambre looked from the Chief to Palea and back. Usually, the combat trainer took time to change and refresh before presenting herself before any of the royal family but not today it would seem. *Odd... and then some.*

Iambre more heard than saw Palea shut the door, her eyes centring on Eso Mehadja's taut features, a sucking sensation now disturbing her belly.

The Chief was travelling as part of her retinue, on and off, sometimes ahead of Iambre's arrival in a new place, sometimes leaving well after she and her people had moved on, but though the woman had an unpredictable way of coming and going, the presence of the King's security advisor at this hour was still perplexing. *Indeed, when last she'd received the Chief, it had been to hear word on the sighting of a renegade gang operating out of Imkarah, but they'd never encountered any conflict.* Watching Mehadja now, Iambre's head spun with questions. *Now what? She did not have time for this!*

Undoing the laces of her long rain-blackened cloak with incidental efficiency, then slinging the once forest-green oilskin casually across the back of the pale upholstery of the nearest Iddian sofa, the Chief raked a hand back through her salt and pepper bob, water dripping off the dark ends but seemingly not caring about this discomfort either.

Not meaning to, Iambre frowned. A gutter-worn smell accompanied Eso's presence – *again odd* – and the princess hid a slight premonition of alarm, though not the second frown as Eso paused in front of her like a miniature shadow.

"Apologies for the intrusion Your Grace, but I must have words," the Chief stated politely correct, though she did in fact still not look particularly sorry. With a sidelong look for Palea's presence, she added, "This does not require an audience, Princess."

Audience? Palea was hardly classed as 'audience'.

Doubly worried now, Iambre looked past the Chief to Palea. The handmaiden dawdled of course, seemingly shocked and intrigued by the Chief's appearances. *No audience?*

"Mistress Palea," Iambre spoke with care, slightly absent-minded because she was too-aware of Eso Mehadja, "please would you call for some towels and perhaps a pot of something hot for the Chief to fortify herself?"

Palea offered the Chief a quick look and curtsied quickly, "But of course, My Lady."

"Highness, I thank you, but I must decline," Eso spoke up before Palea could move a foot, leaving the young handmaiden hovering with uncertainty suddenly, and Iambre found herself staring at the Chief in quiet wonder even as she slowly waved at the handmaiden to withdraw.

Palea acquiesced without a word, her already big eyes suddenly impossible large in the doll-like face, yet whatever questions she must harbour remained unvoiced for she was well-versed in decorum, and – mercifully – also still doubtlessly keen to get underway with her given task.

In turn, Iambre took a beat to compose her face before she offered the Chief her attention. *Was it her imagination or was the set of the woman's brow a little harder than usual? The slant of the mouth a little tighter?*

With Palea gone to her dressing room, it was just Iambre and the Chief in the large salon and suddenly she felt cold beyond weather and anger. *The Chief always took time to dress before presenting herself; did she think it acceptable to slacken procedures just because they were so long out of Etruia that the capital seemed but a distant dream?*

Iambre didn't think so. Eso Mehadja never went slack on anything. Yet here she was. And clearly not to spread good cheer.

The Princess felt her stomach bunch up. *This... this would not be good.*

Solancei's Memoirs

The Province of Tarléon.
Ocean's End.
Autumn of 780 P. C. W.

I thought I was ill.

By the time the funeral was halfway done, I felt sick to my guts: sick with strange new concerns, sick with cold, sick with fluctuating sadness: courtesy of the Veranto and my lacking perception of what I was doing – but mostly, I was sick with confusion.

When the disaster had claimed my parents, their small party had been returning from a simple two-week business trip to the still-undamaged ice fields of Ilandor Meadow, less than two dozen leagues to the north.

I didn't get the connection with 'murder'. They'd had these trips so many times before: Ilandor, Ilsuldarh, Iquenthalarh... it hadn't much mattered which town, nor how many days; always I'd not missed their presence in Ivanor, but...

Well up to this point I'd simply thought the Gods had a hateful sense of humour: Taliana had rarely been asked to accompany my parents. *Why had she had to go this time?* I hadn't liked it and I had prayed for the whole fortnight that the Gods would return her safely to me – but curse them, they hadn't.

Now suddenly to top that, I knew exactly why people had been whispering in corners only to turn from me in weary silence whenever I'd incidentally walked too close or been drawn by curiosity.

But why would Rainan have lied about the manner of their deaths? My father's steward was a steadfast, solemn man with a silly droopy moustache and a good heart: one of the few to tolerate my 'wicked' independence. *Why?*

To the nearest hour, fifteen days ago, I had stood there by Rainan's side, receiving the bad news and forgetting how to breathe, all while the brute words had cascaded from my father's aide with a never-forgotten lilt of horror – *and yet I hadn't known?*

"But this is a damnable catastrophe; a flecking disaster!" That had been the exact phrase exploding out of Rainan as his face turned white, then semi-see-through, a purple vein pumping like a bloodworm under the skin at the temple as he snatched the messenger's wax-sealed missive with a gesture of brusque anger that had almost unseated the travel-worn man.

That had been fifteen days ago. *Fifteen days… and an eternity… and a dozen people still dead: all perished in that same disastrous event. Fifteen days…* and the investigation ground to a halt, all leads gone supposedly colder than newly solidified pack ice. *Fifteen days… and forever…*

Perhaps he had sought to spare me further grief? I was till then only aware that there'd been an accident: he knew my care for Taliana, and might have sought to shield me? Yet in hindsight, I should have known this had not just been about the accident. For one, father's steward had seemed a stranger from the moment that message was delivered; people whispering in corners about something unholy should have been my second clue – but Taliana's death had filled me: made me oblivious to the way people would catch me watching and quickly break off topic or hurry on with business. *What can I say? I was seven for fleck sake. Was I not permitted to suffer a certain level of naivety?!*

Still, at the funeral, I must have looked at Rainan then. I recall his presence to my left like a wraith standing sentinel: pale and silent in his white leathers, fur-trimmed mittens and tall boots, the only sign of life in him the puff of air issuing with regular speed from his nose.

The memory of him is another thing I recall so easily, so vividly – *I 'blame' the Veranto for this too* – for as he returned my gaze with a grim frown, strange emotions trailed through me, bordering on something prescient. *I had felt new anxiety already; now suddenly I also feared the unknown.*

But that was just a child's imagination, you might say – nothing more than mood-enhanced fancy. However, I would tell you that as if to underscore the feeling, out of nowhere, like the petrifying breath escaping a vast dragon, a hard snort of air gusted sideways around the erected screens, shaking the attached carabiners as though to test the mettle of the ice spars driven into the frozen waters to offer the mourners a little shelter whilst in situ, and I nearly vomited fear then.

I was used to the wind's painful bite, but this new air felt like acid on the few exposed patches of skin, and I knew in my heart then, that this 'whatever it was', had only just begun. For real, I sensed a change in more than the weather approaching, and there'd be nothing I could do about it – that was as certain as my dead parents in their iron-lined caskets of costly white-lacquered wood.

Then the Prefect called my name and I realised I'd shamed myself, for I had no idea what he'd said.

"Duchess Solancei del'Isthalani Calverhana?" he repeated, a furrow of question ploughing from his weather-burned forehead into his gravelly, formal voice.

And Gods... I'd done it again then, hadn't I? Not quite managed to act according to expectations!

For a blink, I utterly cared. Then the Veranto floated me away on a lily-pad of serenity, taking even the new feelings, to anchor my concerns beyond reach for yet a short burst of indeterminable time.

I remember thinking that it was just as well. *A funeral was not the place to question Rainan about truth – and besides, I wasn't willingly going to explore further the thing that made my insides clench with unwarranted fear if I gave it half a blink of credit!*

Solancei

Grim Discoveries

He should have known by now that nothing ever worked quite as planned.

His head hurt. *It shouldn't, of course.* But neither should the commonly-simple spell have all but collapsed on itself in the way it had done, upon he and Ambar'Zadron crossing past the Boundary into Ostravah.

He supposed under differing circumstances, such an experience might just have left him sweetly bemused, but then again…

Having been trapped like a fly in the crushing web 'in-between': for moments forced to endure a gut-wrenching, soul-polluting attack of the expanding Weave as it tore away at the universe of his insides, he was, most assuredly, anything but bemused.

In fact, if anything, he was simply painfully aware that he and his companion had been saved from certain entrapment, only through speedy ingenuity and the raw strength of his powers; he wasn't sure if the disaster would have killed him had it come to the crux, nor did he know if such a thing would have even been allowed in the grander order of the Old Creator's Will, but nevertheless…

Still unsettled by the odd experience, he'd forced himself to pick at the details ever since: yet warring at the skeleton of his constructs, his Weave, his execution, he'd learned little from which to stand encouraged that this had not been the result of a permanent glitch wrought by the sundering of the Astral Aide.

And such a thing stood to reason, of course. He'd already known this near-failure to pass unscathed into Ostravah had not been due to some twisted haemorrhaging of concentration or error in his ability to Persuade the flows into the correct construct.

In a strange way, this truth half-sawed at him, though. Indeed, could it only have been something simple like that, it might perhaps have seemed an easier problem to accept, but then again: never had he been one for casual mistakes or slack Weaves. Never had he been left wanting on any Tier, and to start now…

A gush of air sifted through the trees, stirring branches and hustling a few early-turned leaves till they released purchase and fluttered like festive cheer in the breeze. Then picking up, rushing down to sway the meadow-side grasses and wild herbs, momentarily lifting the ends of his hair with invisible fingers, the wind lapped for one heartbeat longer at the spare cloth and long functional ties of his coat before releasing with a hollow mewl.

Another rush ruffled his hair, and another. *Buffering his frame, the formerly-soft breeze was picking up now…*

Knelt upon the dry grassy ground in concentrated focus and opened senses, he ignored the weather though disenchanted with the ripening changes. *The rolling landscape was still lush but everything was different now. The magic, the people, the climate, the Upper Circle, the stakes, him…* - in comparison, the blustering insistence of autumn seemed a droll coincidence.

Staring at the sloped-backed hill cupping the horizon, his a far-seeing gaze didn't miss a single detail, and he let cool sobriety fill him to smother the imagined taste of oil and ashes in the back of his throat. *The boundary spell should not have worked like that; it should not have turned like that! It was of a loop-construct, tied to its own anchor: innate unless activated with the correct spell, and bound to perform only one action…*

He exhaled, feeling the air flow past the tip of his nose. *Innate, yes… what a joke that seemed: his small, simple activation-spell had evolved right at the time of his passing – impossibly, as though something had given it a* *grain of self-awareness – and for moments he might as well have been any untried Affinity playing with a 7th Tier Persuasion, because he'd been unable to adapt fast enough to follow the erratic change of Weaves, and then-*

He remembered how it felt when attacked by the product of other Weavers; recalled too, how it stung to get burned by the backlash of your own stupidity when a Weave went awry. The first he'd usually been strong enough to walk away from, the latter hadn't happened very often, yet both categories were not something any Spell-Weaver was wont to forget, and still…

Well, this had been something new. This had been different. *Water versus blood, different!*

He grasped a handful of wayward hair and slowly settled it back over a shoulder, caught yet again with a building urge to dissect the event.

He imagined it might stem from the fact that he could still feel the exact way the magic of that spell had turned and slipped from his grasp as if it was bound by no Law or Weave. It had been brutal and instant – the two simple constructs merging, then spinning like a ferocious snake to coil around its prey before sinking-in magical fangs for the kill.

He mentally twisted from the lingering unease, unwilling to allow it purchase. *The subsequent way it had leeched Power from him – as though trying to empty him, before Ending him…*

He knew of spells that might do such… *things*… - and they were dangerous beyond sanity, of course – but this 'event' had shifted beyond even that. *Destructive spells were always searching for an outlet or a target, but Weavers directed the outcome: chose the aim! For certain, he did not stand the unwitting mark, only this time…*

Perhaps he could have been any trespasser, he allowed. Perhaps the spell had not reacted to him per se, but in the ensuing fight for control, it had certainly seemed personal. The magic had pushed him back, but there had only been one path open for pursuit: the path meant for him and his companion, and since he hadn't been willing to sacrifice his need to reach their destination to a spell-gone-rabid whilst he, in turn, remained trapped, maimed, or worse – he'd bound the link on a whim and a thought, knowing the danger and cost, but also the possible benefit.

He rubbed the tender surface of the Maker's rune across his temple and the corner of his eye, unsure when he might begin to feel less head-sore. *Danger and cost… not to be advised, but floored by lack of saner options, he'd stalled the rogue spell's end product: using his own body, first as a vessel for its containment, then as a conduit for its subsequent destruction.* It had been unwise, yes. Of course, it had hurt like the touch of a Blight Rider multiplied hundredfold, and it had proven one of the longest moments in his already rather wholesome existence because the magic of such Persuasions would naturally build in Power until released – but it had worked as intended. *Sort of…*

Mentally flayed, chewed up like old leather, his struggle for supremacy had ended as abruptly as it has started: with a wrenching lurch and a pull, followed by a searing pain along the spine, but then it had been over: he on his knees in a shallow beck on the edge of a birch grove and Ambar'Zadron twenty yards removed, skittishly brimming with distrust whilst seemingly set aglow with some kind of after-effect that had only just faded by nightfall. *Had he not been a Guardian with the Maker's power flowing through the runes, then-*

Of course, the fact that neither he nor anyone of the Upper Circle had ever been forced to fight the very fabric of existence as it buckled and twisted into something wholly unrecognisable all around, was in truth an issue for debate – but not now. *Not whilst he still harboured a kernel of twisting unease and grating contempt deep within. Not while he did not feel quite in control yet; not when he had no answers; not-*

He raked a wayward skein of hair from his face with curt impatience, the black-upon-black symbols of insignia upon his Spell-Weaver cloak flashing under the still-warm afternoon sun – now more the haunting jest of times long past than a full set of honours-awarded.

Narrowing his eyes momentarily, he crinkled his nose with distaste. *This damage wrought by old disaster spread wider and deeper than initially expected or perceived. It drained his energy and it made him feel unbalanced; made him feel…? Feel… testy?*

Chewing on the concept that anything at all should successfully stir old sentiments, he released a breath. *Testy?* He hated the word, just as he hated the way things had unravelled so quickly already.

He knew magic; knew how to manipulate or persuade it with spells great or small; knew just how it behaved; how it moved; what it tasted and smelled like – black hex he virtually 'owned' magic! For a fact, he did not lose control or get trapped. He most assuredly did not feel testy; did not waste time on dead feelings – perhaps with the exception of 'hate', that was, this being the one remaining sentiment he'd polished, and treasured, and saved, for the sole purpose of pursuing the Mad Ones and their ilk. *But 'testy'…?!*

Derision fuelled denial. *Feeling testy was as unprecedented as the Boundary Spell turning; almost as unnerving as looking a Vessel in the eye, and worse so, because he couldn't even begin to remember when he'd last felt this way; didn't want to, because that-!*

Almost as if in response to the stress, a muscle jumped in his jaw but he ignored it, glad of the wind suddenly, as it clamoured for attention and seemed to clear his head. *Was this what others might refer to as 'unhinged'?*

The thought was disturbing on a base level and he pushed it from mind as though it held a contagion. Perhaps, he amended, it was because the event had been so unpredictable. And perhaps it was because it had served to remind him of everything that was changed; of everything that must be salvaged – *he didn't know* – but something was off. *Off beyond his Affinity to pinpoint...*

A shimmering eel of impossible vibration slithered around his bones, chilling his muscles from within – causing him to imagining that he could still feel the lingering touch of fey magic deep inside his core. *He could not of course, but still...*

How could he escape the fact that for moments he'd carried something akin to Sentient Magic within; something akin to what might be found within a Neidar Ba'raie perhaps? He'd wrestled it and lived. *Danger and cost had not outweighed need, but maybe in spite care, it had stirred a certain part of his Heritage, so how could he take pride in the achievement?!* To do so, would of course serve to humour the illusion that this was the weirdest thing that had happened since the Quickening, but it was not. *It was most assuredly not, for the sense of loss alone...*

A new slash of derision filled him at the thought. Sadly, he was not cowardly inclined and he opened himself a tad wider to the broken magic surrounding him – if only to prove that he was prepared to leave one small mishap behind in favour of a much larger, challenging problem. *The Twins and the Astral Aide. Those were of prime concern. Yet without magic...*

At the acknowledgement of Truth, it seemed the wind offered blunt agreement, though with a harsh bluster of warning.

He didn't care. The weather was only an afterthought; the construct that bound magic together was in a whole other dimension of complicated. And it commanded respect. *Much more so than a lingering sense of wrong, or an ability to shrug-off unease, or a pandering to the concept of subsequent testy feelings.*

In a heartbeat, the sense of loss intensified, the tart ache in him since crossing the Boundary, almost rising to near pain. *Of the Ostravahn flows little remained but a few tangled tatters: some ruined, some stunted.* Had he been a kinder creature, he might have wept for the waste, but instead he'd experienced only a heightened sense of chilling objectivity and sallow impatience that could not be alleviated. *He wished he had time and right to address this conundrum, but he didn't, black fell, he just didn't!*

The testy feeling vanished, washed away under a wave of new sangfroid detachment.

This was the final blow that made Richarmarlan Envalair's actions seem nothing short of treachery. *Not only had his former friend and Guardian shattered the Astrolabe, he'd somehow 'torn' the magic – both destroying the old, and in a sick way also inadvertently creating something... other.*

He didn't know what to call *this other,* though. *Gods' curses, even the Elvern would have no word for this change. The twins would need protection: more than a couple of swords worth! To locate and mend an artefact like the Astrolabe, required more than compass and glue! And Marlan had 'given' them... other?!*

A bitter smile graced his lips for the challenge not allowed him to pursue, for the question of the broken magic represented a puzzle to stir his otherwise limited capacity, or willingness, to engage with anything other than that which he'd been Reborn to do.

But that was not his purpose here. As a matter of fact, some might argue that without the magic at his call, he did not have time to consider matters anyway, and yet…?

What was he supposed to do? Though unsanctioned to overstep his mark, was he supposed to ignore the grinding facts?

As he'd viewed only since arriving, the disaster had produced an altercation of the cardinal substance from which all was made; designed; woven. *He was a 7th Tier Spell-Weaver without magic! Was it not inconceivable that he should not address the problem? No matter the words spoken in the Upper Circle on the day of the Quickening, should he not attempt his damnedest to bring order to what had been left – both for prosperity and for need?!*

He exhaled sharply, multiple issues pressing, layering. *The common Signifier appeared to have been wiped: lost; the Cipher washed from existence. Dear maker, but he should be able to figure this out; find a new common signifier with which to bind the tatty remainders into something of worth; into something… useful.*

He grimaced but mostly because it was something – *apart from feeling testy* – that he could do. The flow of magic had been misshapen and diminished before, but it had never failed to fall back into normal alignment, even after a great Weave or upheaval had rocketed the Realms. *Why had it not healed? Was it Alérathnar?*

For a beat, such possibility made his stomach turn – something of heavy duality descending, as though he'd tried to take on too complex a spell; as though he'd reached for the impossible to spin death into life, or suns into planets – then practicality overruled. The maker's power still flowed within him and he visualised instead Richarmarlan Envalair in his mind's eye, the image as sharp as it had been a near millennium ago.

There had been no shift in the other Guardian's persona; no altercation to warn!

With everything the Upper Circle had ever done, they'd also rarely found the need to shift or vary their strategy - and then had come this magnificent hammer blow. His fallen friend had been a Human 6th Tier Spell-Weaver and canny to boot, but whatever Marlan had done in those last fatal moments, he'd excelled himself beyond Tiers or Affinity, and then some: in one sidewinding feat of stunning deviance, they'd found themselves betrayed by one of their own; by the one person who'd fought the Chaos with as much avid loathing for its existence as himself, and it beggared belief.

Marlan might have moved on the edge on multiple occasions but he'd never risked Thessilia! In spite of the Oaths and the woman's stunning ability to safeguard herself, old promises stuck deep, and Marlan had still felt some kind of chivalrous need to shelter her. *With his actions, evidently something had changed, but what?*

It was another thing that made no sense, but at least that was Rhindarhlar and Sinuhé's business now – just as coping with this 'lack', had now attached itself to him. For mercy, if the flows did not conform, there were always other ways through which to gain what had been temporarily lost; other options: artefacts and-

'Commander! First Guardian! Come back to me – I am losing the link! Please, I cannot do this alone. Keep with me!' The velvety voice echoed in his mind with enough concern to sway him back to task as requested.

'Fine, Guardian Emara, fine,' he relented, yanking a mental hold of the Power in his core and casting a little more of his barely renewed strength

into refining the link of communication they'd erected between the leagues and Veils that separated them.

'*So what happened then, Commander?*' prompted Guardian Emara, fellow of the Upper Circle and Protector of the Realms, this time directly offering concern into question.

'*You have withstood the power of destructive spells before; you are no stranger to their Weaves. Why should this have been different – even with the circumstances being what they are?*'

He shrugged. '*I have watched waves of magic destroy and annihilate, yet none of those violent moments could've compared. This was different: it was as though I did not know the construct. As though it was composed according to an entirely different set of rules than the ones we stand privy to. For a fact it aggressively counteracted my presence as though I were the enemy; as though it did not recognise my link or right; as though... as though it had been corrupted and was searching-out the destruction of anything live.*"

'*Commander, this is most worrying.*'

'*It is a disaster,*' he admitted. Bluntly. '*I fought the destructive construct, then neutralised it. Still... the backlash expelled me from the Boundary only because I twisted its Weave, manipulating it with everything I own! You know my Affinity... know my power...*

'*Guardian Emara, I had to cling so tightly to this alien Weave that when it came to part I found it hard to let go. It was in me: a rogue force, grown fearsome and strong out of mutation and from what felt like an almost unending supply of Matter. Fortunately it lacked finesse and I had more, but nevertheless...*'

'*But how?*' Guardian Emara enquired, ever-practical, ever-investigating. '*The Veils are not damaged.*'

'Ah, who knows? Ask the Story-Makers; ask the Mad Ones; does it matter?'

'Oh Commander, you know that everything matters.'

'Well then,-' he remarked with dry self-deprecation, *'-in that case, perhaps it matters too that I tell you more. Guardian Emara, old friend, it raked my insides to gain free and believe me: the ensuing waste of energy was colossal. It left me feeling... weary.'*

'I taste your distress through the bond,-' Thessilia Emara sounded nonplussed, *'-but surely you don't think it that bad?'*

'Surely not,' he echoed sardonically, *'But then again, you were not the one who nearly got ripped in half coming here. I have been delving and meditating for days and days now and still nothing. Guardian Envalair's schemes have ripped the place apart: destroyed the common ciphers and erased the flows. It's as though Chaos is already ruling this realm and as if that wasn't bad enough, the stench of the Mad Ones rides everywhere!'*

'My! Malandar old friend – aren't we tetchy?' Thessilia's friendly banter held an echo of what once was. It irked him for a blink, then he forgave her: had there been more than the two of them involved in this conversation, he knew she never would've allowed herself this level of familiarity – yet now however, he could almost see her face before his mind's eye; could almost imagine how her copper hair shone a colour a little too vivid for nature and how her onyx eyes, likewise a little too black, would glitter with mirth in favour of distress. Strange perhaps, but even in her Guardianship, certain things had never altered with Thessilia and in the light of certain disastrous events, the Guardian Commander wondered if perhaps such a small mercy was not to be seen as a good thing. That was but a personal theory though – not meant to be shared – and his bond reflected only purpose.

'Then, you think the task as difficult as the Guardian Speaker would have it?' she pressed, a hint of vexation in her voice. *'You think that he was right then and that we should have waited for him to deliberate and meditate upon the state of things?'*

'Perhaps,' he allowed, not really believing himself of that very conviction even as he said it. *'Our blindness aside, everything is so much worse than we could've ever anticipated. Perhaps we would've had time to wait – at least a small time. Guardian Cahmerhin would've been happy then, Guardian Mehand'Arun would have had less reason to feel hacked-off, and-*

'

'Is that so?' Thessilia cut his string of thoughts with an edge of velvety danger. *'But surely, you would not have allowed Mehand'Arun such reprieve! That Elvern Twit is of no use except in a good fight against the Mad Ones, and even then he goes his own way. Does he not deserve to spend a little time with the break-aways? Even if all it does, is to help him recall his place?''*

'Undoubtedly, that is your personal conviction, Guardian Emara?'

'Drivel Commander Denarlin! My conviction. Everyone's conviction. I dare say: even yours, for surely you don't pretend to care about Mehand'Arun's feelings now?'

'The man who became the Guardian, is no longer my enemy, Thessilia. In this, our past is oblivion; in this, we are all allies! He is the Flight of Fire; he is of the Upper Circle. That is all now!'

'Well and good then, Commander Denarlin. Let's just hope that Mehand'Arun sees clear to extend you the same sort of gracious courtesy and leave it at that! Tell me instead what else stirs in the Lands of Ostravah?''

'*What else?*' Malandar killed a mirthless grin. '*My dearest Thessilia Emara, where would you wish me to begin? I guess I had hoped for something salvageable; anything; but so far my efforts have turned up little. I am inspired to think of myself like a blind man hoping for a sliver of light to indicate where next to place his foot along the ledge of the precipice – hoping, praying with each new step, that his instincts will not betray. What can I say that hasn't already passed between us: the damage is extensive, without structure, without laws; some flows lie dead or stunted, others are live but void of all recognisable traits.*

'*Thessilia, this experience... none of this will prove easy. I breathe in air, yet find myself starving.*'

For a long moment, Emara kept her own council then, but he could feel her frustration now overlaid by concern, and no wonder. This would all be prompting her to think about the events leading up to the disaster. Events unforeseen that must still prompt anger, for she was strumming tension now.

At length, she enquired, '*And what of it if you enlist the aid of focal exercises to strengthen a Persuasion? Can you not revert to basics? Can you not use gestures or words to Persuade the flows that remain? Surely something must be of use to us still?*'

And there it was again, the word 'surely'. It might as well never have existed for all the good it did him.

The First Guardian shook his head to himself even as he mentally conveyed the negative sentiment behind the gesture. '*No Guardian, there is nothing. It would seem the irony is most perfect, don't you think? For someone who's never been without magic, the concept is still staggering to me. I fear that everything will be different now. There are too many variables to contend with; too many changes.*'

And the Twins?' she prompted with grim frustration, *'The mission? You know what comes first.'*

Malandar Denarlin's re-occurring frown twisted his brow though he said, *'Glad to hear you jest again! Guardian. I am compromised, not dead, nor senile.'*

'Good.' Thessilia smiled sheepishly, a weak concession to her fleeting doubt. She would be able to feel his smouldering contempt for these circumstances through their link, but though he sensed shared feelings, she still had no real way of understanding; no way of relating. The weakness in his bones was new: something near forgotten, but it had a hook in him somehow – the lacking energy of these dying flows no longer enough to sustain – and for someone who'd fought Chaos this immeasurable amount of time it seemed not unlike a physical slap in the face. With the benefit of hindsight, perhaps this might even have been what the Speaker had tried to spare him by attempting to strike the thought of caution into all their minds, but like anything since the Quickening, he no longer knew exactly how the route forward might plan out.

Still, in a sense, it mattered not.

He was in Ostravah; for now, Thessilia was tucked away within Heirah-Noor and would not feel the restrictions as he did.

It was a respite for her. All considering – even with his father's people for company – it was!

Unwelcome News

Iambre suppressed a shiver and drew herself up.

The severe hairstyle, kept so meticulously short that it never reached past Eso's narrow jaw, seemed currently sleeked tight to the woman's skull in such a way that the Chief's already-straight strands appeared to have grown a good inch longer than usual. It accentuated Chief Mehadja's ever-gaunt features, somehow making her appear hollow-cheeked and older than the fifty-odd autumns she carried to her name.

Iambre shuddered. The rain was coming thick and fast against the panes behind her now. It fed her imagination, raising visions of alarm that she sought to hold a bay with reason. *It was raining: the Chief had been outside... nothing wrong with that.*

For a blink, Iambre could almost make herself believe it, but the Chief's leaf-green leather-wrapped breeches and scuffed leather doublet were mottled dark in patches where water had penetrated the great-cloak — something even the princess knew most felt-embellished leather unlikely to forgive. *This was not typical of Eso at all. Not at all! Why had she not changed into dress-uniform? Why had she allowed herself to become so bedraggled in the first place?*

Oddly-strange thoughts flicked through her mind, faster than fleeing sparrows before a hawk. She had a right to be offended by the Chief's obvious neglect, but should she be?

Rallying some steel for her backbone, Iambre fused her mouth into a smile of polite concern. "So Chief... no refreshments?" The princess drew her shoulders back, widening the smile to include a sliver of wry spirits as she deliberate rolled her gaze over Mehadja's form with just a brief flash of her mother's cooling disdain. "One might be inspired to wonder at your fortitude? In fact, one might even speculate as to the reason you did not appropriate time to dress or even afford me a few moments to take a knee in a semblance of respect? Well… never mind. If report you must, then… report."

The Chief swallowed, the sudden acerbic sentiment in her dark eyes and a tilt of the chin not inspiring ideas of chagrin over the chastising words, but rather of smooth tolerance marred by just a thimble of impatience. Something was not right and as she perused the Chief's waspy expression Iambre knew a moment of mute fear as something foreign curled itself in around her spirit.

"Chief, the night is dripping by." Voice rendered harsh from odd emotion, Iambre made a semi-flouncy gesture to point out her own state of affairs. "As you recall I have a banquet. Is this important?"

The Chief shifted minutely, a tiny wry smile bending her lips, then vanishing.

"Your Grace is not in an affable temper, I see." The Chief stated with a twist of features to convey how ill-received Iambre's misguided performance had been. "Now sadly, My Lady, I do not have much of a humorous streak in me today, otherwise I might have felt inspired to see how far you could drive this childish behaviour, yet as it stands – either find the grace to listen or else forgive me for redirecting my time to better service elsewhere!"

Iambre dropped the haughty mien as though someone had slapped her. Just about, she managed to squeeze back the words of embarrassed apology that clamoured to be spoken out of sincerity, but only because the Chief looked too preoccupied to care for further gestures of sad behaviour.

With a flash look for the bedchambers where Palea had disappeared, the Chief returned Iambre a sapient look, the brown sharp eyes drawing her in. From 'anyone', it would have been considered bold behaviour, but the Chief was not quite breaking protocol because, in matters of security, Eso Mehadja fairly outranked everyone but the king himself. *Why in the fifteen provinces had she tried to pull the Chief up on stupid trivia? Stupid! So stupid!*

This time it was Iambre who swallowed, though with a different sentiment than the one the Chief had shown her.

'In an emergency one cannot have time for all that bowing and fawning – that is a thing of the Senate and the council chambers – not for emergencies!'

As Iambre sought composure, out of nowhere, she suddenly recalled her father's words, and with a touch of self-induced bruised dignity, she looked at her hands. She also remembered her mother's disapproving face and how those beautiful features had been touched by fury veiled in sweet politeness as she'd argued with her husband not to take that view. *The Chief had backed her mother on that day. Death and daffodils, what was happening?*

Searching Chief Mehadja for a clue, Iambre shrugged self-consciously. The Chief was over a full head shorter than she, yet Eso had always seemed taller regardless, and today the commonly serious set of that thin mouth appeared to have twisted a good few knots tighter, rendering it within the category of 'severe'. The woman didn't blink under the scrutiny but her permanent frown lines looked more like frozen furrows of a ploughed field than human features of character – and whatever the reason, Iambre suddenly did not think her personal behaviour the primary cause, a notion that disturbed almost as much as her faulty attitude.

The Chief could wait all night. Probably would, or else just leave. Iambre's blunder would cost her more than permanent ignorance: it would kink her standing with the Chief, not to mention warp the older woman's impression of her unless she salvaged this sharply.

Iambre found herself swallowing again. Softly, she ventured, "Chief, I find my own company disagreeable too these days, but please…"

Uncommonly lost for words she gestured silently, another cold trickle of premonition sending a shiver down her back as she regarded the Chief with guarded question, aware that she was catching her own breath just a tad now. *Report? That could be on anything, yet she had that strange feeling twisting down her spine; was that reluctance she spied behind Mehadja's too-official mask?*

Perhaps reading Iambre's now earnest expression, the older woman offered her a tight smile then. "My Lady, lessons come in all shapes and forms. Your Grace is still learning, yet next time try to separate personal grievances from official matters. It's important to distinguish the two, as Gods only know they may soon enough tangle of their own."

"Chief." Iambre concurred, a frown growing.

"My Lady, again I regret the unfortunate hour, but I would of course not have come unless I deemed it important. This… this is not easy news to breach. I will make this brief."

Important? Brief? The Chief had put an unfortunate slant on those two particular words. Iambre blinked, anxiety now raising hollow cold trails in her veins.

"But of course, Chief," she managed.

Then pealing her eyes sideways, she added, "Please Chief, would you not come sit by the fire? Would you not accept a drink or perhaps something… something anything?"

Something anything? Gods she was making a pig's ear of this!

Without waiting to see if Mehadja would come, Iambre covered her creeping embarrassment and ambled towards the enormous set of furniture flanking the cosy blaze. Why had her heart started trotting? *Keep your calm… breathe… just keep calm…*

"Your Grace is kind now, but again I must decline," Eso spoke politely behind her, but with an edge of strain that took away the relief it otherwise was to realise that the Chief had not left her dangling. It attacked her with a sense of hollow dread as she halted before the twin set of finely-upholstered divans, squaring up like game pieces before each other across a low table of pale Kheltian marble.

"Please, would you at least not sit?" she managed, though she wasn't quite sure if she actually meant the courtesy as much for herself as for the Chief. Surprisingly, however, she sounded calm and ignoring the fact that the older woman's soaking attire was bound to ruin the fine fabrics of cream and gold, should she in fact aim for a pew, Iambre gestured for Eso to relax her formal stance. *There was a vibe in the silence.* The fire was blazing merrily but Iambre felt only colder. *Why had she not asked Palea to fetch her a dressing gown?*

"Forgive me, Chief-" she sank onto the nearest seat a little too eagerly, bracing herself to look up at Mehadja. *Swallow. Smile.* "-Forgive me, but I must press: what ails you? Is everything all right? You seem… Well… out of sorts. Are *you* all right? Is everyone on my staff all right? Or is it…"

Realising that she was babbling nearly as badly as Palea sometimes, she let her voice trail off and stared blindly at the pale Kheltian marble crowning the low table before her. It was striated with pale grey lines that reminded of Dragon Silver the way it drew the firelight. *Could Dragon Silver grow in marble?*

Iambre pushed away the odd thought, slightly worried about the way her heart continued to speed up.

"Your Highness, this… this is delicate, but please, I would ask that you remain calm." On her part, the mature woman who faced her remained strictly professional – and as Iambre nodded in puzzled accord, she was suddenly very pleased with Eso's ability to stay focused. *At least it made one of them!*

As though vexed, Mehadja's brow knitted, hazel eyes locking onto Iambre reminiscent of a hawk homing in on its prey, mirroring no mercy. Then without any further preamble, Mehadja simply said, "Your Highness, I am here on duty to inform you that Solancei Calverhana has... has disappeared!"

Simple words. Simple sentence. *Huge impact!* For a few endless heartbeats, Iambre could do nothing but stare in surprise at the security officer.

The thought occurred to her almost instantly that this was surely a very untimely jest of sorts – only it was not the Chief's style to play tricks – and for lack of better, Iambre raised her brows in wordless question. *Normally, Eso Mehadja would never speak on matters concerning Solancei; not in such a forthright manner. This… this was all too irregular; too concerning. Good Gods!*

"Disappeared?" Still failing to understand, she managed to press the word out, well-aware that she sounded nothing more than mildly displeased. *Disappeared? Had she really angered her friend that one time too many with her stubborn disregard? Lancei had told her: either Metavo goes, or I do – but no! No, it wasn't possible…*

Silently, Iambre nurtured growing incredulity. The Chief was not immediately forthcoming with answers to her outburst and as questions started pressing, the princess' initial surprise soon faded to numbing dismay.

"With all due respect Chief Mehadja," she started again, very much less civil now, though she kept the edgy tone reigned back in memory of earlier. "But what…? What exactly do you mean?

"Disappeared? Disappeared how?"

Glaring at the older woman as if it might help further her understanding, Iambre attempted a different tack, "I mean… she went to train with you less than a handful of hours ago and now she is gone? How can that be? Is she angry with me? Has something upset her? If it has, then she must come and speak… and speak of it…"

Words trailing off, Iambre wallowed a burst of confusion. Eso looked grim, giving nothing away. This was beyond their disagreement about a certain Captain on loan to her from the King's Legion, she realised. *Surely it had to be! Solancei did not sulk, and Iambre had only truly known her to hide from the world once. Surely… surely Lancei's oaths would stop her from leaving? Surely…*

"If she's on an errand for you, you have but to tell me, Chief. I will understand-" Iambre began again, but this time Eso shook her head, a little too quickly killing that idea. *Too suspicious…*

The Chief made as if to speak but suspecting now that the two of them were in it together, Iambre overruled the older woman, "Chief, I've had it to my corset straps with this! Are you two not aware that I have a state banquet to attend tonight? Don't you know that I require Solancei's services! Has she twisted your mind? Put you up to this? Because it will not do!"

As though in a daze, the stupid words had left her mouth – *sharply like a hiss* – before she could think to remain calm, and the Chief looked strangely disquiet now.

Startled at her own emotions, Iambre sat back. Aware of her totally selfish concerns, the unbidden thought fleetingly crossed her mind that *now* she really *was* going to be late, and Bilan-

Mentally she shook herself for a fool: despite Zanzierian sensibilities, her lateness would prove of no real consequence – and certainly, it was nothing in comparison with the Chief's statement about Solancei.

"I don't understand," she repeated, ruffled temper cooling, then settling.

What to make of this? What to think? Solancei gone? It seemed ridiculous!

For split heartbeats more, Eso regarded her with what appeared to be studied calm. Then she drew a deep breath, "Your Grace, you must listen now…"

Expelling the breath, the Chief continued in sober tones, "What *I mean*, Princess Iambre, is that Solancei attended to *some training* in town today, and that she is now gone. I apologise. It was perhaps not clear?"

"Yes verily."

Something about the Chief's tone numbed: chilling the blood. Iambre knew well how to play her words to step around the true nature of something delicate, and to her, Eso's words reeked of caution. Indeed, in all likelihood, the Chief was attempting to sidestep one issue in order to hide certain particulars regarding others. *It was what she'd do…*

She returned Eso a steady gaze. Attempting to read her, Iambre decided she might not want to know the full details of Eso's delicate omission, but nevertheless…

Lancei's well-being had always concerned her, just as she knew hers concerned Solancei. She wanted the truth. Even if unpleasant! Breathe… Keep it together…

Knowing that she was about to discover something unsavoury, Iambre took a moment to steel herself. Suddenly she had the strongest feeling that Lancei was definitely *not just* missing because of a disagreement about the choice of escort for the evening; Lancei was not petty by nature; she would have come, Iambre belatedly realised. *She would have come, had she been able!*

The clear-sighted deduction sent a pang through her body. Ashamed by her own behaviour all over, Iambre's heart started speeding once more. *Lancei would have come - and Iambre had been ranting like a child, when really-*

"Klaasinah Eso Mehadja", she began, using the Chief of Security's full name to instil power to her words, just as her mother had taught her, "I command you on your Oath, to explain the exact nature of this disappearance to me. I command you to reveal the precise sort of *training* we are referring to here, and I command you to sidestep any concerns you may think you harbour in regards to the protection of my 'delicate' sensibilities. Drat Chief, I thought we had an understanding that she should not train too hard on days where I need her as my handmaiden. Do you forget my parents' expectations that she always accompany me on first appointments?"

Eso's tight expression quivered, but this time it did not look to be in anger over Iambre's direct words.

In a strange voice to match, the Chief said, "Your Grace, I forget nothing."

Iambre's stomach cramped. "No, I didn't think you did. But then what? How will it look when Solancei is not by my side tonight? How will my parents feel? Sure, I appreciate that Solancei may not be familiar with the city of Zanzier, but I have also never known her to get deliberately lost no matter where we go. Kindly acknowledge my command and right to know the details of this; kindly enlighten me as to why she is so suddenly losing her way now?!"

Her temper about to gain free reins once more, Iambre stopped to prevent another verbal onslaught on the Chief of Security. Fuelling anger would assuredly not aid, yet it sure did bolster, and riding a fine line, the princess pinned the Chief to the spot with angry question – aware too that in light of her earlier attempts, it might have been a ridiculous thing for her to push the Chief again, but...

Well, if Eso could be pure steel, then so could she – and right now she'd refuse to back away from a straight answer!

The Chief gave her an odd look and for a blink, Iambre was wholly certain she'd overstepped every line in the book. Then, as though she was overcoming her own reluctance, the Chief nodded to herself and looked at Iambre with a sigh of what sounded like capitulation. "As Your Highness commands, so I obey. Yet I also predict she will not appreciate this knowledge! This will... well this may take longer than I anticipated. May I sit?"

Sit? Iambre nodded curtly, unwilling to relent under the Chief's steely countenance as the woman moved stiffly to occupy the edge of the sofa opposite. Whether in consideration for the fine upholstery or whether in mental discomfort, the Chief seemed disinclined to make herself more comfortable whilst she appeared to hover on the brink of speech. *Time warped…*

"Very well." Eso steepled her hands, resting her arms on the thighs of her vet breeches as she leant forward, encapsulating Iambre's attention with the strength of her presence. Then she said, "Now with due respect to Your Grace, I will speak bluntly here because this is what you desire of me, but know this: what I am about to tell you, it…

"It will not lend you the peace of mind you imagine. Are you certain now that you wish me to continue?"

Waiting to see the reaction to her declaration, Chief Eso gave her liege-lady a penetrating look that was stripped of comfort or illusion; a hard look which promised no compromise, yet rather than falter on her own demand, Iambre stuck out her chin and met the Chief's gaze with unwavering authority. *Whatever the Chief said or however she felt about the matter, she would have an explanation. Keep calm…*

Silence lingered but a moment, then Eso offered her a hard smile to match the look in her hazel eyes; the furrows on her brow seemed to deepen, then…

"Well, My Lady was always brave." Mehadja capitulated, the corners of her mouth tugging sideways in a weak smile.

Iambre nodded but found she could not bend her own lips to serve.

Eso did not appear to care. For a long beat, a silent pause seemed to grow between them, wherein Iambre got the distinct feeling that Eso was weighing her words, then…

"So you know how Solancei must train," the older woman stated. Her tone was tactfully neutral but Iambre detected just a hint of dissuasive smoothness that did not match the set of Mehadja's jaw, as she carried on, "In fact lady Iambre, you seem to know this better, I think, than Lancei herself. You see, My Lady, you ascribe her efforts true value even as she debases it to little more than a simple fact of life, and so you understand. I mean… truly understand.”

Iambre nodded again, intrigued in spite of herself. *It drained a little of her anger…*

As if she didn’t notice, Eso rocked a smidgen on her perch and carried on, “Princess, Solancei is talented. *Very.* And so perhaps My Lady might also understand that given enough time, Solancei is set to prosper into an extremely skilled Master of her arts – which, as you also know, has of course been our goal all along, for that is what a true Shield must aspire to; what *you* might need from her when you eventually ascend the throne: a shadow and protector that will move as circumstances require.”

Eso paused, straightening a little and drew breath, then continued, “But of course, even gifted people must learn and develop – otherwise how else can they achieve the ultimate result? As you already appreciate, My Lady, only training and focus will lead her to complete success.”

Iambre nodded again. *Death and daffodils! She was very much aware of just how much training Solancei did, but where was the Chief going with this?*

Chief Eso offered the princess a tight smile – as if to say ‘patience My Lady’ – but she did not dawdle; nor did she hesitate. “Now with these facts in mind, My Lady should know that whilst we’ve been travelling the realm these past eleven months, Solancei has been testing and honing her skills in the jackal fights where opportunity allowed.”

The jackal fights? Iambre’s breath caught in her throat, utter surprise turning her near-instantly from disbelief to horror.

Without looking in a mirror, she knew the exact moment all colour drained from her face, for it was closely followed by a rush of prickly goosebumps all over.

The jackal fights!

Her breath caught again. And stuck. *Gods but you cannot give in to the panic! Breathe!*

Feeling faint but ignoring the discomfort, Iambre forced each breath in and out as she sought for the right word or gesture to convey her emotions. Of course, she failed, the words 'jackal fight' echoing in her head with false impish levity: rumours and stories giving her an inkling as to what these 'games' had once entailed for the participants, but-

But this archaic sport had been terminated, branded illegal and abandoned since a long time past now. In fact, since a good fifteen years, if her teachers were to be trusted.

How? Why? What?

Suitable words escaping, a slow incredulous anger began to simmer in their place. Mercifully, it released her ability to breathe freely but that was not to anyone's benefit right then.

Part of her sat disbelieving. Part of her knew the Chief didn't lie. *Dear Gods… what had Mehadja been playing at? Indeed, what had Solancei been playing at?*

Reading her reaction, Eso held up a placating hand, stalling the words Iambre hadn't been able to formulate anyway. "My Lady, I have told you the truth as you required, now please extend me your courtesy and listen. I have given you this information in confidence and in the hope that you understand it cannot be casually divulged no matter how Your Ladyship might feel."

Iambre only stared. It took a moment for her to understand the sounds coming out of the Chief, and yet another to compose herself – then icy disdain crept forth, killing all other emotions.

"I see…" she heard herself whisper, "Well, in that case, Chief Mehadja, pray tell a simple girl what else she should know."

Eso pulled a face as though ill-touched, then her grim features assumed a fierce quality. "Well, for one, you should know to be very proud of Solancei. In every Province, in every city visited, she has entered the challenges of the jackal fights with the specific purpose to gain experience with a number of different combat styles and opponents. In result, she has gained… *gained much.*

"Indeed, she's… well, that is to say, *her skills,* have grown immensely since we left Etruia, and… and well… My Lady, they are not without merit."

"I see," Iambre repeated, unable to trust herself with more words, "And today, then?"

"Today she went to a fight near Crow Square," Eso told her. "I believe it finished as planned but then she failed to report back. I regret to inform that's all there is to it, Highness."

Solancei's Memoirs

The Province of Tarléon.
Ocean's End.
Autumn of 780 P. C. W.

No, a funeral was not a place to go raking up the truth about the manner in which Taliana or anyone else had died, be it accident or murder. Indeed, I tell you, I wasn't even sure if I'd be brave enough to ask at any given later time – but apparently, a funeral was *very much* the place for me to begin acclimatising to my new illustrious title as 'Lady of Ivanor'.

"Duchess del'Isthalani Calverhana? Lady Solancei, dear child?"

I felt light as snow. *They wouldn't leave it.* A kindly-faced priest gently touched my shoulder, a gesture that landed me back within myself with a semblance of guilt. I'd been to other funerals, yes. I might not have heard the official request, but I understood I was required to react, for as head of the family I was expected to say something of worth and value to honour the people gone Beyond, but what could I possibly have to say?

With the relentless sting of the immovable ice cap penetrating my boots through the layers of cloth, leather and fur, the urge to stomp my feet became strong, but I refrained. At the time, instead of honourable words for my parents, I thought of praise for Taliana. *I couldn't help it. My mind wandered.*

Absurdly, I remember thinking that she had always warned me to eat more; that she had warned me that I didn't carry enough fat on my bones and that I'd remain forever a slip of a girl if I did not start putting on more weight. *Had the Iddian woman perchance been right?* I'd never been this cold before, but now, even sheltered by the mass of people, as well as by the temporarily-erected sailcloth, the cold was inescapable, freezing me into muteness like the water beneath my feet. *I always ate a lot. How could I possibly begin to eat more?*

The wind howled, the high-pitched moan of a hungry wraith, and no one spoke. On the other side of the makeshift windbreaker, capricious winds caught the canvas, warring the cloth as though one of Osari'Chi's pale Sa'brans had snapped its jaws around the expanse in a fit of rage against the life still assembled and it shifted the mourners' attention, giving me a blink of reprieve.

It wasn't long enough.

They were used to such display and though a few pinched faces grew white as spirits, I felt those many eyes return in moments. Respectfully patient, they watched me: waiting for me to issue some form of regret or tribute, yet all the while the combination of one dour-faced Prefect, the most-holy priests in layers of fur and silver cloth, as well as the two hacked out ice-wells containing my frozen parents, seemed to make the task nigh-on impossible.

Solancei

As the Raven Flies...

'Commander! First Guardian! Pay attention!' Thessilia hissed through the mental link without the slightest attempt at being civil this time, and Malandaar'Vahran Denarlin Cor'Esardan snapped back out of his fourth relapse to re-solidify his mental bond with his fellow Guardian. Thessilia's spiky irritation radiated down the link and he conveyed an image of regret, something which only appeared to rub her further the wrong way.

'Old friend! You digress!' she remarked with a noticeable tang in her velvet voice, *'please desist or you will have me worried. Are you sure you are wholly recovered from the ordeal of crossing? Perhaps you ought to take a few days more: meditate, leave the flows alone, soak up the sun, regain some equilibrium?'*

'Guardian Emara, you forget your place! All is well with me – why wouldn't it be?! Yet you see that I have much to contend with and more than a few gritty choices to make. I want to go hunting Venzoians and yet I can't if I wish my presence to remain obscured – it's a strain! If you expected to find me unaffected by this taint, you remain blind to reality!'

'But of course I'm not, Guardian.' Matter-of-fact understanding flowed his way. *'Any one of us would've been struck off balance too – even Guardian Isavelia Cahmerhin, I dare say. The mere fact that there are surviving Venzoians in this realm is unbelievable – this situation cannot be rushed; take your time.'*

Take your time...

The First Guardian gritted his teeth as a flash of cold anger rolled through his core at this needy development. Having long since dispersed with useless emotions and treasonous feelings so to assure unclouded judgement and actions, he nevertheless still couldn't quite banish his feelings when it came to the thoughts of the Enemy. Only *they* were to blame for this atrocity facing the nine realms of Dallancea and he thought them pests – *them* and their minions and their chaotic, selfish desire for destruction and war. He wanted the illegal Venzoian presence gone from Ostravah; it mattered not where the monsters met their demise, nor how! Ripped to pieces; burnt by magic; eaten-up by their own hatred – anything to render their already dying world Aellnaron nothing but air and ashes, he cared not! With the Venzoian race obliterated, maybe then they could finally turn to face the Mad Ones themselves! *Take your time?! Did Emara not imagine the slight he must feel?!*

That he existed now solely because of those insane Gods and their cruel machinations was as inconsequential as the act of breathing. Because of one, the other had become a necessity. They sought to unleash the Age of Dust; sought to kill the Realms: to change them beyond recognition till all were enslaved, ruined. *Did Thessilia so easily forget their past? Did she seek to sweep aside that Malandar carried with him the memories of a time when the fighting had been rife, the chaos of the enemy's thriving and the only certainty of the morrow, a song of violent magic and the stench of death?*

Marlan Envalair had tried his very darkest to destroy what sacred oaths should have protected – but it would not deter; Emara should know better than to smooth his disposition. The Veils would not fall to allow access the chaos of those mad, false creatures who styled themselves Gods!

'All good and well then.' Thessilia's voice rang clear in his mind as though his raised level of determination had served to lend some extra clarity for the purpose of maintaining the link. *'Now before I go and lose your connection for good, tell me – what is the plan?'*

'The plan?' he echoed, in spite all, semi-charmed by her chosen change of conversation. *'Pray, why would you assume that there is currently any kind of plan other than to investigate the flows and to search out the Tarvia and the Alscara?'*

'Ah Commander, what do you take me for?' Thessilia's smile reached him through the bond, *'I know you better than you know yourself. Of course, there's a plan – always were: always will be. Now tell me I'm wrong?'*

Malandar remained silent.

As expected, she would see it as one of his 'habitual' quirks, and she did not comment with more than a defective sigh, then prompted, *'Well? Do you have a plan?'*

Malandar closed his eyes for a blink, smoothing out the crease of unease within, but she deserved an answer.

'No Guardian, I do not have a plan,-' he revealed, though with a certain slow reluctance, for the near-lie hurt his head, *'-instead I have a theory, but since I am not yet of a clear mind, I am disinclined to share my thoughts on the matter. It is perhaps a little vague for your taste but you will need to trust my reasoning.*

'Anyway, regardless of appearances I am not without Power and I wish you to know that magic or no magic, the Tarvia and Alscara will be made to perform their duty. Yet would it comfort you to know that I would drag them along if required? Would you feel comforted to hear me pledge before one and all that I will do whatever it takes: confound them by compulsion or whatever nefarious spells I might possibly discover still work? Rest assured: on the Day of Reformation the Twins will be present in the Upper Circle to perform their duty to the Veils and the Realms.'

Malandar felt Thessilia pause. *Did she actually feel sheepish and sad? Curses…*

Face twitching, Malandar sighed, relenting and abandoning his coarse attitude. *'Guardian, the Artefact will be whole again and the Natural Magic restored, Alérathnar the Maker will see to that, so I swear by the ancient blood in my veins and the spirit of my rebirth. Good enough for all times sake?'*

Silent for a few beats, Thessilia signed too. *'So you have picked up a trail for the Twins then?'* A hint of hope sprang down the link between them, eviscerating the traces of shared discomfort.

'Not yet,-' he allowed, and it was the truth – after a fashion; the half-weak spoor he'd picked up did not count, *'-but I will!'*

Uncertainty stood in his way though, and allowing candid doubt to enter the equation for the first time, Guardian Denarlin wondered how exactly one could fight off the entire Parthenon of mad creatures whilst also holding back the river of their spawn without the aid of more magic than that which currently flowed along his runes from the Maker Himself. It seemed… ambitious.

'Malandaar'Vahran Denarlin Cor'Esardan!?' Thessilia scolded, inadvertently causing another lapse in formality by using his name rather than his title, *'Alérathnar's fury, what are you not telling me?'*

Edged question underscored by suspicious pique transferred sharply down the link. *He sensed the crooked frown now plastered to her mental image, but of course it was just as well…*

Truth of the matter was she had small patience either – and thinking them long past the need of formality anyway, he ignored her familiar conduct, if not the bold demand for clarification.

'Thessilia, old friend,-' he warned, though without heat, *'-don't push me for you will not like it!'*

'Oh but there are many a thing I don't like – even now! Something's amiss Malandar, and not knowing about it…? Well, let's just pretend that I would like some kind of nasty surprise even less!'

Though insight had never been a crime, for a blink he almost cut her off regardless, and Thessilia hissed like an angry cat.

Malandar, pray enlighten me: where is Ambar'Zadron?' She threw him the question like a shuriken pulled from her sleeve, and this one struck him to the core.

A ripple of unease dancing along his spirit rune, he froze their mental link blank, seized by surprise and discomfort. It was an odd experience for he had not felt such depth of emotion in a long time and the realisation burned him uncomfortably – something which must have spread – for though Thessilia would not feel his state of mind in this very moment, the shared bond with the Eikyr offered no such luxury.

Alerted to the flux in equilibrium, Ambar'Zadron suddenly brushed against his mind, the First Guardian receiving the impression of the beast, as it tossed its great head rebelliously to set the long mane dancing. *Not happy. Which made Malandar even less happy.*

He rapidly soothed the Eikyr, mentally striking up calm, yet clenching his teeth, knowing he mustn't fall prey to doubts. Then he let Emara back in.

'Commander!' Thessilia immediately pressed for a response. *'What's occurring? This link is of worse reliability than a carrier-pigeon! Where is the Eikyr, did you say?'*

Guardian Commander Malandaar'Vahran Denarlin Cor'Esardan emptied himself, wondering why he hadn't just refused the Maker all those aeons ago. *Persistence. That was Thessilia Emara's forte, but right then he wished it could have been anything but!* Why did he not possess the Speaker's neat trick? His fellow Guardian's naturally calming influence had saved many a deteriorating situation from escalating beyond salvage and Malandar could have used a little of this gift right now.

Reluctantly, he said, *'If you insist on knowing, then I will tell you that Ambar'Zadron is not presently with me.'*

Pause. Then…

'He's not?' Emara sounded utterly confused.

'He's not,' the First Guardian confirmed and felt his natural link to the Eikyr flicker with a rise in regret. Attuned, from some place leagues off, Ambar'Zadron flicked his lethal tail with a soft swish that could be sensed across the distance, the animal's interest brushing like a soft presence against Malandar's mind.

'Calm.' He told the Eikyr in sentiment more than word, and Ambar'Zadron's ears pricked forward, contented once more. Then the animal relinquished interest, Malandar receiving a soothing impression like a return-to-sender: a breath of an image, which showed his companion returning to graze on the carcass of a freshly-killed deer.

In turn, the First Guardian redirected his full attention to Emara. By way of explanation and to allay her growing concern, he said, *'Zah is well but he's not here. I sent him away.'*

'You sent him away?' Incredulous, Thessilia repeated the words as though she'd misheard, then she rallied to question, *'How? But why? Surely, if the Deck of Persuasion no longer works, then you cannot afford to be without Ambar'Zadron! I… blessed… I…*

'Well pox on the Mad Ones! Commander, with all due respect: are you utterly mad?!'

Mad? Well there was a question…

Malandar shook off his darkening mantle of unease. He found himself in a vexing state of mind: un-centred; unbalanced; something fey pecking at his senses: a disquiet digging in the back of his mind, toying with ideas. *It seemed peculiar to contemplate the thought, but was Thessilia perhaps more right than she could possibly suspect?*

Relinquishing the clawing possibility in favour of rational thought, he smiled for the brief fancy. He did not believe himself mad but once made privy to the contents of the plans simmering in his mind, perhaps Thessilia Emara would find herself disinclined to concur.

'Well, Commander Denarlin?' Bristling concern struck his mind, Thessilia mentally prodding him for the lack of a forthcoming answer – not a thing he appreciated – and cross the leagues the Eikyr snorted in agitation as though in concert with his sudden affliction of ill-hidden nuisance.

'I am not mad, Guardian,' he refuted in hard dismissal, *'At least, no more so than anyone else and I'd thank you not to get hung up on banalities. It's nothing. Ambar'Zadron was causing too much of a stir with the locals; he was attracting too much attention. It was my judgement that it would've forewarned the Mad Ones of our Quickening. Now with the Natural Magic garbled like an old hag, I am – as previously stated – not yet ready for a fight.'*

'But even so? Banalities? Commander, leaving behind your Eikyr is hardly what I'd refer to as a 'banality!'

'Guardian Emara, understand that there was little choice.'

'Verily you must have seen it thus, but could you not-'

'The further I went, the more obvious the disaster,' he cut in, *'I am no charlatan; I tried everything, but Eikyr are still not susceptible to magic no matter what the need for camouflage – in the end, these people…'*

Malandar paused, searching for the right manner in which to convey the ill truth. He could tell her these Humans had turned as irrational as the Mad Ones: these false Gods they now worshipped with such ill-suited faith – but in reality the lie would burn his spirit, so he said, 'Well I guess it's just too long since anyone has set eye on an Eikyr.'

'But you call separating from Ambar'Zadron the better choice? His speed alone-'

'His speed means nothing if the Mad Ones gain knowledge of our return,' he remarked with dry sarcasm and felt Thessilia's ruffled state of mind hit him in response to yet another interruption. He didn't care. *'That the magic has definitely been torn from the realm is well beyond question and seeing the effects for myself, it is clear too that it was not done by gentle action. A haze lies in the air: a subtle mist you might call it. It obscured my physical sight for a few days – but my point, Guardian, is that there is no disguising the violent imprint left behind by Marlan Envalair's hand – and it taints, affecting everyone, though of course these people know no different.'*

'That... that is yet more worrying news, Commander.'

The First Guardian snorted, bemused by Emara's feelings. *'You should have seen! One look at Zah and people scurried like rats from our path as if we were a pair of Shadow Crawlers! These Humans, they...*

'Well I dare venture they don't know us anymore Emara – yet black fell, do they think they know the Mad Ones! The world reeks of their obnoxious belief; reeks of falsehood. I could not-'

Malandar broke off, biting back his lingering disbelief. To control his lapse, he drew a harsh breath, exhaling equally hard. It did nothing to alleviate his senses. The air exuded an alien pressure that felt draining and put him in mind of wading through silt to the knees. Sacrificing the Eikyr's speed in favour of sustained stealth had been a poor, but necessary, choice – that Thessilia failed to comprehend spoke volumes and he realised it irked.

However, in truth, he remained still far too annoyed about the incident that had sparked the decision for him to leave Zah, and he did not wish to make the lengthy verbal account required either. Thessilia must be made to understand though, or he'd never escape her questions, so he quickly sent her the gist in pictures and memories: the round-eyed shepherds, the farm 'incident', the bucking draught horses, the split-open crates of new wine packed for market, the farmhands running for their pitchforks, the screeching young woman nearly fainting and naming him 'Demonai-spawn'… *it was really rather simple!*

Feeling a sliver of anger stir at the indignity of having had to flee a bunch of pulp-headed farmers; at the frustration of them not knowing of his kind; of them not 'remembering', the First Guardian severed the memory.

Thessilia sounded shocked, *'I see… how unfortunate: must have been gaping simpletons the lot! No doubt this was an incident that couldn't have been helped, though now I fear our task may yet fall prey to failure if this is the kind of welcome we can expect from now on.'*

Malandar shifted an onset of irritation before it could settle over his spirit too. *'Guardian Emara, we will not fail and the Chaos will not win!'*

'No,' she replied, unfazed by his terse tone, *'No we will not fail Commander. On that, I stand ready to sacrifice what is required.'*

Uncommonly weary, Malandar sighed. *'I will not let Zah run wild forever – Gods hate, I have barely made headway to speak off since separating, yet it is most certainly too soon for the enemy to learn of my presence. Should word reach the wrong people, it would endanger the Twins, perhaps even the general population, and it would play into the Mad*

Ones' hands every advantage we would not wish to grant. Ambar'Zadron is not of this realm; alone I have a chance – but I need horses.'

'*I see your point,*' Thessilia Emara sounded as frustrated as he. '*Time is a fickle thing when you first set foot back into the Realms, I know that. What is your present location?*'

'*As the Raven flies, approximately 20 leagues from the border between Kretoria and Zanzier: on the outskirts of some insignificant town. As soon as we are done, I intend to be on the road, mounted.*'

'*That is well then,*' Thessilia commented, but with a lack of conviction.

'*Emara, I would charge you to assemble the Black-Eyed Army soon!*' Malandar urged her suddenly; on a hunch, '*You cannot linger in Heirah-Noor for long. You must not. We need recruits and you will be needed here, I believe.*'

'*Your will, my action.*' Thessilia answered with a curt incline her chin so to underscore that she understood. '*Until later then, Commander Denarlin! Intriviatu al hastriviatu! May Alérathnar the Maker guide you!*'

'*And you also, Guardian Emara. And you also,*' Malandar breathed and broke the mental link to his fellow Guardian with curt efficiency as he looked to the low, late-afternoon sun.

He judged the time somewhere around the hour of the whistling winds already, and the setback cut. With Zah he'd made splendid progress, but on foot…

There was of course not much he could do about that. However, that didn't mean he couldn't affect progress, sooner rather than later. *And he intended to. Once he was mounted again.*

All there was…?

For a few blinks, the ensuing silence ate warmth from the room. *All? All there was…?*

"Bloody rats, Chief!" Iambre ignited with vehemence, her mind twisting with a profuse number of questions ramming themselves forward like pearls on a tightening string that might eventually strangle unless clarification was had. She drove her gaze to Eso's, aware that present feelings left little goodwill in their depths.

The Chief didn't flinch. Her mature features were composed in the curious detachment Iambre had seen before when state affairs and poor news was relayed and deliberated upon, but like a hunting cat observing its surroundings with flat, onyx eyes of luminous coiled danger, Mehadja seemed the untarnished master of them all, revealing no emotional ripples to mar the surface of her self-possessed calm.

It was both reassuring and infuriating. A revelation of this magnitude seemed to warrant more, somehow, still it was not lost on the princess that no matter the context, the old woman was presently trying to measure the effects of her confessions. *Because that's what the Chief did. Observe, evaluate, formulate…*

She drew a smooth breath. *In. And out. In. And out…*

Lowering her gaze, mouth working briefly as if she'd been trying to dislodge a tiny piece of toffee stuck to her teeth, Iambre attempted to re-channel her focus, but there was a hint of pressure building in her chest again and the usual breathing pattern didn't seem to be working. *All there was to it? Well wasn't that a pip! All there-*

The new rush of anger came out of nowhere, engulfing her like a tidal wave that momentarily dragged her far enough off course to throw caution into the whirlpool as it seemed to rip at her physically.

"All there is to it, you say?!" she spat in disgust, pleased that a solid table stood between them. "Well, don't you have an odd way of describing certain matters, Chief Eso! A very odd way indeed!"

The Chief shrugged – *actually shrugged* – her entire bearing retaining that carefully neutral position in the face of the princess' outburst – and as the real truth of Solancei's absence asserted itself, Iambre felt her internal flame ignite hotter, evaporating the tidal wave beneath something of scorching simplicity that made lethal intent writhe to escape her body like a separate entity. *Gods help her: she'd thought Solancei petty for failing to attend her. How very, very wrong she'd been! If the Chief shrugged one more time… if she did not show more symptoms of remorse…!*

Iambre's throat constricted but she was too angry to care; she was shaking all over now, a kernel of chill slipping into her core below the striking heat to make her feel feverish. *It did not matter.*

"My handmaiden – nay, my best friend – is partaking in illegal sports with the blessing of the realm's prime security officer-" she summed up, voice spilling tight with anger-made-subtle by lilting restriction to allow for a shadow of incredulity that just did not seem as severe as she might have wished, "-and you… you make it sound of small consequence! What were you thinking?! I tell you now: confidence or no, Chief Eso, you mark my words: Father will hear of this!"

Eso Mehadja offered her a thin smile that seemed harder than a punch in the guts, but then she appeared to relent a fraction, the lines bracketing her waxen moderate lips slightly softening to convey a sense of forbearing disappointment. Shaking her head, the action tenuous, Mehadja's voice held candour, as she said, "My Lady, have a thought now, then tell me: who do you think sanctioned Solancei's training in the first place? I carry clout, but sadly not that kind of power…"

Eso let the sentence hang but Iambre gave her a blank glare, just about managing to haul back on the smoulder, as it waxed and weaned.

The Chief shrugged again. *Too infuriatingly casual.* But as Iambre leant forward to argue, the older woman paused her with a tired look that seemed to stretch her ascetic features. Voice sounding bruised, Mehadja stated, "My Lady, the King already knows."

"Father *knows* about this?" Iambre squeaked in dismay.

Clenching her fists as she stared to the ceiling in effort to stop herself from physically pouncing on the Chief, for a blink she wanted to shake the older woman till her skull rattled on her lean neck. *Had the whole world gone mad?*

Controlling her less than pleasant urges, she drew a deep breath and slowly, so very slowly, the need for violence subsided, though the horror did not. She didn't have to think long about any of this before it all made perfect sense. *And not in a good way.*

"Oh merciful Diekima'Chi!" A small sound of spiky ironic mirth escaped her. "But of course father knows! Why wouldn't he? And Lancei agreed to this? No, don't tell me – of course she did! The wretched woman is mad in the head!"

Shutting her mouth lest she might utter some rather regrettable truths, Iambre flung Eso a withering look, yet within her grief, she knew to be careful. With her temper so ruffled, she wouldn't put it past the Chief to walk out if she thought the princess unable to cope, and it was of course the last thing Iambre would wish for.

With no small effort, she composed herself – the many hours honed by her mother now finally paying off. *Breathe… in… out… in…*

"Chief, what would you have me do? What would you have me say?" She enquired at length, feeling lost as the heat began to fizzle out. "It's all so ridiculous! How was anyone ever in agreement that this was a perfectly acceptable avenue of pursuit? How come no one sat back and thought, *'Hey, pray think now! Perchance this is too dangerous a pursuit, not to mention morally wrong! Hey, pay heed now: let's just forget about it!'*

"Dear Gods, what's the matter with you all!? Death and daffodils, you should be ashamed! You should… you should apologise!"

A nerve in her cheek twitching as though bemused, Eso cocked an eyebrow at that, then looked down as if to contemplate the state of her own boots. *Those quiet frown lines were deepening. Perhaps her words might just be getting through…*

"Highness, you're angry." The Chief appeared to choose her words, perhaps with a little too much care. "Indeed, I am able to appreciate your position, My Lady, but…

"But you should also know that I cannot, and will not, apologise!"

Eso perused her boots, then met Iambre's eyes with the same kind of unrelenting light sometimes spied in Lancei's, adding, "Solancei needs to be prepared for every eventuality and we haven't much time left. Your safety has always been paramount: to the Realm, to your parents, to me, and most certainly to Solancei. The fights have seen her grow; have seen her develop – but most of all, it has helped prepare her for duty in a way that would otherwise have taken additional years, and that My Lady, is something which should not be atoned for."

"But I thought it had already taken years," Iambre blurted. "Surely you're all too paranoid. She's not only just 'T'lexara Corunan Vitalioni', you know!"

"My Lady, that she is not!" Eso agreed, mildly tilting her chin to concur, "But first and foremost that is her duty, nonetheless. Before anything else, she is your life-shield and it remains not an oath to be trifled with! Now, with respect Highness: Solancei knows this even if you sometimes seem to forget."

"And so you have drilled into me since I was but a girl three feet high – but the jackal fights? You should have told me; good Gods Chief, they are illegal! And now Solancei is reportedly gone. Where the rats is she? Daffodils, how was this ever a good plan? How? When?"

Eso sighed, hands gesturing slightly as though to avert further infraction. "Oh, believe me, Highness, the decision to enter the fights was not easily agreed upon. Your lady mother was against it from the start, but 'needs-must' made even the Queen amenable to sense. Eventually..."

This surprised, but for now Iambre didn't have time to dwell on her mother's unexpectedly contrary attempt to protect her charge, as Eso continued, "I have of course taken great precautions to keep our secret covered; Solancei's identity remains ever-undisclosed; she fights with no distinguishing heralds or colours; no glorious equipment – and that is how it must be. Now whilst I regret the deceit certainly, surely you do see that we could not in good conscience have told you about any of this before."

Iambre sniffed dismissively and Eso's voice took on a pinch of dry levity, "You do not approve – I appreciate the fact – but your knowledge would have stood in our way; in the way of Solancei's progress. My Lady, oblivion is not always a bad thing; your reaction notwithstanding, even as we speak, I regret the need for a conversation on the matter, but the truth will out as they say – and you must trust me Princess when I say, that the jackal fights were the only way. *The only way!”*

Eso paused, then added with resigned candour, “We each do what we must Crown Princess. You, I, Solancei; but she is your life-shield! You need but to look to the future to admit the prudence of our decision.”

Iambre opened her mouth. Words of abusive ire bubbled like caustic fire on her tongue but Eso didn’t give her the opportunity to speak before she forged on, “You are travelling the widths of our realm; you are outside walls and in foreign locations. Out here, you do not have the entire garrison of Castle Servangar to regard your safety. Out here, we are only a few handfuls of people to protect you, and it is not… not… well, My Lady, it may appear an easy task to you, but it’s not, and as you grow older, your role will become ever more public. I do not wish to cause you alarm, but to be safe, you will need every skill that we can arm Solancei with, make no mistake!”

With the first open expression upon her lined face since she’d confessed this nightmare, Eso appeared honest and unveiled, and Iambre realised the woman allowed herself the grace to look a touch unhappy then, not for the Chief’s own sake, but for hers.

Brow furrowing – three lines across the forehead to give her a forbidding countenance – Mehadja caught Iambre in the sturdy embrace of hazel eyes. “Now be upset if you must but I personally urge you to let it slide before people read the difference in you and start asking questions. Need I remind you of the attempt on your life when you were just seven summers old? Need I remind you that in the last three hundred years, six of your ancestors have been assassinated and four sorely wounded? We live in the Enlightened Age, but not everyone sees it thus: Solancei trains for you, My Lady. Don’t begrudge the methods that one day might save your life!”

And what was there to deny? The Chief was right of course, wasn't she? Because as the future Queen and ruler of the realm, Iambre's life remained by default worth more than Lancei's – or so they all kept telling her! By now, and by similar default, it was only too-clear that Eso was painfully right and Iambre was not! *And, as Lancei would say: there is not a ruddy thing you can do about it, so just accept it!*

Iambre sat deadly still now, her fingers chilled and motionless in her lap. She wanted to argue and she was trying to deny the sound reasoning behind Eso's words, but sadly she could find no point of opening. It flustered her further to know that she was just a sigh away from relenting to the Chief of Security's logic; frustration pushed at her anger, and anger fought back, even as concern intermingled, colouring it with emotion.

Eso meanwhile, continued to look her in the eye: something beyond duty finally permitting her a licence to remain a little less reserved. "Surely Highness, you will not see this as-"

"Oh enough!" Iambre barked with an authority borne out of years of training too, and Eso complied.

Mehadja's soft release of understanding seemed worse than the shield of serenity she'd showed earlier and for a moment the princess could look nowhere but the rug at her feet. She still wanted them all to be wrong, but the respectful change in Eso did not alter facts. Iambre had seen the relentless look in the older woman's eyes; had seen her lack of compromise. The Chief of Security was never going to be in the wrong about this and Iambre would have to concede the point. *But her father be damned! How could he?* Sure they might all be right with this mad-scheme, but what about her? *What if she didn't actually want saving if it meant her friend standing in the way of danger?*

Iambre ground her teeth, trying to study her emotions rather than give in to them. Right then, she was not sure if she was capable of forgiveness but nevertheless a small part of her knew that she must. She was Crown Princess. Heiress to the 'Future'. She had no choice. Anger still patrolled her insides but even if she hated to admit the hard-faced truth, she saw their reasons. *It had been the right thing to do. And curse it: she was ever about doing the 'right thing', was she not? For a fact, Solancei would often joke that Iambre ought to make it her official 'Code' to go below the Coat of Arms; that if Iambre was not careful, she might one day brush her teeth with it! Ah, Lancei…*

She let go of the strand of hair she'd been twisting into a tight cable around her finger. Realistically, she was overreacting, but worries about Lancei aside, there were the official concerns to consider – and if cutting it right back to sheer legality…

She was 'The Realm'; the Future. Already she was tempting fate with her illicit feelings for the Captain of her guard, but this…

If news of the jackal fights became common gossip, it would top the biscuit by a league! Society had her on a very tall, very narrow pedestal and they'd not take kindly to her falling off. Those fights had been deemed barbaric and unnecessary in this modern age and they'd been eradicated – *supposedly.* Of course, Eso and Solancei had been right not to inform her about their sordid affairs: they'd protected her as was necessary; as they saw fit and proper. And still…

Still… right then, what did it matter? In this very moment, she resented them both with a vengeance, not only for their extra-curricular activities but also for excluding her: protection or no!

The princess peeled her front teeth across her bottom lip, grimacing without thought for pretty airs or manners. *Was it possible to resent the fact that even should she be entitled to fuel resentment or not, this also didn't matter either?*

Iambre's face soured like the state of her thoughts. *Hoops to them all! Solancei mattered above her own standing! Even if she was not allowed to think that way, she did!*

"Highness, you needn't worry yourself."

As though reading her mind, yet also part-misinterpreting, the Chief gave her an oddly assuring smile, "As I have already explained, we have ever taken the utmost care. True names or identities were never once divulged. The name 'Solancei' was never mentioned or entered onto any parchment; all money – be it for services rendered or for winnings – was ever paid in coin and handled by a third party. Trust me, no one could ever trace this back to you."

Iambre nodded, aware it was what the Chief expected but… *the secret might be safe, but Solancei was still gone!*

"My Lady, perhaps this is enough for now?" Using her hands for leverage, Mehadja shifted on her seat, gathering herself in preparation to stand. "I am aware that you have not much time before duty calls, and I should-"

"Duty be hanged, Eso Mehadja!" Iambre interrupted impotently, though with enough lingering vexation that she knew she could not let up, "I am not done here! You shouldn't have taken her to those fights! She shouldn't have gone – do you hear!?"

For a heartbeat, Eso looked taken aback, then she eased back onto her seat. With a subtle crease of the silver-laced brows, she said, "My Lady… we could discuss the subject all night without finding an accord, I'm sure. However, as someone who knows little of the Steel Path, I appreciate you must labour to comprehend how benefits can outweigh risks. You should appreciate now that Solancei understands she is sworn by King and Blood to protect you. Could you deny her the destiny she is chosen for?"

'The destiny you chose her for', she felt like saying, but Klaas' voice was so full of reason.

Iambre scratched her forehead, one fingernail nervously responding to an invitation of her mind that told her to win time. Pulling her hand away, she swallowed, angered with herself to have given in to pursue this small tell no matter how insignificant.

"Highness, I could teach the girl only so much – sparring partners to hone such skill require commitment: we tried it once but it did not work out to our benefit nor advantage. As it tallies, sadly even I could not guarantee total secrecy, even had such a scenario been deemed worthy of a second attempt, and imagine if you please, if Solancei's ulterior role were to become known? All the years of secrecy will have been for nought! She'd be the first they'd take out: poison most likely… and then you'd be alone: exposed!"

Iambre swallowed again. Eso spoke eloquently and she had no reply to the logic, yet she felt like a traitor to let the matter die so easily: a traitor to Solancei, and a traitor to her own principles, never mind the Realm!

Would it have been so bad if the Realm had known about Solancei's duty? Would it have been so bad to let it finally be known that people would have to cut their way through her lady-in-waiting should they wish to harm the Princess of the united Ostravah? Gods, but seventeen years ago she'd simply thought Solancei was going to be her friend, and now it was so much more complicated than she might ever have imagined as a seven-year-old. *Solancei might like this – but Iambre sure didn't!*

She sent Eso a withering look borne of frustration, but this had been built over years, too strong a construct to tear down with a few angered words. She had no power to change that which her father had writ in blood and gold on a sheet of hammered Dragon Silver one particular morning those many winters ago. She'd been a child. Her parents had wanted Solancei to be a secret, a mere shadow, like a unique defence against the ultimate threat and Iambre had only been too-keen to keep Solancei close; too keen to please her parents that she'd never argued.

No, the arguments had come later, but even then it had been more of a spoilt grumble than a true voice of complaint, because it had never been this real before. Perhaps she should have tried harder – *yes, she definitely should have!* – but she could not deny that her parents had moved to take this extraordinary step of precaution for a reason. *Would any parent not, if there might have been a chance their child stood likely to get hurt?* They might live in 'enlightened' peace times but as Eso had pointed out, there were always people who did not agree with the majority: history could easily repeat itself and a bit of foresight had never gone amiss when considering the safety of the Royal House.

With all thoughts about lateness and dresses forgotten, Iambre clutched the fabric of her undergarment in a white-knuckled grip. *She couldn't stop it. Other questions pressed...*

"Was this... this 'venture' also about money?!" A sense of absurdity washed through her when she said the words aloud and yet she had to ask. "You mentioned something about 'payments', did you not? Did you gamble, Chief?"

"Well... not exactly Highness." Eso's words trailed off.

Pensively massaging her pointy chin, the Chief observed the sudden decency to appear uncomfortable, and Iambre's eyebrows climbed in shock as the impossible went unsaid. *Why had she even asked...?*

"Chief?" She pressed in a relentless tone.

"We… we might have thrown in a few gambles," the older woman allowed at length, "here and there… *you know*… not much, but enough. Sometimes we'd get paid for representation… that kind of thing. See, what Your Highness must understand is that it's sort of part and parcel of the jackal fights. If we do not gamble, it will only raise suspicion."

"I see." Eso's meagre explanation did nothing to placate and the princess purposely pressed her lips into a thin line in effort to salvage the threads of her melting equilibrium all over again. *Thank Ishjah that what she'd taught Iambre on regal iciness still prevailed. It seemed all she had left.*

"I see," she repeated. Moments ago, she'd never suspected a thing like the jackal fights could have survived into their modern age and now the Chief was giving her facts and details as though it was one of the most common things in the realm. *It was madness!*

On a whim, she asked, "And Lancei gambles too?" *Please say no…*

The Chief looked momentarily surprised. "Well, My Lady, what does it matter? It has no consequence, surely? She can hardly be said to care about the money."

Iambre stared at her Security Chief and didn't manage to suppress yet another waspish, 'I see.'

She rubbed her brow. As though the action was somehow the instigator, another thought occurred to her.

Recalling to breathe – *just* – she gathered her thoughts so that the question she knew must be asked, did not escape her on a whisper of dread.

"So, on a different note, Chief… Since you appear to be such an outstanding expert on this 'sport', tell me now: how does one avoid injury? I mean, it's a tough game is it not? I… I imagine it was outlawed for a reason? How… how does one survive in one piece?"

Iambre tilted her chin, scrutinising her security officer, who stared back with mute sobriety. *What Eso said next would explain a good many things she might not actually want explaining when it came to the crux, but-*

"I am uncertain how My Lady would prefer me to answer that particular question," the Chief finally replied, "You are no child, Princess…"

The words might have been considered impertinent had they been spoken by any other member of her household, but coming from Eso, they held a candid potency that made any notions of slight fade to grey. Iambre's overactive mind made the connections all too easily and the cold travelled from the pit of her stomach to encase her heart. *She'd been a fool.*

"So many times…" she sighed softly, "So many times, you told me that she had received those knocks in training and I never suspected…"

In retrospect, she felt soiled by her own naivety – still it winked to nothing when another idea brought her eyes sharply to the Chief's, cutting, as the line of her heart plummeted with further understanding. *Suddenly she was lightheaded – and so very, very cold.*

"Oh merciful Gods Chief! Don't… don't tell me this is what I fear? I mean…? What are we *not* saying here? Don't tell me you think Solancei is hurt! Tell me that is not possible!"

The Chief kept a smooth face and blinked just once as she shook her head, refuting the concern; it wasn't really a tell, but a shadow of something unrealised in Mehadja's eyes, nearly robbed Iambre of breath regardless. *The Chief was worried!*

Notions of anger and of betrayal seemed to drain in a heartbeat. *If the Chief was worried…*

Feigning control, she directed a stern stare at nothing in particular and folded her arms to stop her hands from shaking again.

"Very good then," she croaked, paused to swallow, then tried anew, "Chief, this is not over! I can condone none of this, but-

"Well if it's not too much trouble, I'd appreciate it if you could go find my life-shield and bring her home safely. Sooner rather than later now, you hear! Solancei is maybe nothing to you, but to me, she is most definitely so much more than a simple Shield!"

Eso inclined her head in accord, but something flashed in her hazel eyes. On a tight breath of civility, she said, "With respect... My Lady, has no need to remind me of her feelings on this matter! Indeed, please do not mistake my objectivity for a lack of care. Solancei is... is dear to us all."

"I am glad," Iambre managed, garbled by a need to bite, but Eso held up her hand, indicating that she was not done.

"Now before we part: My Lady has been forthright, so allow me to reciprocate?"

Iambre inclined her chin mechanically, nearly immune now to the iron in Mehadja's unblinking gaze.

"My Lady, in as much as it's worth, I extend you my unreserved apologies for the situation we face,-" the Chief sounded strained, then her tone firmed, "-it was of course never our intentions to lay such burden on you – however..."

Iambre cocked an eyebrow. "What?"

The Chief didn't even blink. "However, if My Lady harbours need to pick up the conversation on rights or wrongs again, I must inform her that I stand disinclined to oblige. Highness, I am commanded still by the grace of your good parents to see to the matter of your protection and so I cannot always make you privy to things – good or bad they may be. Hence, should My Princess possess any unresolved 'issues' in regards to Solancei's training, I would thank her to address these matters with her parents, not me."

And there it was! Iambre almost cringed. *Eso didn't mince her words. Never had.* And the old woman had just made it plainly known to her that she was able to usurp Iambre's authority if she deemed it best for King and Realm! Iambre might be next in line to the throne, but she was yet not on it and that made a whole lot of difference. *A whole lot...*

"Well and good then, Chief," she allowed, feeling spent. "But please, before you go and leave me stressed with worry, could you... could you tell me all you know about Solancei's supposed disappearing 'trick'. I will not preach, but... but as her friend, I think I have a simple 'need' to know!"

Eyes flicking to the water clock, the Chief cleared her throat, looking wholly as though she was about to walk into the Goddess Ulvaro'Cha's pit of fire – the stealth of worry drawing tight the lined face, even as she appeared to mentally tiptoe around the steel spears just about to descend on her position.

Was that honesty or show? Iambre hated that she still couldn't tell with the Chief, but then, drawing a deep breath, the old woman shifted to hold her future liege's stare: the details surrounding recent events as requested, then delivered without flinching.

And Iambre listened. She was aware that it was perhaps at best a threadbare account, barely worthy of the Chief's usually-impeccable attention to detail, but what the Chief of Security did include in her sketchy report would not have been better received if wrapped in pretty gauze. For mercy, Iambre kept her promise and stayed quiet, just like she recalled to breathe steadily throughout, but it required fortitude.

Solancei was gone, and Chief Eso Mehadja without a single concrete lead. Iambre already did not like Zanzier; this news did not enamour her further!

Solancei's Memoirs

The Province of Tarléon.
Ocean's End.
Autumn of 780 P. C. W.

"Gods defend you!" I recall the priest muttering then, squeezing my shoulder in what might have been meant as reassurance, but felt only like the claw of a Blue-Wing attaching itself, and I think he must have misunderstood the reasons for my delay, for with the next breath, he whispered, "It is done child. If you have words to add for the honour of the people gone Beyond, then you have a right to speak now – as their daughter and surviving blood."

I know… *even priests can be idiots.* Many of their colourful ilk certainly seem prone to the misconception that I am one fleck bothered about their archaic ideas and foul dogmatic dispositions – and still…

Well, I suppose this one was the least straw-headed of the lot, because I recall the genuine concern for a seven-year-old orphan that I spied in his eyes. He thought me undone, not uneducated, but I had nothing to say, and that's the terrible truth. *I had nothing to say, and I did not imagine anyone would care to hear about the hollow space in my chest, nor the cold in my core, nor-*

Oh but funerals are also not the place to stir offence either – I am not ignorant – so I raised my chin, then my eyes, and said, "May the Gods protect their journey through the Void. May they find comfort in each other's presence and may eternity weigh like a feather upon their spirits until they return."

There! Words of scripture that had been good enough for the Lords of Old!

Of course, I doubted they were good enough for my dead parents – even gone Beyond, they no doubt require more, always more – but that was their dilemma now, not mine. And besides, I was hungry; the streak of Veranto kept flexing. *Was it wrong to sweet-talk the dead and living both, just to see an end to this hours-long funeral process?*

I guarantee, the seven-year old me, didn't think so – and, as luck you have it, the now twenty-six year old doesn't much see the problem, either. It was done. The rest of the procedure became a blurred event that I don't much recall. But mercy… it was done.

And mercy, so was I.

Solancei

Thank you for reading☺

The story will continue in Episode 2: Unexpected Bargain

Available now

****

Post Script from the author

Hi there!

If you enjoyed this book (or any of the others ☺) I'd really love you to spend just two minutes leaving a review on Amazon/Goodreads/Bookbub/ etc.

Why?

Because feedback on my product is invaluable for me! Not only does it help me learn and grow as an author, it may also help other readers discover the book, and – very importantly – that it's okay to take a chance on an indie publication.

And don't forget...

For extra insider info, updates, freebies, exclusive offers and giveaways, you can also allow me to keep in contact by signing up to my **newsletter**…

Just visit www.llthomsen.com and follow the link

Acknowledgements

This list is by no means exclusive, but I cannot praise the help and support of the following enough:

To the most talented fantasy writers in their own right - LinaBean, IngThor, Gabrias & RealBitsofLemon – thank you for sticking with my crazy, purple-edged story. Indeed, thank you for all your invaluable comments and honest feedback, which helped me see the purpose of this manuscript in a clearer light. You taught me so much about writing, and about my style, just as you made me aware of many new and wonderful facets that I hadn't previously been aware of!

To one Sue and to another Sue: both amazing women whom I love for all your kindness and support. Thanks for lending an ear and offering good advice. You are in my heart forever.

To my husband for his patience and support. Though not a geek or lover of fantasy like myself, your trust and generosity means the world and this work would simply not have been possible without you.

And finally, I can of course not neglect to mention the most important people of all: my children; my muses; without whom my imagination would undoubtedly still be slumbering in a deep subterranean cavern. When I spend hours at the computer you still cheer me on – never lose the magic!

And finally...

Curious about the world of Ostravah?

For glossaries, maps, and more, please visit my official author website on

www.llthomsen.com

Also feel free to contact me via

https://www.facebook.com/themissingshield/

https://www.facebook.com/linda.thomsen.12979

https://twitter.com/LLThomsen1

https://www.instagram.com/llthomsen/?hl=en

https://www.pinterest.co.uk/llthomsen7589/

The Missing Shield - Order of Episodes

This story begins in Episode 1 of The Missing Shield.

Below is the full list of books in the series in order of release.

- A Change of Rules – Episode 1
- Unexpected Bargain – Episode 2
- A Perspective of Death – Episode 3
- Running the Gauntlet – Episode 4
- Notions of Risk – Episode 5
- The Final Card - Episode 6
- The Lure of an Ancient Fable – Episode 7
- All in a Day's Work – Episode 8

And coming up soon...

- The Way Star –Episode 9
- All Thieves' Honour – Episode 10
- The Neidar Ba'raie – Episode 11

This will complete The Missing Shield – Vol 1 of 'The Veil Keepers Quest'.

***

New!

Also NOW available: **The Missing Shield, Part 1** - Author's Preferred Edition box set, which includes episodes 1 – 6.

***

*****

Concept Drawings

ART BY ABE7280 (DEVIANT)

ART BY ABE7280 (DEVIANT)

ART BY ABE7280 (DEVIANT)

Art by Yukimi Wintel / SketchJunkie (FB & Insta)